THE IRON SHIRT

Also by Frank B. Linderman

The Iron Shirt (2004)

Henry Plummer: A Novel (2000)

Wolf and the Winds (1986)

Quartzville (1985)

Montana Adventure: Recollections of Frank Bird Linderman
(1968)

Recollections of Charley Russell (1963)

Blackfeet Indians (Out of the North) (1935)

Stumpy (1933)

Beyond Law (1933)

Red Mother (1932)

Old Man Coyote (1931)

American: The Life Story of a Great Indian, Plenty-Coups,
Chief of the Crows (1930)

Kootenai Why Stories (1926)

Lige Mounts: Free Trapper (1922)

Bunch-Grass and Blue-Joint (1921)

How It Came About Stories (1921)

On a Passing Frontier (1920)

Indian Old-Man Stories: More Sparks from War Eagle's
Lodge-Fire (1920)

Indian Lodge-Fire Stories (1918)

Indian Why Stories: Sparks from War Eagle's Lodge-Fire
(1915)

THE IRON SHIRT

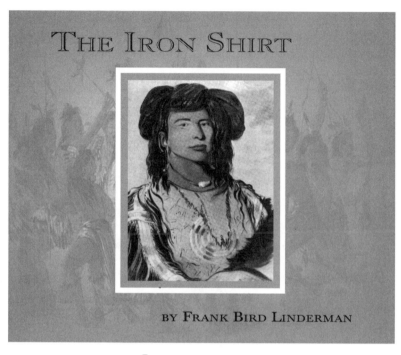

BY FRANK BIRD LINDERMAN

INTRODUCTION BY
SARAH WALLER HATFIELD

HOMESTEAD PUBLISHING
MOOSE, WYOMING
SAN FRANCISCO, CALIFORNIA

ISBN 0-943972-76-0

Library of Congress Control Number 2003096400

Printed in the United States of America on recycled, acid free paper.

First Edition

ILLUSTRATION CREDITS
Cover: Ha-wón-je-tah, first chief of the Sioux, by George Catlin, courtesy
Smithsonian American Art Museum, gift of Mrs. Joseph Harrison, Jr..
Page 13: Fort Union, Mouth of the Yellowstone, by George Catlin.
Page 18: The Steamboat "Yellow Stone" leaving St. Louis,
by George Catlin.
Illustrations, courtesy the Schreier Collection.

PUBLISHED BY
HOMESTEAD PUBLISHING
Box 193 • Moose, Wyoming 83012
& San Francisco, California

For other fine titles in the AMERICAN WEST CLASSICS, contact:
MAIL ORDER DEPARTMENT
HOMESTEAD PUBLISHING
BOX 193 • MOOSE, WYOMING 83012
or www.homesteadpublishing.net

INTRODUCTION

WHO WAS FRANK BIRD LINDERMAN?

On January 2, 1924, Churchill Mehard wrote to J. K. McDonald, in care of Hollywood Studios, to introduce McDonald to Mr. Frank Bird Linderman. The introduction–wholly Mehard's–was to spark the idea to make a moving picture of Linderman's recently published historical novel, *Lige Mounts: Free Trapper*. In his letter Mr. Mehard stated:

> Mr. Linderman is an old timer in Montana, and is, I feel safe in saying, the greatest living authority on the old days and history of the northwest–Mr. Linderman has been prominent in Montana for many years and has written several books–He has made history of the old west his life-work, but only recently has he attempted anything seriously in line of a novel.

Linderman started his intense study of the old northwest when he came to the remote unspoiled wilderness of Montana Territory in 1885. Years later in 1920, he wrote his friend Ralph Edgerton that he was a trapper in the winter and cowpuncher in the summer, and was the first white man to winter on Swan Lake. During the next seven years he also worked as a guide, and ran the ferry at Holt. He became intimate friends with mountain men and many of the native Indians in the area. He established relationships of trust with old full-blood Indian chiefs and medicine men and, being an adept sign-talker, learned with great interest their customs, stories of creation and hero tales. In 1915 Charles Scribner's Sons published his first recording of this vanishing culture in *Indian Why Stories: Sparks from War Eagle's Lodge-fire*, a volume of Blackfeet, Chippewa and Cree legends, illustrated by his close friend, Charles Marion Russell.

Frank Linderman left his wilderness life in 1891 and married Minnie Johns in 1893. He subsequently followed self-taught careers as an assayer, miner, newspaper owner, Montana state legislator, assistant Secretary of State, and general agent for Germania Life Insurance Company of New York. To fill pages of his Sheridan, Montana newspaper in the early 1900s, he wrote true short stories from his experiences, poetry, and sage sayings under the pen name "Uncle Billy."

Born in Ohio in 1869, Linderman had a boyhood love for the woods around his Elyria and Lorain homes where he spent most of his holidays, studying and learning to talk to the animals and birds, or hunting squirrels with his sawed-off musket. He once experimented with taxidermy and ruined his freshly papered bedroom with his stuffed birds.

Nearby Lake Erie and later Lake Michigan, when his family moved to Chicago, provided young Frank with the wonders of steamships. On April 15, 1962 Linderman's youngest daughter, Norma Linderman Waller, wrote to Dr. Harold G. Merriam, editor of Linderman's autobiography, *A Camp Kettle Career*, retitled *Montana Adventure: Recollections of Frank Bird Linderman* on publication that:

> After the move to Chicago he found a friend whose father owned a tug, and the two boys used to ship out with him [on] summer vacations and sail Lake Michigan. There began his love of the water and boats.

Linderman's first ambition was to attend the Naval Academy at Annapolis. An accident, however, took the sight in one eye and changed his focus to become a trapper in an area removed from the contamination of civilization. He loved adventure, and night after night he endlessly studied a map of the United States to locate the area of his dreams. Many years later Linderman stated in a biographical sketch for the Junior Book of Authors: "Perhaps the blood of earlier Lindermans who pioneered in New York State, Pennsylvania and Ohio, was somewhat responsible for my boyhood desire to go west. It came early and never left me."

In March of 1885 Frank left Oberlin Business College and, with his parents' reluctant permission, set out with two traveling companions by train, stage and steamer to Swan Lake at the outlet of the Bigfork River. The area, he decided, was the wildest and most untamed in Montana Territory. The wilderness was too much for his companions and, a few days after building a crude log cabin, they left sixteen year old Frank alone, and returned to "the States." Totally without fear, he remained in Montana the rest of his life.

After his first book was published in 1915, Linderman set out to fulfill his dream, germinated since his trapping days. He built a large log home on the western shores of Flathead Lake at a favorite early day campsite, and moved his family back to the wilderness in 1917. There he devoted his remaining years creating a permanent record of the passing Western frontier in pen and ink, and sculpture–a duty he felt he must fulfill. E. R. Edgerton quoted Frank in his article, *Makes Solid History of Frontier Days* (circa 1917), as:

> I am not lonesome here with my family and my work. If only I could write the old days into a permanent niche where time could not steal them–if only I could tell of those days as they were, so that men would appreciate them and not forget, I'd be satisfied with life. My aim is to try to tell and not to cheat in the telling; to perhaps lend firelight, but in lending it, keep from drifting from off my chosen range.

Linderman's best known books, perhaps, are the classic first person accounts of two Crow Indians recorded in *American: The Life Story of a Great Indian, Plenty-coups, Chief of the Crows* (1930) and in *Red Mother* (1932). Another popular publication of Crow legends is *Old Man Coyote* (1932).

Linderman was a keen observer of the customs and environment, and obtained firsthand knowledge of plainsmen, mountaineers, Indian people, trappers, traders and miners. He learned stories of early day road agents from men who knew and hanged them. He felt compelled to make a meticulous record of that waning era in several historical novels, and he first started *The Iron Shirt* in 1918, as evidenced in an August 5, 1918 letter from Charles M. Russell to Linderman:

> Little Joe [De Yong] got a letter from one of the girls that said you are working on the Iron Shirt from what you told me I think it should be easy for you.

In 1921 Frank wrote to Chick Rossister in Sheridan that he was half done and stuck. But by November 23, 1923, again working on the manuscript, he wrote a letter to Joe (?):

> I must thank you for your letter and the description of Fort Union. I shall find need of it a little later in telling of the country 'round it. And I'm only a day's run from the old fort right now.
>
> Yes, Dave Hilger already sent me the dope I needed, but yours will come very handy, too. It isn't the same sort as the other...yours takes in more of the out of doors. The story is coming along pretty well and I'll finish it this winter easy enough.

Further research found in estate archives includes a lengthy typed text from Audubon's Journal, v. 2, p. 180-188 entitled *"DESCRIPTION OF FORT UNION, by Edwin T. Denig. July 30, 1843,"* that provided information Linderman needed for several of his books.

Novels based on historical fact were Linderman's main focus in 1920. He recorded a collection of true mining stories (many unpublished) that were told to him by the "company" doctor, O. M. Lanstrum, of Helena, Montana. In a February 5, 1920 letter he stated to Ralph Edgerton:

> I have also about finished a collection of short mining stories of the old Marysville District and the Drumlumon Mine. I may call the collection 'The Doctor and I' but as yet have not submitted them to a publisher.

One of his last major works incorporated a half dozen of these *Doctor and I* stories into *Quartzville*, a mining novel centered about the real Montana town of Marysville.

During the same period Linderman also started a story about Montana's infamous sheriff and leader of a band of road agents in the 1860s entitled *Henry Plummer*, and another, his "pet book", *Lige Mounts: Free Trapper* based on his own experiences and those of Lige Mounts, a fur trapper who was the first white man in the vicinity of Bigfork.

In 1923 Linderman came upon economic hard times. To replenish his bank account he took a sabbatical from his full time writing career for three years to become proprietor of Hotel

Kalispell. As time allowed, he worked on manuscripts, and on December 14, 1923 he wrote to his friend, Charley Russell:

> My 'Iron Shirt' isn't finished, and now I can't finish it for some time, but I will finish it someday.... Going to work out something on January 1st, and this is most likely the last letter from Goose Bay.

On December 21, 1923, Frank advised Mr. Burlingame at Scribner's Sons:

> I am obliged to abandon writing and to go back into business while yet I have chips to make the ante. My camp needs the meat. I have a novel The Iron Shirt half done. It's a tale of early fur trading days at Fort Union. But it will have to wait until I 'kill' again.

Roger Burlingame's January 7, 1924 reply was positive:

> I hope you will surely let us see 'The Iron Shirt' when you finish it, and hope you will not find it necessary to put off finishing it too long.

Poet Lew Sarett, a stimulating friend of Linderman's, wrote him in June, 1925 that: "I like the title 'The Iron Shirt.' It's magnificent, paradoxical, provocative—has everything a title should have."

In the fall of 1926 Russell wrote his last letter to Frank, saying: "I'm glad you are getting along with Iron Shirt. I think it will win."

Thus encouraged, Linderman submitted The Iron Shirt to Scribner's Sons, and they replied on October 4, 1926:

> We have read as promptly as possible your manuscript, 'The Iron Shirt,' and are free to say that it 'goes against the grain' to have to return it to you, as we value our association too sincerely to regard with anything but regret any interruption of it... It seems to us, however, to belong in a class of fiction that just now is a little difficult to get a hearing for, the current competition being extremely exacting and of not only a volume but of a character too different in spirit and appeal to make successful headway against. The interest of your story

seems to us in the main the interest of quiet charm and atmosphere, historic color and pioneering data, the picture of the
frontier full of verisimilitude and real value, but the whole in-
sufficiently dramatized by its romantic element to make its
material background and its action (save at intervals) striking....
The plot being exotic as well as 'old-fashioned' and as an 'ex-
pedient' artificial and the narrative 'realistic' and natural, the
elements seem welded rather than fused. We fear we should be
unable to find our own interest in it shared by the somewhat
heedless and pampered public....

Such a rejection caused Frank to sour on a work he thought
important, but on November 15, 1926 he wrote to his daughters:

I'm working on the stories and I'm in the middle of one
long yarn I don't like. If it were not for its why feature (why
Indians had blue eyes) I'd throw it out. But that why is worth-
while, I guess.

However, when demand was great for more "Lige" stories,
Linderman abandoned submitting *The Iron Shirt* to publishers and
incorporated several of it's pages in *Beyond Law* (1933), as a sequel
to *Lige Mounts: Free Trapper*.

Two of Linderman's three daughters were college students at
the time he seriously started his writing career. Wilda (with a focus
in teaching) and Verne (majoring in creative writing and journal-
ism), often critiqued or helped edit his work, and their comments
are evident on manuscript copies. Wilda Linderman, when she
was in her late eighties in 1981, stated that she was always sorry
her father abandoned *The Iron Shirt*, as she thought it was a much
better story than *Beyond Law*.

Fourteen books were published in Linderman's lifetime. From
his own personal experience in the world of nature, Frank wrote
two animal stories: *Stumpy*, (for the Junior Literary Guild) about
the habits of a chipmunk, and an unpublished manuscript, *Big Jinny*,
illustrated by Elizabeth Lochrie. In 1934 Linderman wrote to Dick
Walsh (John Day Company) that he had "finished typing a kid's
story, the autobiography of a grizzly bear (Big Jinny tells her own
story) that contains much information not generally known."

In the mid 1930's Linderman wrote *Wolf and the Winds* (1986),
a historical novel based on the life of a Gros Ventre Indian friend,

and considered it his finest work. The *Iron Shirt* is the sixth posthumously published Linderman book. Frank was first a poet, and more than 200 poems, several manuscripts of Indian legends, historical novels, short stories, personal letters and lectures remain to be published. Some day these will reveal more personal experiences of Frank Bird Linderman, and of the vanishing frontier life he sought to save in pen and ink.

Frank Linderman's German and Scottish ancestry, his own frontier experiences, historical studies, and his wife's avid interest in reading mysteries no doubt stimulated him to write *The Iron Shirt*. It is a novel of adventure and mystery that transports the reader from ancient Scotland to a trip up the Missouri River to Fort Union in 1833 aboard the American Fur Company's steamship, *Yellow Stone*. The company of travelers includes young Donald McLeod, new chief clerk for The American Fur Company, and true life characters naturalist Prince Maximilian from Germany, and Swiss artist Karl Bodmer. On board is young Miss Jane Strongford, traveling companion to Maximilian's niece. Miss Strongford searches, as her ancestors have, to find a hidden half-crest that will enable her to claim an ancestral castle, stores of gold and a fiefdom in Scotland. Angus Cameron, a villain who boards the *Yellow Stone* as it steams up the Missouri, tries to solve the same mystery as Miss Strongford, so he can claim her hand and thus her ancestors' fiefdom. Does this somehow solve the mystery of *why* an Indian they meet has *blue eyes*?

While fickle tastes affected acceptance of Linderman's historical novels in his lifetime, today's readers appreciate his contributions in saving the old West's vanishing cultural history. Linderman wrote to Harry R. Cunningham on June 28, 1922 that, "Nobody can tell what an author or his books can do until time has juggled both...."

In January 1930, while Frank was in New York negotiating several publishing contracts with John Day Company, he wrote his son-in-law, Roy Waller: "I'm as full of the old Northwest as a toad is of warts, and I want to tell it my own way, and now I will."

The Iron Shirt is indeed a unique creation written in Frank Bird Linderman's *own way*. It is the only historical *mystery* he wrote before his death in 1938.

Sarah Waller Hatfield
Granddaughter of Frank Bird Linderman.
Goose Bay, Flathead Lake, Montana.

The Steamboat "Yellow Stone" leaving St. Louis, 1832.

THE CAST

Donald McLeod–In *The Iron Shirt Foreword,* a fur trader, age 65– In *The Iron Shirt,* chief clerk for American Fur Company at Fort Union, age 21

J. D. Frederickson–In the *Foreword,* Associate editor of a large Philadelphia daily newspaper

J. D. F., Jr.–In the *Foreword,* J. D. Frederickson's son

Kenneth McLeod–Secretary Treasurer of American Fur Company–Father of Donald McLeod

Mary McLeod–Kenneth McLeod's deceased wife–Donald McLeod's mother

Duncan McDougal–President of American Fur Company–Close friend of Kenneth McLeod

Lord John Strongford–Fourth in line since Bannockburn and Lord of Strongford Castle and fief in Scotland

Bannockburn–Where first Strongford won his fief with a seat at Strongford

Strongford Castle–Ancient castle in Scotland

Duncan Ross–Keeper of Strongford Castle

The Moor's Shirt–Lord John Strongford's armour shirt of fine chain mail

Charles Strongford–Lord John Strongford's only son

Andrew Strongford–Lord John Strongford's only brother

Thomas Strongford–Husband of Mary Campbell Strongford– Father of Jane Strongford–Direct kin of Andrew Strongford

Mary Campbell Strongford–Wife of Thomas Strongford–Mother of Jane Strongford

Jane Strongford–Only daughter of Thomas and Mary Campbell Strongford

Lord Merlin Cameron–Greater Lord to north of Strongford fief in Scotland

Lord Colin Cameron–Son of Lord Merlin Cameron

Angus Merlin Colin Cameron–Nephew of Lord Colin Cameron, grandson of Lord Merlin Cameron

Hawkins–Angus Merlin Colin Cameron's man

Ely Whitney–White trapper

Medicine-coat–Blue-eyed Sioux Indian at Fort Union

Strikes-the-enemy–Gros Ventre Indian

Prince Maximilian of Wied–Great naturalist and hunter from House of Wied, Germany

Hans–Prince Maximilian's servant

Mrs. Margarete Doeffner–Niece of Prince Maximilian

Karl Bodmer–Swiss artist traveling with Prince Maximilian

Northwest Fur Company–In Canada

Hudson's Bay Company–In Canada

American Fur Company–In the United States

Yellow Stone–American Fur Company steamship

Captain Crook–Captain of the *Yellow Stone*

Sandy Campbell–Old American Fur Company Engineer

Captain Burwin–In charge of Fort Leavenworth

Trapper–American Fur company steamship

Chippewa–Steamship–Name of an Indian tribe

Arickara or *'Rees*–Name of an Indian tribe

Fort Union–Located on Missouri River

Sooty–Blacksmith at Fort Union

Tallow–Sooty's dog

Dunshire House–In St. Louis

Eliphut–Mr. Dunshire's man

Old Mose–Mr. Dunshire's slave

THE IRON SHIRT

Fort Union, Mouth of the Yellowstone, 1832.

Foreword

I t was the year of the great Centennial Exposition in Philadelphia when I was living in a small, but very comfortable hotel on the city's outskirts, that I met Mr. Donald McLeod. He, like thousands of other Americans, had come to the Exposition, not so much to see the sights it presented, as to acquaint himself with that portion of his native land which had been the nation's cradle. I came to know him quite intimately inasmuch as, once he had established himself in attractive rooms opposite mine, he always returned to those quarters after his travels to other areas which had figured in the country's early history.

I had seen him when he came first to the hotel. It was in the twilight of evening, and the gas was lighted. I remember that I had at once attributed some of the features about him which had so attracted me to the lights, but tall, very erect, and thin as a wafer, he did attract me. Indeed I am sure he would have attracted anybody, especially if one saw him wearing his high beaver hat which made him appear taller and thinner than the popular caricatures of Uncle Sam, and which with his snow-white mustache and goatee did seem to mark him as an extraordinary individual. Besides, he carried a heavy cane that had a round knob of gold for a head. Remember that I have said he *carried* a cane. Mr. Donald McLeod never deigned to use his cane while walking, he never swung it idly when he stood, nor toyed with it when he sat. He carried it, always, head down, beneath his left arm like a weapon, and if it ever touched the ground, pure accident occasioned the touching. It was as much a part of his careful toilet as his close-fitting frock coat, and he would as readily have trailed one as the other in the dirt of the city's streets. And he wore boots, which style had passed in Philadelphia. I could sometimes distinguish their tops beneath his trouser legs when he sat down, but he would not have been himself without them, nevertheless.

But even without these peculiarities, and they were just that, I believe his eyes would have attracted anybody's attention. They were gray, and piercing for a man of his evident years, and they were confidently cool without being cold. Set rather deeply beneath brows white as his hair, they missed nothing–nobody, and yet after measuring you, they left you the feeling of a fair appraisement. I needed not to be told that he was genuine, and a gentleman, nor that he had seen stirring times. I would have wagered that he had succeeded where success had required great judgment and personal power, and that he could not abide inactivity even now.

I was then associate editor of a large daily newspaper, and utterly alone in the city. My wife had passed away a year before, and our only child, a son, was away at school, so that at first it may have been my situation which lent interest in Mr. McLeod. Anyway, I burned to know him, but he was older than I by more than a score of years, and his bearing, while neither naughty nor vainglorious, was diffident. A fortnight passed before there was occasion.

He had just returned from Valley Forge. I met him in the corridor when he was about to unlock the door to his apartment, and he bowed, pleasantly.

"I have missed you," I said, honestly, glad of my opportunity.

"Have you, indeed?" he smiled, the heavy cane as usual under his arm.

"You left very early this morning, and I had determined to ask you to ride today with a friend and me," I told him.

I saw that he was pleased. "I am sure that I should have accepted, sir," he said, opening his door. "I am a stranger in your city, and being a garrulous old man I require companions, I find. Have you dined, sir?" he asked. "My name is McLeod, and if you have not dined and have no engagement I shall feel honored if you will be my guest for dinner, Mr. ——"

"Frederickson," I supplied, and we shook hands.

"No, sir, I have not dined, and you have delighted me with your proposal, Mr. McLeod," I said, looking forward to a pleasant visit with him.

"I thank you, Mr. Frederickson," he said. "I shall be ready in a few moments. Come in, please," he invited, laying his hat and cane on a table, and lighting the gas.

"You will find this chair very comfortable," he bowed, showing me a rocker by the table, and when I sat down, he excused himself to go into his bedroom.

I could feel him. The apartment, itself, had taken on an air that was his. I could see his trunk in the bedroom. It belonged to my grandfather's generation, and was lost here in the City of Brotherly Love. The gaslight shone down on the bright knob of his cane, and I thought that a pair of the flint-locked dueling pistols might well have been there, too. Even his gray gloves, not tossed carelessly beside the hat, but placed exactly together across the cane, were expressive of calm preparedness and precision. I could almost hear someone, in the gray light of morning, intoning one, two, three, fire! And what was the round, flat thing on the table? I leaned forward. A snuffbox; a beautifully ornate snuffbox, black and smooth as a shining jet, and with inlays of gold around its jeweled rim. I ached to examine it. Dare I?

I could hear his stirring in his bedroom. If he had stepped out wearing a powdered wig, a skirted velvet coat, knee-breeches and a sword, I should not have been surprised. The light was still burning in his bedroom. I would chance a look at the snuffbox! Rising, I picked it up, its velvety surface and weight attesting its price. "Exquisite," I breathed, turning it to better light that I might read this inscription set in golden letters on its lid:

"Donald–
    Better be a dupe to faith than a grinning skeptic.
    No tale is true to incredulity, and the incredulous
    are never pioneers.
                              –Jane"

His light went out in the bedroom. Guiltily I laid the snuffbox on the table, and sat down, the old aphorisms running in my mind. I felt that I had willfully peeped at privacy. But I was curious now. Who was Jane, I wondered? Had she sought thus aphoristically to guide him in his youth? No, the inscription was on a snuffbox. She could not have been his mother. Jane had lived to see him touch his goal. Her words, set in gold, had been inspired by his attainments. She had taken them from his own measure, I felt certain.

"I have kept you waiting." My host came straight to the table. "Now for amends," he smiled, picking up his hat and cane.

I saw the snuffbox disappear into his side pocket, as tucking the cane under his arm, head downward, he reached to turn out the gas. "Now, then," he said, cheerily, and we were off.

He gave his hat to the man at the door before we entered the dining room, but he kept his cane, I noticed, and I was secretly glad, since to me it was part of him, and I wanted it with us.

"I have enjoyed a meal or two here, Mr. Frederickson," he said, laying his cane on the seat of an extra chair at our table, its heavy knob away from him. Somehow it always reminded me of a ready weapon.

Reaching into his breast pocket he drew out a pair of spectacles. "I can no longer see without their aid," he sighed. "I'm sixty-five, sir. Now, let me see," picking up the card on the table.

He knew exactly how to order a good dinner, and an hour had gone when I remembered that as yet I knew nothing whatever about my host, excepting that his home was in St. Louis, and that he knew all there was to learn about me. He had seemed impressed when I told him my vocation, and I had thought that he wished to discuss my work, but something had turned the talk away.

Twice after this I dined in his company, and each time I got closer to him until he finally fell to talking of himself, as I hoped he would. He had been a fur trader on the great plains of the Northwest, and my deep interest in his adventures pleased him very noticeably.

"Why do you not write what you have been telling me tonight?" I asked him, over our coffee.

"I have, that is, I have written a story of my first visit to Fort Union," he said, embarrassed by the admission.

"Where is it? What have you done with it?" I leaned over the table in my anxiety. The tales which he had told me that evening had fired my blood.

He was drawing back into himself. I could see this. "Where is the story, Mr. McLeod?" I asked again, hoping I might keep him going, at least.

"I think I might find it. I did nothing with it. I am a fur trader, not a writer of books, Mr. Frederickson."

He looked at his watch. "Nearly twelve o'clock!" he said, surprised. "I have kept you from your bed, sir."

I never saw him again. When I came to the hotel on the next evening the clerk handed me a letter and a package which Mr. McLeod had left for me. The letter expressed deep regard for my friendship, and promised another to be written from his home. It explained his hurried departure from Philadelphia, and mentioned the package in exactly these words: "I have left you my story. I have given it to you to do with as you please." It ended with a promise of another visit to Philadelphia.

But even while I was reading his letter he was lying dead—killed in a wrecked train over in the state of Ohio.

J.D.F.

—————————

The foregoing, in my Father's handwriting of fifty years ago, I found only last fall in an old trunk in the attic. It was folded with the manuscript of *The Iron Shirt*, which story has in no way been amended or abridged by either my father or myself.

J.D.F., Jr.

CHAPTER ONE

I can see the steamboat *Yellow Stone* even now, when I close my eyes. How the smoke from her stacks thrilled me with promise of wild adventure on that early April day in 1833 when, with a letter from my father to Mr. Duncan McDougal, Esquire, safe in my pocket, I boarded her at the St. Louis levee. She was bound for Fort Union, six and a half miles above the mouth of the Yellowstone on the Missouri River, with trade goods and supplies for the traders there. In a certain way I felt myself to be a part of her consignment, since I was being sent as Chief Clerk to Mr. Duncan McDougal, President of the American Fur Company, always referred to by my father as "the Factor."

My position as Chief Clerk had been arranged by my father with Mr. Duncan McDougal upon the latter's visit to St. Louis earlier in the spring, and while I felt elation over so great an opportunity I, nevertheless, had been a little miffed because I had not been consulted beforehand. I felt that I had known Mr. Duncan McDougal all my life, having been born in St. Louis where he often paid visits to my father's house, but only once in my remembrance, and that lately, had he ever seemed to take any notice of me whatsoever there.

It was on the occasion of my twenty-first birthday in April, just past, that when I had been formally introduced to Mr. Duncan McDougal by my father he had appeared to notice me. I did not know at that time I was being appraised by the great man, who I thought evinced more than ususal concern in the state of my health, my education and my general industriousness, all of which was attributed to the close friendship existing between my father and him.

My father and Mr. Duncan McDougal had been warm friends since early manhood when both had entered the employ of the Northwest Fur Company, where I doubt not both experienced dangerous and sometimes wicked service, since the warfare between their employers and the men of the great Hudson's Bay Company was carried very far indeed, so far that my father and Mr. Duncan McDougal, sitting beside our fire, often whispered of it, nudging each other over their Scotch whisky. More than once when I was young, too young they believed to understand or remember, I had heard them till my blood ran cold at their reminiscing. Man, I could not sleep of nights for a time afterward for thinking of what even to my child's mind were wicked deeds done at awful risk of the law. And yet, when their heads were close together over their toddies, in the library with the fire sparkling beneath the portrait of my paternal grandfather, there was something fascinating about it all—something that held me huddled upon the slippery horsehair sofa across the room in spite of my grandfather's cold eyes which seemed always to disapprove of my presence when my father and Mr. Duncan McDougal talked of the fur trade. How I struggled to not look up at my grandfather—to watch the firelight that streaked across the polished floor through the wide doorway into the hall where the round brass pendulum of the tall clock caught and reflected it with a flush every alternate swing. I well knew that every minute on the black sofa would provide new and exquisite material for wilder dreams, but so keen was I to become a fur trader I even then dared to dread my mother's coming to pack me off to bed. But whenever the clock whirred to strike, shivers ran up my back, and to save my life I could not keep my eyes from meeting grandfather's.

Both my father and Mr. Duncan McDougal, quitting the Northwest Fur Company (I know not why) had come out of Canada together, and in St. Louis had invested their store of money, saved from their erstwhile service, in the new American Fur Company of which Mr. Duncan McDougal soon became the head, and my father, Mr. Kenneth McLeod, who was more given to the counting of money than collecting furs in the wilderness, its Secretary and Treasurer. Both had prospered, and both were held in high esteem in St. Louis where my father married and set up a home in perfect keeping with his high position in the great and prosperous American Fur Company.

My mother, a gentle woman of finer clay than my father, whose devoted partner she was, knew that he had destined me to follow him in the fur trade, and while not seeking to turn me against such a course she nevertheless cherished a hope that I would choose to enter the practice of law instead. But when I was ten years old a team of pacers belonging to Judge Whitehall, who lived next door, ran away with Mrs. Whitehall and my mother, and from that day until she died two years later, my mother was an invalid, patient and loving to the end. Perhaps if she had lived I might not have entered the fur trade, for I loved her dearly, as did my father who remained a widower for the rest of his life. Anyhow, because of a promise she exacted from him I was sent to school in New Orleans where I stayed for three years, returning to enter my father's office in St. Louis.

I have been reared in the atmosphere of the fur trade. As a child with mates I had played at hide and seek in the dim warehouses among the hundreds of odorous bales of buffalo hides and tongues shipped to us from up the great river, and always with a deep feeling that here in every bale, every dried and twisted tongue, was a story to stir the blood if only it could be told. I knew the idiom—even some of the tricks of the trade before I could understand them and, like my father, believed the fur trade to be the most lucrative of all human endeavors, and the most honorable. The first, by long years of experience, I have proven to be true; the other, like many borrowed beliefs, is true only so far as conscience is permitted to *save* honor. In my day conscience seldom succeeded in finding its way so far up the Missouri as Fort Union, so that experience has obliged me to alter my earlier opinion respecting the fur trade there.

My father had sent my baggage aboard the *Yellow Stone*, and at the breakfast table where, as usual I sat opposite him, I was suddenly conscious of the loneliness which must be his when I was gone. I had no brothers or sisters to take my place at home. There would be nobody in the house with him excepting old Andrew and his wife who were not slaves, and therefore might take themselves off if they wished to leave him. My father had never owned a slave, and indeed hated the institution of slavery with a bitterness that had made him a few enemies in St. Louis. It had never before occurred to me that anything could affect my father. But now I was troubled with the thought that he would be alone. He must have seen dejection in my countenance and no doubt attributed it to fear of being put upon my own resources, since he began to talk interestingly of the voyage of the *Yellow Stone* and to glorify adventure on the plains.

"You will have very distinguished company, Donald," he added, eagerly, as though he would prevent my speaking in opposition to the venture. "No less than a Prince and ladies will go with you into the wilderness!"

My father seldom joked. There was only seriousness in his eyes now. "A Prince and ladies, sir?" I inquired, astonished.

"Ay, Donald, lad, a Prince and ladies," he nodded, gravely pouring the tea. "And there be a bit of deep mystery in the baggage, I doubt not, sin' the lass, Jane Strongford, hersel', be one o' the party," he added, the Scotch burr in his words betraying, I well knew, a guarded interest.

The word "mystery" as used by my father, roused me out of the discomfort occasioned by my thoughts of leaving him alone. I even, for the moment, forgot the prince in my sudden interest in the girl my father spoke of as mysterious. "And are you acquainted with the lady, sir?" I asked, as old Andrew withdrew and closed the door.

"Ay, lad, in a way," he nodded, his blue eyes narrowing as they did when his mind was shrewdest. "I knew her father, ye ken, and her mother, before her, Donald—in Scotland."

Would he go on, or must I content myself, and wait another time? I knew my father well. His aversion for inquisitiveness was extremely deep, and he would go out of his way to defeat it. If he was minded now to tell me what he knew I ached to learn—about the "mysterious baggage" and the lady—he would do so. I drained and passed my teacup, determined not to press him though curiosity should consume me.

"A pretty, saucy lass, her mother," he said, pouring my tea.

I scarcely breathed as I took the cup. "She was a Campbell," he went on, and I knew I should hear the story to the end.

"*Mary* Campbell," he said, softly, as though the name "Mary" were a crown. (My mother's name was Mary.)

His face softened into a smile. "Mary Campbell would ha' been a bra one in the old days," he said, slowly. "She always turned and spat spitefully when she pronounced the name *McDonald*. No Campbell ever hated a McDonald more than did Mary. She married

Thomas Strongford, and it is of the Strongfords the story is, so we'll leave the Campbells in their modest house to peep at the ancient castle of the Strongfords where, as a bride, Mary Campbell went to live."

"Strongford Castle was a picture, lad; a little more, since it had fallen into ruin a hundred years before Mary Campbell went there to live. Long, ay, very long before that even, the Strongford line had been broken—its estates lost by the mad, romantic act of the head of the house who was fourth of the line since Bannockburn, where the first Strongford won his fief with seat at Strongford. In my day the folk about marked distance by the old castle, and it was by the castle's towers that my grandsire swore, solemnly, that happenings of his youth were true. Strongford Castle was a ghost of perished grandeur, lad, and venerated by the aged ones about it as only old folk can venerate and respect a past which is ever nearer to them than to irresponsible youth.

"Lord John Strongford, fourth of the line since Bannockburn, had one son, Charles, and one brother, Andrew, both of whom became involved in a quarrel with Lord John through the agency of the king, himself, it was claimed, although nobody in my time knew the true story of the trouble between them. I only know what I learned from Mary Campbell Strongford, herself, and a painted picture in the old castle. The picture, which hung in the great hall near the staircase, was a life-size portrait of Lord John, fourth of the Strongford line, in armor, a grim-visaged, bearded Scot whose high, narrow forehead, closely set gray eyes and sensitive nose prepared one for the verse painted on the canvas with his crest.

"The verse ran thus:

'A quarrel, and by ye king arranged,
Hath mine from me for aye estranged;
But pride hath teeth; our line be old;
Let fate, not I, its future mould.
My father's crest I now divide;
One-half I wear, one-half I hide.
(Armed lions couchant, twain,
Proper, gules, vert champagne)
And who of brother's blood, or mine,
Man or maid of Strongford's line,

Shall find ye half of Strongford's crest,
That man or maid shall claim the rest
Of Strongford's lands, her castle-hold
Her vassals, and her store of gold.
Let none complain, nor cry "Unfair,"
Since fate alone thus names my heir.'

"'Twas thus it ran. And 'twas signed, mind, 'John, Fourth of the line of Bannockburn.'

"As though the verse were not enough to prove the man mad, a golden chain, piercing the canvas so as to appear to encircle his neck held half the divided crest like a locket below Lord John's sandy beard–a silver shield divided lengthwise, and with only one couchant lion upon it. Gad! I could have choked him for beggaring the like of Mary Campbell. (Though 'tis true she might never have been a Strongford but for the madness of Lord John.)"

He stirred his tea until the spoon rattled in the cup. I feared he would not continue. "Was the hidden half of the Strongford crest ever found, Father?" I asked, breathlessly.

"There's the rub, lad, there's the rub. I do not know; nor did Mary Campbell, although she believed it *might* have been found by Lord John's son, Charles, as big a fool as his father, if Mary Campbell's story of him be true.

"Mary got the tale from her husband, Thomas Strongford, and he from his father. The story is old as the picture, lad, and nobody knows if it be true or false. But have it, as I got it, garbled and with pieces gone, and make what you can of it.

"'Twas said," he continued, "Lord John, after dividing the Strongford crest, swore never again to wear armor, nor to couch a lance, come weal or woe. In his mad tantrums he had the portrait painted and rigged with the half-crest, as I have said. And then, that all men might know that he was forever done with arms, the madman placed the wooded manikin of a knight in the great hall of the castle, clad from head to foot in his armor–the armor of Lord John. I never saw the figure. It was gone long before my time, but 'tis said the shirt of chain mail underneath the corslet was so fine that it was known throughout Scotland and England as 'the Moor's shirt.' None there was that was like it. None so fine, or so impierceable as 'the Moor's shirt.' And wrought upon its breast was a star and crescent, or some such emblem foreign to any we know as European.

"No doubt but that it came from the East, but of the Holy Wars, most like; filched there, or won honorably by a Strongford in battle with some infidel prince. God knows. They were a hardy, canny lot that fought for the cross, and not over-honest; though fight they would, and did. Ay, they surely did. However the Strongfords came by the shirt, it was true that no other knight in Scotland or England had one the like of it, and that Moorish, Saracen, or whatnot, it was known by all men as 'the Moor's shirt.'

"Within the year after the effigy was rigged by Lord John somebody entered the castle at night. Whoever it was he was no common thief, since he disturbed nothing but the Moor's shirt, which he took away with him. It has never been seen since that night, though the thief left something which he intended to be taken as a clue to his identity, whether a true or a false one, nobody knows. The dagger of Charles Strongford, Lord John's only son, was left sticking in the breast of the dismantled manikin. No man about the castle had seen Charles Strongford for months (or so they testified). He has never been seen since. But Mary Campbell Strongford believed that 'twas he who stole the Moor's shirt, and that he may have found the hidden half of the crest, and scorning his father with the intensity of a half-wit carried it and the 'Moor's shirt' away with him.

"Mary, romantic beneath her witchery, had only wild stories to conjure with. Many a day I've seen her and auld Duncan Ross, the keeper, sitting by the moat in the shade of the castle and kenned what was going on between them. Those who have been long associated with an institution *must* know more that concerns it than strangers, even though they pretend a good deal. Auld Duncan, white of beard and bent like a dried herring was superstitious as a fishwife, and as garrulous. Born there, as was his father before him, he was an oracle to Mary Campbell. And Man! Man! The tales he told her, (as a Strongford, mind) were enough to turn her queer.

"But there is sense in her belief that Charles Strongford went to the foreign wars, and was killed there, since he never returned to Scotland. And if it was Charles, himself, who left the dagger sticking in the breast of Lord John's manikin, then it was he who stole the 'Moor's shirt.' Ay, and he may have found the hidden half of the family crest, as Mary believed.

"Of course, she had no proof that he did. 'Twas auld Duncan put the notion in her head, auld Duncan Ross, whose hooked nose had been in every nook and cranny within a mile around, and who was yet searching for a silver bit Lord John had hid before auld Duncan's great-grandsire was born. Man! Man! What a game the old devil, Lord John, played them a'. No doubt auld Duncan only searched where a Ross had searched a hundred times before, and to as much purpose. But those who are born to a hobby will ride it, and riding alone, as they must, makes them crotchety and queer as dizzy ducks. Quick youth may snatch a morsel of inspiration for a song or story from such as auld Duncan Ross, but if it sits too long by their fires it will gain no good. It must listen, laugh in its sleeve, and be off.

"Weak heads are often on strong bodies. Maybe 'tis the head that wears men out. When the back had sweat the body will rest, but used to labor, the mind knows not when the sun has set. Lord John lived to be old. When he died the Strongford fief passed out of Strongford hands, and remained so for more than a generation, when claim for it was again made by a Strongford, blood kin of Lord John's brother, Andrew, who, after the quarrel had gone to Germany. The claim was easily established so far as blood relationship was concerned, and at last a settlement was made with Thomas Strongford, the new claimant, which included the old castle and the stony lands about it. The Lords held that without the hidden half of the Strongford crest the expressed will of Lord John Strongford, the head of the House, a knight and noble, could not be carried out, and that *until it was found and produced*, the fief, or that greater portion of it not now given over to the new claimant must remain escheated to Lord Merlin Cameron, whose lands adjoined the Strongford fief on the North, and who was the greater Lord. Great or small, he was no fool, and at once offered ten thousand pounds for the hidden half of the Strongford crest in order that quiet title to the escheated fief might forever rest with the Cameron. His offer, attested by the Lords then, stands now, so that to find and produce what old Lord John hid away is worth a hundred packs of prime beaver, lad. But 'tis gone beyond discovery, or the Strongford who came out of Germany to the old castle, or his heirs, or the Rosses, or Mary Campbell, herself, would have found it.

"It was into this family, the new claimant's family, though of pure Strongford stock, that Mary Campbell married. And 'twas she who took the half-crest from the portrait of Lord John in the castle hall and carried it wherever she went till she died. (That was long after I had come to America.)"

My father poured more tea, and sipped it. "I doubt not that this lass, Jane Strongford, is carrying it now," he said, thoughtfully, "and that she is looking, as her mother looked, to find the missing half wherever she goes. It has crazed many a man since Lord John's time, and it made even Mary Campbell a little queer. No doubt 'tis the same with Jane, God help her. And that's the story, lad, an old Scotch tale that many a granny has told over her toddy by the fire at night, and in the very shadow of the old castle itself. Thomas Strongford is dead, and Mary, and auld Duncan Ross, though mayhap another of that name is watching over the ruin and turning stones to find what his father could not, while the devil roasts Lord John."

The tale, so full of the romance of feudal days in the land of my father, impressed me more than I would have him know. "May I ask, sir, by what circumstances does Miss Jane Strongford travel with the prince and his party in so wild a land as the upper river?"

"Ay, 'tis a natural question, Donald, and any man would ask it, but it is not difficult to answer.

"When Lord John's brother, Andrew, went to Germany during the quarrel that played the devil, he set up a house there—in Wied, it was—on the Rhine, and not far from Coblenz. The province, or principality, or whatever they call it there, was Wied, and the ruling House was of that name. Andrew, through services rendered in war, firmly established himself in the friendship of the House of Wied, and ever since that time a Strongford has been held high in its esteem wherever or whenever met. When Mary Campbell died (and 'twas not long after her husband, Thomas, passed away) Jane, her only child, being practically penniless, went to Germany where she has lived with her father's relatives in Neuwied ever since. She has come here now as traveling companion to the niece of the German aristocrat Prince Maximilian Alexander Philipp of Wied-Neuwied, a former Prussian army officer and a trained naturalist. He is a great traveler, and a fine man he is, lad, and a great hunter all over the world. He comes now to study the primitive character of the natural face of North America, and then to write a book, and has brought a skilled illustrator with him.

"Mr. Astor wrote me from New York that they were coming, and I made ready for them as best I could. The Prince and his

party, which includes a Swiss artist named Karl Bodmer, are the
Company's guests, and while the ladies will not stay at Fort Union,
but will return on the boat to St. Louis, the Prince, with his painter,
will remain at the Fort as long as pleases him." My father looked at
his watch.... "Lad, 'tis time we moved toward the levee," he said,
rising.

We did not hurry, but walked leisurely toward the levee, my
father chatting lightly of the buffalo hunting on the endless plains.
It was like him to keep to himself the news of the coming of Prince
Maximilian and his party. Perhaps it was wise, too, since he must
have feared that at the last moment I would decide to remain
in the office at the big warehouse. Now, after he had told me, I was
so full of the story and the promise of adventure, that the smoke
from the *Yellow Stone's* stacks only thrilled me with delight and
anticipation.

Chapter Two

T he *Yellow Stone*, although built expressly for the freight of the fur trade was more pretentious than the other steamboats, the *Assiniboine* and *Trapper*, belonging to the American Fur Company, having rather comfortable staterooms, six on either side of the saloon, so that considering the time and circumstances, the Prince's party had ample accommodations on board her.

My father presented me to Prince Maximilian and the ladies, and Mr. Bodmer, the artist, in the saloon where the party was already reading or lounging when we were announced by Captain Crook of the *Yellow Stone*. I had felt a little secret dread of meeting a man so high and mighty in the world as the Prince. My reluctance, however, had been no match for my curiosity, and now in his presence I felt my embarrassment slipping away. He was so apparently happy and eager that his very manner seemed to deny any distinction over the rest of the group in the saloon, and in a minute we were all talking and laughing easily. I felt immeasurably relieved especially when the Prince welcomed me as 'a very valuable addition to his party,' and graciously included me in his conversation with my father. He was short and squat, a man of about fifty, a little gray at the temples, and with very earnest brown eyes that were everywhere, yet direct enough, and unafraid. He held a feathered fedora in his hand as he popped one question after another to us. He could scarcely wait for complete answers, but seized what his scientific mind needed. I do not mean that he monopolized my father, for he did not, and when I heard the deck hands covering the hatch my father easily found opportunity to excuse himself and to talk only to Miss Jane Strongford. "I knew her mother in Scotland, Your Highness, and there is now but a moment left before you sail," he explained, bowing himself away from the Prince.

The Prince, also bowing, walked a few steps toward the window, engaging me in conversation, so that quite naturally I followed him, thinking him a good sort to put value upon my youthful opinions. "I have been informed, Mr. McLeod, that American plainsmen are marvelous marksmen. Have you witnessed their shooting?" he asked eagerly.

"Only at targets, Your Highness, in St. Louis where often during the fall and winter time there are matches. A turkey's head at seventy-five yards is the usual mark, then."

"At seventy-five yards? Astonishing! I should like to witness such marksmanship," he declared with enthusiasm. "But then," he added, with a shrug of his stocky shoulders, "the American has done much to perfect the sporting rifle, and therefore it is quite natural that he should be more efficient in its use than others. A turkey's head at seventy-five yards," he repeated, wonderingly. "Such marksmanship is splendid!"

I thought that he half disbelieved the possibility of such accuracy, and that he was anxious to hide his doubt from me until he could investigate further. I began wondering if his compliment to American rifle makers was sincere, but in another minute I knew he was incapable of pretense. I heard something strike the wall over my head, and then fall to the floor. Stepping back a little I discovered a large beetle lying on its back, its prickly legs kicking out in all directions in a wild effort to right itself.

"Ah!" Prince Maximilian stooped quickly, and picked up the bug, his interest in rifles instantly transferred to the kicking beetle which he held lightly between his thumb and finger.

"Margarete," he called, like a boy delighted by a new toy. "See, Margarete, the *Carabidae* are also here!"

Mrs. Doeffner, who had been talking animatedly with Mr. Bodmer and Captain Crook of the *Yellow Stone*, excused herself, and hurried to her uncle, the Prince. "Yes, Your Highness," she bowed, "and what have you found?"

She bent over his hand. "How exquisite!" she exulted. "*Where* did you find it?"

"Here on the floor. It must have flown in through the door. I heard it strike the wall and, looking down, I saw it on the floor."

He turned the bug to the light, and I saw that its shining back was vivid violet-green bordered with red.

"A large family, the *Carabidae*, Margarete," he said, thoughtfully. "This is indeed a fine specimen of the larger variety, fully one and a half inches. He is a killer of caterpillars, this fellow. See, he is gorgeous in his colorings, and armed. Is he not beautiful, Margarete?"

"Yes, indeed, Your Highness; very beautiful. Shall you retain it? Shall I call Hans? Or shall I prepare it for you?" she suggested, eagerly.

"No, no. Hans is a bungler. His fingers are clumsy. I will, myself, attend to this specimen. Come, Margarete, you shall assist me–If you will excuse us, Mr. McLeod," he bowed.

And then, speaking happily in German together they went into the Prince's stateroom with the beetle, as genuinely chummy as two persons could be. He was not at all like the prince I had imagined. He was democratic as anybody, and vitally interested, even in American bugs. I knew I should like him.

As soon as Mrs. Doeffner had quitted them Captain Crook and Mr. Bodmer had gone outside to watch the last freight come aboard, and alone now I turned to look at my father and Miss Jane Strongford who were rapt in their conversation. I thought Miss Strongford exceptionally fine looking–slender, though I could see she was not really frail, only lithesome where the German lady was stocky. She was nodding her head spiritedly as she talked with my father, who looked pleased with himself. She might easily have been a princess, I thought, and the German lady *her* companion, although the German lady was much older than Miss Strongford. My father's story of Mary Campbell had led me to expect a rather gloomy-looking young person who would probably not have much to do with the other passengers on the boat. I had expected to see in her face and bearing at once that she had turned over stones with old Duncan Ross. I had somehow imagined her to be dark and peculiar-looking, perhaps with a hook-nose, though a feminine one, like old Duncan's own. How different was my impression of the real Miss Jane Strongford who was sociable like girls I had escorted to parties in St. Louis, only more so, it seemed to me, and she had bright, abundant hair, which even if her whole manner had not been gay, would have dispelled quickly my former thoughts of a gloomy nature in her. She must have spoken to my

father of me, for he turned, smilingly, and I believe with the intention of inviting me to join them. But just then Prince Maximilian
came out of the stateroom, and as though our conversation concerning rifles had not been interrupted by the green bug, he said,
"I have been told, Mr. McLeod, that American marksmen prefer
the round ball to the slug. Is this true?"

"Yes, Your Highness. Marksmen declare the round ball to be
more accurate than the slug."

"I should think the slug, though, would carry farther, and that
its execution would be greater, with the proper charge of powder
behind it, than the round ball. Would not you?"

"Yes, undoubtedly, the slug is more efficient in killing big game
than the round ball." And just then the sun from the skylight fell
upon Miss Jane Strongford's hair, making it shine like burnished
copper. She seemed wholly radiant, and I could scarcely restrain
myself from staring openly.

"I have ordered a Hawken rifle made for me here in St. Louis.
The Hawken is famous, and I must have one of the weapons. Besides, I have ordered moulds for both the round ball and the slug
to fit it. I will show you a fine German rifle."

He stepped to the door and spoke rapidly in German to his
servant, Hans, who brought the weapon. It was a beautiful gun, I
thought, though the sights were coarse, unlike those used by our
hunters.

I said as much.

"Yes, yes. I have myself noticed that. My new Hawken will
have the regular American sights. I think them better for fine shooting."

Captain Crook, cap in hand, came into the saloon, smiling.

"All right, Captain," said my father, knowing the time had arrived for the boat to sail. "*Bon voyage*, all." He shook their hands,
and taking me by the arm drew me along with him to the gangplank. "Good bye, Donald, lad," he said, his hand on my shoulder.
"Take care of yersel', and be a man among men—a McLeod. That's
a' I ask o' ye, lad."

"I'll do my best, father," I promised. "Good bye, Sir."

"Good bye—and mind the letter, lad."

"I will, Sir."

He looked at his watch, rubbing the crystal with his thumb,
"Mister Duncan McDougal is a dour, gude, mon," he said, slowly,

and went down the gangplank to the wharf where already the lines were being cast off.

The *Yellow Stone* swung out into the stream, her wheels churning the water into white foam. We felt her quiver with the strength of her engine that like a great heart within her gave her life, and power over the Mississippi's current. My own heart leaped at the thought that now and, with the boat, I was part of the American Fur Company in the open field of its activity and that like her, I must put forth the best that was in me in its service.

Father was still standing on the levee. I waved my hat, a lump, dry and bothersome in my throat. He answered, and then as though ashamed of his show of affection, he turned away into the crowd and was quickly lost. But just when his hat disappeared among the jumble of others, I recalled the last words he had spoken: "Mister Duncan McDougal is a dour, gude, mon," he had said. Never had I heard my father use the word 'dour,' and it bothered me now.

The stream of passengers from the boat just landed was moving up the dusty street. I looked for my father, and at last discovered his tall beaver hat towering above a small man beside him as slowly they walked together, with the hurrying crowd pressing and passing them in its eagerness to reach the hotels or its homes. I waved my hat again, but my father did not see my signal of farewell, and I felt suddenly as though I had been cut off from his household, that I had in fact already begun to be a man among men as my father had demanded.

The *Yellow Stone* gave a blast from her whistle, startling me into new interest in my voyage. A steamboat was churning down the Mississippi, and as they came from the saloon to see the passing boat which to them must have been a strange craft, I heard the Prince's party speaking in German on the deck above my head. There had been no time to ask my father anything of his conversation with Miss Jane Strongford. I would not see him again for perhaps a year. I needed to talk to somebody, the oncoming boat, having whistled in answer to the *Yellow Stone's* signal, I went up the companionway to the boiler deck where upon my arrival the Germans at once changed their speech to English, and greeted me warmly.

"*Chip-pe-wa.*" Miss Jane Strongford pronounced the name of the boat nearly abreast of us, her decks piled high with bales of buffalo skins and beaver fur.

"What a pretty name!" she said, unpinning her veil and letting it stream out on the breeze, a friendly banner of soft gray, like webs of spiders in the sunshine. "What does it mean, *Chip-pe-wa,* Mr. McLeod, please? It's *so* pretty."

"*Chippewa* is the popular name of a great Indian tribe, Miss Strongford," I replied, stepping a little nearer the rail over which she was leaning. "But," I added, feeling thankful I knew so much, "*Chippewa* is a corruption of the word '*Ojibwa*' which means literally, *to roast until puckered,* and refers to the peculiar seam on their moccasins—*Les bottes savages.*"

"How interesting! Did you hear, Your Highness?" Miss Strongford asked turning to Prince Maximilian.

"I did, indeed. Have you learned to speak the language of the Indian, Mr. McLeod?"

"Only *Sioux,* Your Highness. My father engaged a *Sioux* to teach me in St. Louis. The language enables me to talk with the *Assiniboine,* also, since they are really *Sioux* with a slight tribal dialect."

"How many languages are there among the Indian tribes, and do they differ greatly, one from the other?"

"Nearly as many distinct languages as there are tribes, and they do differ greatly. But all the plains tribes use the sign language which enables them to converse quite easily one with another even though no two of them speak a word of the other's tongue. And a proficient sign-talker can say anything with his hands, which spoken words could make plain."

"Most remarkable! I should like to know how such a language became common among people speaking different tongues and so widely separated."

"I can not tell you that exactly, though probably it was necessity which brought it about. Frequent contact incident to war or barter necessitated a means of communication, and the sign-language grew little by little to be the recognized medium of conversation between strangers or enemies on the plains."

"Do you understand the sign language also, Mr. McLeod?"

"Yes, Your Highness."

"Proper names—names of persons? Could you make them known in the sign language?"

"Easily, if I knew them in *Sioux,* Your Highness."

"How would you express Miss Strongford's name to a plains Indian, for instance, please, Mr. McLeod?" The Prince smiled graciously at Miss Jane Strongford.

I felt my face grow hot, but instantly made the signs I should have used under the circumstances named by Prince Maximilian, and was more than half-pleased that I had the opportunity to do so. I am not sure that he noticed my brief embarrassment, but Miss Strongford did, and I thought I observed in her a quickened interest in the conversation of the Prince and myself.

"Interpreted literally, Mr. McLeod, what do those signs mean?"

Now I *did* blush. She might believe them flattery. She would, I thought. But holding myself against an outward show of the panic I secretly felt, I answered, "A stranger must be given a name. It must be like the sign-language itself, comprehensive, and naturally suggested by some peculiarity of hearing, expression, or personal characteristic quickly and easily discernable. The signs I made to express Miss Strongford's name mean, literally, 'Pretty Woman'."

Miss Strongford was blushing now. She laughed, putting the gray veil again over her beautiful hair.

"A pretty compliment, Miss Strongford," said the Prince, seriously. "Very, very pretty, indeed. How extremely interesting!"

I glanced quickly at his niece, deciding I would not get into deeper water. An Indian would have named her 'Fat Woman' but I should not. I would call her 'White Teeth' if he asked her sign name. But he did not ask. "How long shall we be on the boat before we reach Fort Union?" he enquired, filling his pipe with the air of one well satisfied with the world.

"The *Yellow Stone* has made the trip in forty-five days, Sir," I answered, glad to be excused from a further explanation of the sign language. "We have plenty of water now, but a month hence the river will be lower, and the boat is loaded heavily," I added.

He only shrugged his shoulders, a mannerism of his I had discovered. "There will be much to see," he smiled.

In another minute the *Yellow Stone* had turned her nose Westward, entering the great tributary of the Mississippi where at once the swifter current was noticeable. Feeling it, she seemed to slow down as though loathe to face so long a voyage into the wilderness, but like an unwilling horse held stubbornly to its task and bound to go on, began resolutely to forge ahead, the foam whitening at her bows.

Miss Jane Strongford was turned toward St. Louis. "No wonder," I thought, "when no white woman has ever been half so far up the river as Fort Union." My father had said that her mother,

Mary Campbell was a little queer, and I had gathered that the Strongfords all, were a queer, willful lot. Miss Strongford was different from any young lady I had ever known, but still I had been unable to discover that she was in any way queer. She was feminine (I remembered the gray veil). She seemed to me also to be unusually independent for a woman. She might be willful, too, but I did not think so. Rather there was a little air of decision about her that seemed to make her more charming than other young ladies. Possibly this had come about from so much traveling and being a companion, and having to adjust herself to people, and different ways of living. She had acquired a grace in doing all these things, a poise that was noticeable to strangers, and which I decided was very pleasing.

Chapter Three

 ur Congress had lately passed a law which was be-ing strictly enforced by the Federal authorities pro-hibiting the transportation of liquor to the Indian country. The American Fur Company had lost a large quantity of high wines and whiskey through seizure by United States officers in Leavenworth. Mr. Duncan McDougal, Esquire, felt that without liquor to trade with the Indians he could not successfully compete with the Hudson's Bay people who were not thus hampered in their traffic. He had openly defied the law under the belief that Senator Benton, whose power in Washington was considerable, and whose friend-ship for himself and the Company was very warm, would some-how stay the hand of authority.

My father, while acknowledging the justness of Mr. Duncan McDougal's argument against the new law, which *did* seem to give a great advantage to the British traders and which *did* seem to discriminate against Americans engaged in the fur trade, was nev-ertheless opposed to the surreptitious transportation of liquor by the American Fur Company to the plains. He maintained that so flagrant a violation of United State's law would be quickly turned against the company by its enemies, who were numerous and ex-tremely jealous, and that great disaster must eventually result there-from.

Mr. Duncan McDougal, however, had not listened, and in spite of repeated warnings by friends besides my father, men high in political affairs and deeply interested not only in the American Fur Company itself, but personally attached to Mr. Duncan McDougal by friendship, he had secretly carried liquor to Fort Union more than once since the Congress had passed the law.

Knowing all this, and that this trip would hardly be an exception, I began to speculate on what would transpire if there were liquor aboard now and the *Yellow Stone* should be stopped and searched at Fort Leavenworth.

The free-trappers and traders, slipping up the great waterway in their small boats, or traveling by land with pack animals laden with trade drink, could easily pass any point unseen, but the American Fur Company, with its steamboats, and scores of employees, loyal and disloyal, could not possibly evade the liquor law, and was therefore obliged to suffer the discrimination which these circumstances forced upon it. I was somewhat in sympathy with Mr. Duncan McDougal since, by the new law, only the American Fur Company was successfully prevented from trading liquor for fur. Like my father, I sincerely believed that to violate the statute in the wholesale manner necessary to supply our trade would speedily wreck the Company, and if the *Yellow Stone* should be searched and liquor found in cargo I had grave misgivings of the consequence of a second attempt to override the law. The swifter current of the Missouri and the white foam at the *Yellow Stone's* bows reminded me unpleasantly that we were now journeying toward Fort Leavenworth and, if Mr. Duncan McDougal had persisted and there was a supply of liquor on board, that we might have sore trouble.

I therefore excused myself from the company of Prince Maximilian and the ladies and set out to explore and set my mind at rest on this question, or learn the truth for good and all. I went first to the hold where, being known, I was permitted to enter unhindered. I had been familiar with trade goods all my life and easily recognized the great bales of bright colored blankets, woolen cloths, even velvets and silks which had been stored in the Company's warehouses in St. Louis. Lighting a candle I walked aft in the dark hold among hundreds of kegs containing powder, trade balls, flints, and boxes and crates of axes, knives, round mirrors set in tin and brass, beads, iron brass kettles, bars of lead, bullet moulds, small sleigh bells, and countless knickknacks which the Indian covets without seeing even one barrel of liquor anywhere.

The hold was necessarily shallow and divided lengthwise by a bulkhead extending from stem to stern, so that it was partitioned into two compartments, starboard and port. A track ran down the center of each compartment, turning round the forward end of the bulkhead just under the hatchway where four small cars alternately received or discharged the steamboat's cargoes, so that in reality the track was endless. I had traversed the whole length of the starboard hold when, in turning with the track to go back on the port side, I ran into one of the cars at the stern. As though my expecting them to be there had been foregone knowledge, there were two barrels of whiskey on the car, and further investigation proved that two barrels rested on each of the four cars which stood end to end on the track there. We could not hope to pass Fort Leavenworth with liquor aboard, and here it was, and evidently with not the slightest pretense of hiding it from the United States authorities. I sat down on a bale of blankets. The humiliation of being searched was enough to bear, I thought, but to be twice actually caught transporting liquor into the Indian country would ruin the Company. Besides the Prince and Miss Jane Strongford would witness the seizure of the contraband cargo and perhaps our arrest by the officers. What could Captain Crook be thinking of—or Mr. Duncan McDougal? Where were his wits to permit such silly acts? Should I go at once and protest to Captain Crook? No. Somehow I felt that Captain Crook was but following orders, and that I would be overstepping propriety. Perhaps, desperately, some disposition would be made of the liquor before we reached Fort Leavenworth. There was plenty of time to think, since many days would pass before we reached the Fort. In the meantime I would stay out of the hold, know nothing of the cargo. But how I wished my father were on board to handle this affair.

I got up to leave the hold when my eyes caught a queer look about the cars' wheels, and I stooped to examine them in the light of my candle. What an idea! Someone, with little to do, had shod each wheel with buffalo skin, the wooly hair outside, so that they resembled miniature hand muffs. To my astonishment I further found upon examination that all four of the cars had been treated in the same manner and that each wheel had been covered with buffalo hide. And not being content with thus dressing the wheels, whoever it was had named the cars separately; *Curly-Bear, Fat-Calf, Back-Fat,* and so on, each car having an Indian name done in white paint on its end. I smiled at the vagary of the roustabout who had spent his time in thus trimming his cars to suit his fancy, and left them wondering if Captain Crook would not get rid of the barrels they held at Fort O'rleans. Again, I sincerely hoped he would.

As I approached the hatchway the *Yellow Stone* whistled, and I hurried on deck, finding that we were about to land abreast of a pile of sacks. In a few minutes we were tied up to the bank and six stalwart black men began loading these, which I saw held corn, so rapidly that within a quarter of an hour they were stowed below and we were off again.

Corn! Never before had I known of corn being shipped to Fort Union by the American Fur Company. Indian corn or, as we called it, Mandan corn, would grow at Fort Union, of course. But this was a small variety of corn, its kernels white, and blue, and even black, while the sacks contained regular yellow corn, the field corn of the states. The American Fur Company had long ago experimented with field corn. It would not grow on the plains. Mr. Duncan McDougal knew this better than I.

A gay, feminine laugh rang out on the deck above, and I thought of the way Miss Strongford's teeth flashed when she smiled.

"A boat is coming down the river! Mr. McLeod! Mr. McLeod!" she called to me.

I was surprised and a little glad that she had known where I was. I ran up the companionway to the deck where, with the Prince and his niece, Mrs. Doeffner, Miss Strongford was standing near the rail, the ends of the gray veil, as usual, fluttering over her shoulder in the wind. Sure enough, a mackinaw was sweeping toward us, her freight of robes and baled furs giving the craft the appearance of an overburdened raft. Two oars, well up toward her bows, flashed in the sunlight, and I could see the bright green head-silk of the steersman over the piled furs.

"What a picture! Bodmer! Herr Bodmer!" Prince Maximilian ran to the saloon calling eagerly for the artist who met him, sketchbook already in hand.

"A picture for you, Herr Bodmer," said the prince, "See!"

The mackinaw was almost abreast of us when Mr. Bodmer, resting the book on the rail began hastily to sketch the boat and her crew of French voyagers, wearing red cinctures and head-silks of variegated colors, while the ladies and Prince Maximilian exclaimed and exchanged conversation over their picturesque appearance. "Bon Jour, Monsieurs," called the Frenchmen, waving anything at hand, and as they swept past into our wake which tossed the mackinaw crazily, even the oarsmen had unshipped their oars to raise them in salute, staring unbelievably at the white women. "C'est une Angalise!" came back from the tossing boat.

"Vive la France!" Miss Strongford called, gaily, waving her handkerchief. But I am sure they could not have heard her.

"Bon voyage! Bon Voyage!" the voyagers continued to wave and call as long as Miss Strongford's white handkerchief was in their sight, and when the mackinaw swept around a bend in the river the steersman, more gallant than his crew, snatched off his green head-silk and bowed in homage to the first white women to navigate the upper river.

"Do permit us to see you sketch!" Miss Strongford now turned to Mr. Bodmer, her blue eyes full of the lively interest that was part of her. Had she cultivated it, I sometimes wondered, to make her rather dependent condition in life that must, at times, have been irksome, less dull, or was she naturally eager, and high-spirited?

"There was not time. I only got an idea—a study," protested Bodmer, opening his sketchbook, and smiling kindly at Miss Strongford while we pressed about him. He need not have hesitated to show the sketch, since with colors which the finished picture would have, it was the mackinaw and her crew. How the man could have worked so rapidly, so successfully, with a strange scene, and to such detail, was difficult for me, a layman, to understand. The boat was out of sight within a few minutes after he had commenced his sketch. I afterward learned that Mr. Bodmer was recognized in Germany as one of the swiftest of painters and that this, in addition to the Prince's personal friendship for the man, had been a reason for his being chosen to go on this trip into the upper Missouri River country. He had the gift of very quick impression, and the ability to transfer what he saw as quickly to paper, so that his sketches supplemented the Prince's journal with illustrations that were at the same time authentic and the work of an artist.

A sudden blast of the *Yellow Stone's* whistle, so near to us, scattered the group like a covey of frightened partridges, Miss Strongford covering her ears with her hands in mock fright. I first believed there must have been a mistake that we should be landing again so close to St. Louis. Two landings already! My father had mentioned no landings, and I thought he would have if they had been previously arranged.

The bell jingled below, and the gong sounded, and instantly the *Yellow Stone's* speed slackened. I could hear the swish of water under her bows, and ahead of us on the left bank where a road came through the heavy timber to the river I could see oxen yoked to a wagon and several bundles of freight waiting near the river. No sign of a house was in sight and there was no slashing or clearing other than the road itself which ended abruptly on the river's bank. The road, as though having set bravely forth in the interest of civilization and finding its way blocked by the great river, seemed to get discouraged and had plunged in. A strange place for freight, I thought, counting the bundles near the water, and speculating on their contents.

The *Yellow Stone* gracefully swung her nose into the bank as lines were made fast to convenient trees by a white man clad completely in buckskin, and a black man.

"Lively now!" Captain Crook's voice snapped from the pilothouse. The white man and the black man began to load the freight aided, naturally, by the *Yellow Stone's* roustabouts who went ashore almost as soon as the boat touched the bank. My interest centered particulary on the largest bundle which was round in form, and bulky, but which the black man handled easily alone. All the others were dwarfs beside it, though some were quite heavy, and all contained metal I guessed from the sound they made in coming aboard and being stowed below.

Captain Crook, anxious to be off, cried, "All aboard." There was a short, sharp blast, and the lines were being cast off when, as though he felt himself to be of great importance, a white man whom I had not seen until now, stalked as leisurely as you please out of the bushes, stepped onto the gangplank as though it were his own personal property, and followed by the white man who had been helping the black man, came calmly aboard. His very attitude irritated me. He was out of sight in an instant, but he had looked deliberately into my eyes. His face was scarred, his hair was brick-red, and his deep-set eyes were green and cunning. As he looked at me, there had come a flash of instant recognition which I felt sure was no mistake, in spite of the fact that I could not recall him then.

As I pondered who he might be I turned to see if Miss Strongford had noticed the fellow. I found her strangely agitated and deathly pale. Seeing I had noticed her shaken condition she made an effort to ask in a low, strained voice, "Do you know that man?"

I told her I did not.

She leaned against the rail as though she was glad of its support. I was burning with curiosity. "Why?" I could not refrain from inquiring. She feared him, whoever he was.

Instantly, as though my question had enabled her forcibly to expel some abhorrent thought from her mind, she stood clear of the rail.

"Oh, it's gone now," she laughed, lightly. "He reminded me very much of a gentleman I met in Scotland—a gentleman who couldn't possibly be here in America. However," she added, glancing at the companionway as though she half-expected the stranger to appear again, "I do not know where he may be."

"I will learn who he is," I promised. "If he is going with us to Fort Union we shall see him often enough," I added, wondering at the distaste the thought engendered.

"There's the dinner bell, Mr. McLeod! And I am hungry, aren't you?" she asked as though she had put the subject out of both our minds and we should be happy again.

"Yes," I answered, "I, too, am hungry." But I noticed that in spite of her professed hunger Miss Jane Strongford had no appetite for anything brought to the table.

CHAPTER FOUR

he Prince's niece and Miss Jane Strongford did not join us at all that evening on the boiler deck. At dinner Mrs. Doeffner had been indisposed, excusing herself from the dining room almost as soon as we got around the table. I did not see them afterward until supper time, and then only during the meal, after which Mrs. Doeffner again withdrew to her stateroom taking Miss Strongford with her. The Prince entertained us until nearly eleven o'clock with stories of Brazil, for he had traveled widely, and then both he and Mr. Bodmer went to their beds and I was left all alone on the deck. I had enjoyed the storytelling, more I think, because I had expected to feel uneasy in the presence of the Prince to whom Mr. Bodmer and the ladies showed every deference. Their manner toward him, while never servile, was nevertheless always formal, so that I had thought he would be distant. But instead I had found him to be very companionable and kind. The *Yellow Stone* had already stopped for wood at dusk, and Captain Crook had taken on a deck load in order that he might run all night without another stop.

It was an ideal night and being wakeful I went up to the hurricane deck where I sat down and watched the moonlit river and the dark banks. At long intervals, there were small clearings, irregular gaps in the thick timber with sometimes a light marking a cabin, and always a foxhound or two waiting therein to break the stillness with their deep, sounding voices. After one has become accustomed to the monotonous churning of a river steamboat's wheels and the continuous chow-chow, chow-chow of her escape pipes, he can often distinguish sounds ashore where at first they would never reach his ears.

The wind grew stronger and the moon slipped lower and lower over the trees. I fell to watching it, now straight ahead of us, then to starboard or port and sometimes nearly astern, as the *Yellow Stone*, following the river's winding course, kept to its channel, and seemed to be dodging the moon which would not remain in its proper position in the sky. Each time the fireman fed the fires under the boiler far beneath me, a dancing shower of red sparks rained down onto the deck and upon the black water over the side, beautiful to see, but I could only think of Miss Jane Strongford. I would do well to warn her of the sparks which, while not discernible by day were nevertheless there whenever the fireman replenished the *Yellow Stone's* fire. They would burn her clothes. The gray veil! That would catch fire easily. I would tell her of the sparks. Was she sleeping, I wondered. The half-crest! Did she have it with her? I had almost forgotten the story, at times, thinking of Miss Strongford only as she was—as a lady passenger on the boat who filled my interest, and would, indeed, have interested anyone in so unusual a position.

"Good ev'nin' to ye, Meester McLeod!"

The voice was behind me. I sprang to my feet, startled, my fists instinctively clinched as though to meet an enemy. And there he stood—the redheaded stranger who had come aboard with the queer freight—looking calmly at me out of his green eyes. He was taller than I.

"Ye'r na airly ta yer bed, Meester McLeod. Are ye na frichted at the damp, mon? I'll sit, an' ye do na mind," he smiled, lifting a heavy hickory chair by the back as though it were a wisp of straw, and placing it near my own, the same insolence in his voice that I had seen in his eyes on the gangplank.

"'Tis a grond nicht, the nicht, Meester McLeod," he said, sitting down with a motioned invitation to again occupy my chair, "An' 'tis na gude ta be alone, mon," he added with a wag of his red head.

He knew he had startled me, and the thought pleased him. No man likes to be made to jump out of his boots. The dislike is inherent in us. We feel that it shows lack of self-control, and surprised into a sudden exhibition of our weakness, we bristle instantly. It is then that we have truly to govern ourselves or we are apt to do propriety a greater violence than he who startled us.

"It is indeed a fine night," I said evenly, my hand on the back of my chair, "but I find myself at a disadvantage, sir, since you appear to know me and I am unable to recall your name."

He laughed outright–a hearty laugh, though satirical. "'A mon o' independent mink; he looks an' laughs at a' that,'" he quoted, merrily. Then, as I sat down caught by his manner, he spoke more seriously interspersing dialectic words and burring their 'R's' with pleasurable perfection. "A name," he laughed, "such as my own is excess freight in the wilderness where men meet and are measured willy-nilly, each by his own merit, an' ye will marvel at the memory God gave me, na doot. But have the name, man, have it an' pitch it overboard if you like, though 'twould be uncommon hard on the fishes, ye ken. I was dubbed Angus Merlin Colin Cameron when I was too damned weak to protest, or I would have, man; I surely would have. I'm the nephew of Lord Colin Cameron, and grandson of Lord Merlin Cameron, a nobody, and proud, ay, exceedingly proud, when I'm in my cups, Meester Donald McLeod."

His merriment seemed to have vanished with his last words, and their insolence stung me again, perhaps quickening my wits as well, for in a flash I knew him. But no wonder I had failed to recognize him when he came aboard the *Yellow Stone.* Even now I find it almost impossible to associate him with the dandy who two years before had sauntered into my father's office with letters of introduction from a friend in Scotland and who had been introduced to me, a bookkeeper there. He had been intoxicated then, and his condition, together with his evident air of irresponsibility, and no doubt his stylish clothes, had prejudiced my father against him so thoroughly that he had promptly turned the young man away as worthless. He had disappeared as suddenly as he had come to St. Louis, and only now was I brought to recall him bowing himself out of the American Fur company's office, and my father looking after him with mingled emotions of disgust and extreme dislike. It seemed to me, too, as I remembered the whole incident, that my father had been a little abstracted after the stranger left. I had wondered what the letter he had brought with him could have contained that would have so unsettled my father, for the man's condition alone would not have affected him in such a manner. The Scotch are used to intoxication, and while my father had strong feelings against overindulgence for himself, still he had a toleration for those who did not look upon the overindulgence in liquor with the same disfavor as he did.

His clothes of soft buckskin, fringed and embroidered elaborately with colored porcupine quills, his black head-silk, and the scar on his left cheek had so effectually changed the young dandy that it had been no wonder that I had not recognized him.

"I remember you now, sir," I hastened to say, "although I will confess that I might have passed you by a score of times without speaking if I had not been given your name."

"No doubt," he said with biting sarcasm, "not a wee bit o' doubt, being a McLeod of the American Fur Company. Ye're alike as twa farthings, an' mayhap will go as far. 'Tis quite natural that the old dog's whelp...."

"Take it back, damn you!"

"Peace, man, peace! Ye'll wake the watch. I'll take it back, ay, and apologize, if that'll cure it. Sit down, man, sit down. I'm not for war, but peace between us."

I had seized my chair and would have brained him for his insolence. But having apologized he began chuckling in devilish glee at my exhibition of temper. "By the March hare that chased McPherson's hound to cover, ye're easy o' trigger, man, as they say on the plains. I've apologized. Sit down, and let us be agreeable, one with the other."

I sat down, feeling that if he had succeeded with his insult he would have proven an unbearable passenger on the *Yellow Stone*. I did not intend to lose the advantage which I believed I had gained by resenting his insolence. He was older than I by four or five years, but not a whit abler, and I knew that he had carefully measured my fitness also before he apologized.

"May I ask you where you are going, sir?" I asked as genially as I could.

"Ye may," he answered readily. "I am going ta Fort Union. And to save ye breath," he added, his voice again insolent, "I am at present employed on a personal mission for Mr. Duncan McDougal, Esquire, of which I am na at liberty to speak. An' ye?" he asked, "May I know yer errand, sir?"

"I am bound for Fort Union where I shall be employed as chief clerk to Mr. Duncan McDougal, Esquire, a position which, by its nature must necessarily bring me into close touch with the Company's affairs," I told him with satisfaction. But he appeared not to notice it.

"An' the Prince and ladies?" he asked, trying to hide his eagerness to learn about the party.

"I do not know the Prince's plans," I replied, shortly, determined not to discuss the ladies with him. He guessed as much, I think, for he changed the subject, and said, "The 'Rees are warlike again, and may attack the *Yellow Stone*, Mr. McLeod."

He was perfectly serious. The *Arickaras* were a bad lot, sometimes friendly, and then when we had begun to count on their good will, they would suddenly go on the warpath. Living as they did, along the river, they made mischief for us and for all trappers and traders whenever they were pleased to do so. Many a keel boat had lost its crew at the hands of the *Arickaras* and been plundered of goods costing thousands of dollars.

"How do you know this?" I asked, thinking at once of Miss Jane Strongford, asleep in her stateroom.

"They fired upon Sarpy's outfit on its way down an' killed a Frenchman. That's how I know it, Mr. McLeod."

"Have you told Captain Crook?" I asked, anxiously.

"I have, an' all men will be armed before we reach the country of the damnable 'Rees. But 'tis a long way off yet," he added, "and they may have buried the bloody hatchet before we get there."

"I hope so," I said earnestly. The cabin was not bullet proof, and I again thought of the ladies.

"I guess that Fort Leavenworth will be more difficult to pass than the 'Ree village, anyhow," he grinned, bending toward me intimately.

"Why?" I asked—too sharply, I feared.

"Oh, ye ken, the reever is awfu' narrow at Fort Leavenworth, and the *Yellow Stone* may scrape her bonny sides on the banks in passing," he answered sarcastically.

He could not know that I had visited the *Yellow Stone's* hold, or that I knew of her cargo of liquor there. I was resolved, too, not to let him guess it.

"I do not understand you, Mr. Cameron," I said, indignantly.

"Now, I suppose you don't," he laughed. "But I should think that the confidential clerk of Mr. Duncan McDougal, Esquire, President of the great American Fur Company, would know what was in this steamboat's hold, she being a good company ship."

"What is in her hold that should prevent her passing Fort Leavenworth?" I asked, angrily.

"Whiskey! Enough ta send the American Fur Company ta hell if the authorities find it in her cargo. And they'll search her; they'll search her, mon," he chuckled, as though enjoying a joke at my expense.

"How do you know there is whiskey in her cargo, sir," I demanded.

He, too, stood, his hand on the back of his chair as though he expected to be obliged to use it as a weapon. "Mr. Duncan McDougal, Esquire, has ordered me to guard it, Mr. McLeod, and I'll do it, man; I'll surely do it. God nicht ta ye, and pleasant dreams."

He slipped quickly toward the companionway and disappeared, his moccasined feet making no sound on the hurricane deck.

The companionway was to windward, and as his red head, bound jauntily with the black head-silk, went out of my sight I caught the strong odor of beaver-musk which lingered but for a moment, and then was gone on the wind.

Chapter Five

 looked at my watch. It was one o'clock, with the bright moon low, but still lighting the river half way across. The shadows of trees lay far out from the bank on the water, black as ink, and the stars were brightening in the sky. I went quietly to my stateroom and to bed thinking most of the whiskey in the hold, and of Fort Leavenworth where the *Yellow Stone* would surely be stopped and searched by officers of the United States. How could Mr. Duncan McDougal, Esquire, expect his secret agent to dupe them, with the contraband freight in plain sight on the cars in the hold? Could he trust his secret agent? *Was* Cameron his agent, or was the man only lying to me? He was spiteful and bitterly revengeful. I knew this by his talk, and he possessed a grudge against my father and me—the McLeods, as he said. He might be a spy on board with malicious intent to hand over the *Yellow Stone* to the officers at Fort Leavenworth. He would be even with my father and me then. But there was Mr. Duncan McDougal, his friend, or who he pretended was his friend. I could not understand the situation, and snuffed my candle with a will to sleep on it. Fort Leavenworth was a long way off, and Captain Crook was no man's fool.

My stateroom smelled of fresh paint and the motion of the engine rattled the window sash annoyingly. I wondered if they all rattled like mine, and if Miss Jane Strongford would be prevented from sleeping by the noise. I would examine her window in daylight. I thought of her red hair. Cameron had red hair too, but his was coarse hair, like a horse's mane, and brick red. Miss Strongford's was fine as silk and like a burnished copper. I could tell her Cameron's name in the morning. He might be the man she had known in Scotland I thought with misgivings. Then I sat bolt upright in my berth. Angus Merlin Colin *Cameron*! Colin Cameron was the name of the Lord to whom the Strongford estate had escheated! Angus Merlin *Colin* Cameron *must be* the man Miss Strongford had known in Scotland. Had she said *known* in Scotland, or only *met* in Scotland? She had appeared excited when she asked me if I knew who the man, Cameron, was. She must have *known* him in Scotland, and quite intimately to have recognized him so quickly under the circumstances. Perhaps he had recognized *her* and had hunted me out on purpose to make sure of her identity. Anyhow he had failed in this. But he would not fail in the end. He would know her in the morning. How small was the world that two people so differently situated and from an out-of-the-way nook in Scotland should meet on a Missouri River steamboat—and a steamboat belonging to an old neighbor, practically, bound for the wilderness—and one, a woman. What if she loved him?

I slept at last, but fitfully, awakening several times out of wild dreams of Cameron, and of Miss Jane Strongford. When morning came the man, Cameron, was first to find place in my mind, and next, Miss Strongford, just as they had figured in my dreams.

I shaved and dressed with more than usual care, having nothing better to do, and was wondering how I should meet Cameron when his red head with its black head-silk popped in at my open window. "Top o' the mornin' to ye, Meester McLeod," he greeted, merry as a green parrot.

Damn the fellow! I had jumped again, so suddenly had his head appeared. "Good morning, sir," I returned, though I am afraid a little shortly. But if he noticed he gave no sign.

"'Tis a bonny days' beginnin', man," he laughed good naturedly, his green eyes sweeping the room like a cat's, "an' a bra beet o' travelin' our gude ship did in the nicht. Come oot. I'll be waitin' for ye, mon."

He withdrew his head and began pacing up and down past my window, while I finished my dressing. His moccasins, as usual, made no sound on the canvas-covered deck. Well, of all things! Cameron was going to insist upon my companionship. He was singing softly, keeping partly to his assumed dialect:

> "'Oh why the deuce should I repine
> An be an ill foreboder?

I'm twenty-three, an' five feet nine,
I'll go an' be a sodger!'"

I'd meet him half way, and be friendly. It was as little as I could
do, since I was obliged to admit that in his place I would not have
made advances.

I went outside where the song was going through another verse:

"'I gat some gear wi' mickle care,
I held it weel thegither;
But now 'tis gane, an' something mair—
I'll go an' be a sodger!'"

He had shaved clean, and his face while burned by the sun and
winds, was smooth save for the scar on his left cheek. His coarse
red hair, crotchety as his nature, curled and crimped about his
neck and shoulders. There was quality in his voice and a devil-
may-care lilt to his song was pleasing.

"You sing well, Mr. Cameron," I told him, honestly.

"Ay, mon," he agreed, with a wag of his head. Then dropping
his dialect, "The Scotch are all wonderful, the psalm-singing pirates," he chuckled. "Why, there are more promising voices in
Scotland than any otherwhere on earth. Man, they'd promise anything to anybody, though fulfillment would be taken under long
and careful advisement, always."

The Scot may slander the Scot, but I knew better than to agree
with him, since my father was a Scotsman and my good mother a
Scotswoman. I wanted no quarrel before breakfast, and so kept
silent.

The morning was indeed perfect as he had said. The river's
banks, lined with wild rose bushes loaded with blossoms, with here
and there great clusters of white flowers which I did not know,
were like gardens. Tall, ivy-covered trees, and mossy beds, green
and cool by the water invited leisure, and I thought that to spend a
day with them and a good book would be luxury, indeed.

Cameron drew two chairs to the rail. "Sit down, Mr. McLeod,"
he said affably. "The cook is only now making the coffee. Yonder is
the Osage River coming in," he added. "We've come a good way."

"Then we might make Fort Orleans by night," I suggested, looking at the rift in the timber made by the incoming stream.

"Hardly so far," he said, thoughtfully. "We'll have to take on wood by noon, and good, dry wood is the very devil to get. I imagine we will tie up for the night a bit this side of Fort Orleans. Captain Crook will not risk another run by night. I am sure, man."

All his insolence of speech and manner were gone, and he had made no reference to our meeting of the night before. If he had not been clad in the elaborately embroidered buckskin scented with the musk of beavers, I could easily have believed him another person altogether, in spite of his red hair.

"Then we can not hope to reach Fort Leavenworth for four or five more days," I said, watching his face.

His green eyes narrowed instantly and his thin, wide lips parted in a sneering grin. "Himself again," I thought, determined now to go on with him, and not again to permit myself to trust him.

"The wheesky in the hold is pesterin' ye, mon," he said, reverting to his dialect. "But for a' that, an' a' that, be sure I'm a gillie worth me hire. I'm the artful dodger of this holy expedition," he added, cunningly, "an' a common sodger is no match fer the likes o' me, Angus Merlin Colin Cameron, Procurer at Large, an' Laird High Protector of Fire-water to the Honorable Duncan McDougal, an' the————, God bless an' keep them a,'" he broke off, chuckling with his habitual insolence.

He had checked himself before naming my father in connection with the whiskey, but the omission, as made, was broadly suggestive, and I knew he had intentionally made it so. Ought I to let it pass this once, in the interest of peace between us, or should I insist upon an explanation of his inference, and then if he named my father, have it out with him?

"I've aroused your ire again, and I retract my inference that your father sanctions the transportation of liquor to Fort Union, Mr. McLeod," he said, seriously. "He does not, but nevertheless the whiskey goes up the river, since Mr. McDougal will have it. And," he smiled, "of course the American Fur Company profits thereby."

I made no reply to this, and just then Prince Maximilian and Mr. Bodmer came on deck. Cameron rose from his chair, and I presented him to both gentlemen.

"The ladies will be unable to join us this morning," said the Prince, shaking Cameron's hand. "Mrs. Doeffner, my niece, is ill, having had a bad night," he explained.

"I trust Mrs. Doeffner is not seriously ill, Your Highness," I said, wondering if Miss Strongford would be obliged to remain in seclusion all day.

"Oh, nothing of the kind, Mr. McLeod. She will be up and about tomorrow." Then turning to Cameron, "Are you a plainsman, sir?" he asked, scanning the Scotchman's clothes, admiringly.

"Yes, Your Highness," bowed Cameron greatly flattered. "I am a hunter from Fort Union."

"Ah! We are fortunate, indeed! We shall be able to learn much from you, Mr. Cameron. I beg your indulgence, sir, since I am deeply interested in American plainsmen, may I examine the work–the very beautiful handiwork on your hunting shirt, Mr. Cameron?"

"Certainly, Your Highness." Cameron stripped off his shirt and bowing, submitted it deferentially to the Prince who closely examined the quill work which was indeed extraordinary.

"Beautiful. How interesting! And the workman, Mr. Cameron?"

"Was a *Chippewa* woman, Your Highness," smiled Cameron, hugely enjoying the interest his clothes had created.

"Do you use the slug, or the round ball, Mr. Cameron?"

"Both, Your Highness. But the slug does most damage."

"It must! It must! But I am told, sir, that the round ball is more accurate."

Mr. Bodmer excused himself and then asked me to accompany him to the boat's bow where a different view of the river was offered.

"His Highness will talk of nothing but bullets until breakfast," he explained, when we went down the companionway together, "and I care nothing, not a thing, for bullets," he confided, his bright eyes drinking in the scene from the *Yellow Stone's* bow.

He was taller and more slender than Prince Maximilian, wearing a very foreign-looking blond mustache, and I could see that his hands were slender and capable of swift accomplishment. I placed his age at maybe twenty-five.

"I kill nothing," he explained, "so why should I continually talk of bullets–round balls and slugs? Ba! Gott in Himmel! Nothing else. It is eternal."

"There, look–is a jay. A fine specimen of the male bird, and it is now mating time. Do you have the thrush here, Mr. McLeod?" he asked quickly, his eyes on the treetop where the bird he had admired had lit.

"Yes, sir—all the thrushes, I think," I replied, liking him for his interest in the birds and blossoms.

"But not on the plains," he smiled, as though he dreaded them, and had only come to America to earn a needed fee.

"No, sir, not on the plains, but there are birds in plenty, although as yet both they and the plains are strange to me," I said.

Seeing the man who had come aboard with Cameron, I studied him while Mr. Bodmer was engrossed with the beauty of the river's banks. The man was seated comfortably on a coil of rope near the cabin, pipe in mouth, a thin, angular hunter, whose face reminded me of an Indian's. He was tall and straight, with a strong mouth and chin, and ponderous ears in which were small gold rings, often worn by plainsmen of the day. His hair was blond, inclined to auburn, and it brushed his broad shoulders. Seeing that I was looking at him, he nodded. He had fine direct eyes, I thought. I was going to go to him and get acquainted when the breakfast bell rang.

"Ha! My friend, there is the breakfast bell," laughed Mr. Bodmer. "It is in all languages the same, like a bluff. I have an appetite which might easily make a bear jealous. Come!"

We made our way back to the boiler deck where we found the Prince and Cameron waiting with Captain Crook, a fat man of forty with dark hair and very shiny buttons on his ship's coat. As I came up with Mr. Bodmer the Prince was saying, "Captain, I have dared to invite Mr. Cameron to breakfast with us if you are willing to have an extra guest in your dining room this morning."

"Certainly, Your Highness, Mr. Cameron is welcome," replied the captain, leading the way into the dining room.

"More bullets—round balls and slugs, my friend," Mr. Bodmer whispered behind his hand in the doorway. "Sit beside me, out of mercy, Mr. McLeod."

So it was that Cameron came to join our mess, although I am sure he would have managed to obtain the privilege anyway.

CHAPTER SIX

fter breakfast we went to the hurricane deck where, upon request, Cameron brought his rifle for Prince Maximilian's inspection. It was a Hawken, and a beautiful weapon, very long and shapely with a handsome, curly stock. On one side of the stock was a silver spread-eagle patch box, and on the other, a carved cheek piece set with three silver stars. Cameron, himself, had further adorned the piece by covering the firearm of the stock from its beginning at the muzzle, to the trigger-guard, with the skin of a bullsnake. It was a neat bit of workmanship, indeed. The mottled yellow and black skin of the reptile, shrunk tightly onto the wood, ended near the guard with a silver band about a quarter of an inch in width.

His powder horn, too, was handsome, and excited almost as much admiration as his rifle, having an ornamented butt set with shell pearl and silver.

But Mr. Bodmer's interest centered upon Cameron's bullet pouch. This was nearly a solid piece of porcupine quill work matching, in color and design, the embroidery of Cameron's buckskin shirt, but if anything, the art was more exquisite.

The elaborate accouterments, together with a bullet board and starter, neither of which the Prince had ever seen before, shot Cameron high in his estimation. Again and again Cameron must explain the use of the bullet board, which is a flat, triangular piece of hardwood in which from four to eight patched bullets are set in holes. It is placed over the muzzle in loading, and the starter, a short ramrod of perhaps six inches, pushes one of the bullets from the bullet board into the rifle. When the regular ramrod is employed to seat it, it facilitates loading. Both the bullet board and the starter are worn on a thong about the neck, and are common on the plains and in the mountains.

The Prince, having fondled the rifle, next urged Cameron to try his weapon, "A shot at that snag," he suggested, as though he was eager to try it himself.

Cameron, willing enough, took the piece and charged it, using the bullet board handily. The snag, the sun-bleached end of a cottonwood tree as large as a man's leg, was one hundred and fifty yards astern. Aiming quickly, he fired at it.

It was a fine shot. Water splashed at the base of the snag, and the rifle's sharp report caused a quick stir on the deck below. Captain Crook's head appeared in the window of the pilothouse.

"You struck it! You struck it! Remarkable!" exulted the Prince, hurrying to Cameron's side.

The shot had stirred everybody aboard. I heard light footsteps hurrying up the companionway and, turning, beheld Miss Stronghold, her beautiful hair shining in the sunlight, and matched by the gold braiding on her cape.

"What is it—the shooting, Mr. McLeod?" she asked, smiling. "Mrs. Doeffner is—," she broke off, staring at Cameron, the smile frozen on her lips. I saw instead, a strange expression on her face—as though the light that shone there so readily had been suddenly extinguished, contracted by some great emotion, whether love or terror I could not tell.

"Was that a round ball or a slug, Mr. Cameron?" the Prince was asking, his notebook open.

But Cameron, hearing Miss Strongford's voice, had turned, and was now staring at her also, his long rifle held like a staff before him.

For half a second neither of them moved. Slowly, as though confused, Miss Strongford's hand brushed her forehead, and Cameron, at last believing his eyes, removed his black head-silk and bowed gallantly, his long, red hair ruffling in the breeze.

"Angus Cameron!" she gasped, incredulously, her hand pressing her bosom.

"Ay, and at your service, Jane, if I am not daft, and you are flesh and blood," he said, slowly walking toward her, his long rifle across his arm.

I was by her side when they met, and the Prince and Mr. Bodmer came up to the companionway with Cameron as he advanced to take her proffered hand, his cunning green eyes strangely softened. "Old Lord John's ghost would have surprised me less, Jane," he said, lightly, while we all began talking excitedly of the marvel of their meeting there in the wilderness. And then in just a few minutes, it seemed, Miss Strongford had excused herself and had gone down the companionway again back to Mrs. Doeffner.

When she had gone the strangeness of it still kept us going, except Cameron, himself, who did not join in any of the talk. Leaning on his rifle he stared vacantly at the empty companionway as though he had indeed seen a ghost, his black head-silk fluttering in his hand. I thought that besides amazement, there was some mysterious calculation in his green eyes now, though I was prejudiced against him, of course, and might think most anything.

At last, as though suddenly remembering, he made answer to the Prince's question in a manner disregarding completely the conversation that had been absorbing the rest of us.

"'Twas a round ball, Your Highness," he said, turning slowly, and leaning his rifle against his side to tie the black head-silk about his head—"a round ball, and a linen patch dipped in melted tallow, sir." Then he straightened and looked ahead. "I think we will stop and take on the wood I see on yonder bank," he added, shading his eyes with his hand.

The *Yellow Stone* whistled and swung in alongside several cords of wood which I saw was dry and of good quality, and which the roustabouts began loading. While we four went ashore, the Prince and Cameron to shoot at a mark, and Mr. Bodmer and I to walk about the sweet-smelling woods where wildflowers were thick and very beautiful.

My companion's eyes were everywhere and, I think, missed nothing in nature. In a moment he had discovered the cunning nest of a hummingbird, built handsomely of lichens and so resembling the limb on which it had been constructed that I should have passed it unnoticed had I been alone. Only twice since then have I found the nests of hummingbirds, and both times mere chance led me to their discovery. The artist began at once to sketch the nest (he would not take it although I assured him it was a year old). I began picking wild roses and a three-petaled white lily which grew on long stems, exquisite blossoms which were so plentiful that by the time the whistle sounded I had a large bouquet. This, too, Mr. Bodmer admired immensely.

On board again I went straight to the galley where I got a china pitcher, the only vessel procurable that would hold my flowers, and thence into the saloon. Stopping at the door of Mrs. Doeffner's stateroom, I rapped gently.

Miss Strongford opened the door. She wore the dark blue gown with the white lace at the neck and sleeves I had seen under her cape that morning, and the sharp contrast between dark and light made her throat and face whiter and sweeter than usual, though I thought she looked more fatigued and worn than Mrs. Doeffner's slight illness should have warranted.

"I hope I have not disturbed Mrs. Doeffner," I said as I handed her the flowers, and bowed to that lady who was propped up in her berth with a book.

"Oh, how good of you, Mr. McLeod. They are *so* beautiful." She took the pitcher from my hands, looking into my eyes strangely over the blossoms before she turned back to the half-opened door. I left the saloon wondering if Miss Strongford was not troubled, and if she had not been half inclined to confide in me. But I put it out of my mind when I went out on the deck and watched the Prince and Cameron talk intimately of rifles, and Mr. Bodmer, pipe in mouth and hands clasped behind him, pace up and down the deck in that "two is company; three is a crowd" manner which comes when interests are unshared.

The remembered words of Miss Strongford's startled exclamation, "Angus Cameron!" took its place. She must love him. It had not been terror in her eyes up there on the hurricane, but love. I was sure of it now, but there was some trouble connected with it all—she looked upon me as a friend!

"What is the matter, my young friend?" Mr. Bodmer stopped beside me, his kind face solicitous.

I had forgotten about the others, and I felt my face flush as I answered. "Nothing, Mr. Bodmer. Why, sir?"

"Ach, Gott! Your face just then was sad, my friend. But now you smile. It is good! I thought perhaps you were suffering from lead poisoning," he whispered, with a jerk of his long pipestem toward the Prince and Cameron. "Bullets!" he whispered, hoarsely, ducking his head comically, "Slugs and round balls I must dodge eternally on this ship, my friend."

"May I see your sketch of the hummingbird's nest?" I asked, keener now than ever for his companionship.

"Willingly. Come! I will show you many sketches which I have made since I left my home," he offered.

He led the way to his stateroom where, first having produced a bottle of wine and pouring a glass for each of us, he took from his Spanish trunk, of hard rawhide bound with brass, four sketch books which he laid on the berth. "So!" he smiled, refilling both glasses from which only a sip or two had been taken.

Never before had I known an artist of any kind. My father's life at the warehouses had not left him much time for travel, and when he did go away it was always back to Scotland and to the old life of my relatives, so that he had not come in contact with anything that was being done on the continent and, of course, St. Louis was too young to have developed much art. Even if he had had the leisure to seek the companionship of men who were painters and sculptors, there were none there to know. Mr. Bodmer was a celebrated artist in his own country. Most of what he brought out were sketches of places he had seen on his travels, and he talked most interestingly of these, often touching historical facts unknown to me. He had one finished picture, a small canvas, not over six by ten inches, and unframed. It was a portrait of a young and beautiful woman with golden hair and blue eyes of the shade of Miss Strongford's. Brushing the picture with his handkerchief he handed it to me. "She is long ago dead," he said, gently, and sipped his wine while I studied the sweet face he had painted. Somehow I knew that he had loved her, and that her death had changed his life, although he said nothing more concerning her, but turned the talk back to birds.

The ladies did not come to dinner which was therefore much the same as breakfast had been, the Prince listening to stories of Cameron's hunting on the plains, and Mr. Bodmer and I conversing on subjects which interested him.

By three o'clock in the afternoon the sky that had been so bright and clear while we gathered our wildflowers, had clouded over, and by four it was pouring rain, so that all sought the shelter of the saloon, pairing off again as at dinner. The wind was blowing, and although an occasional bend in the river relieved the *Yellow Stone*, her general course was against it, which with the current made her progress slow indeed. Mr. Bodmer and I sat by the windows looking out between the smoke stacks over the boat's bow, watching her fight her way against the squalls of wind and rain, the summer storm filling my companion with wonder and leading him to talk interestingly of his boyhood. I hoped he would come to telling something of the lady of the little portrait, but he did not.

Supper was at six, as usual in the saloon, which was also the diningroom. The saloon was nearly forty-five feet long and round fore and aft. At the forward end there were windows, and the four doors, two on either side, leading out to the boiler deck were of glass, while around the ceiling skylight transoms of stained glass gave a pleasing and ever-changing tint to the white interior whose walls were paneled by the neat stateroom doors, six on each side. The dining table, a very good one of black walnut, was placed near the after end of the room, and always after meals it was cleared so that it could be used for games or whatnot.

Again we were without the company of the ladies. Cameron, having exhausted his stock of stories, both Mr. Bodmer and I were once more included in the conversation of the Prince, who talked, as he had talked one night, of Brazil when he explored the rain forests in 1815 to 1817. This time he related an exciting incident of nearly drowning when the ship he was in wrecked off the coast of Peru. He was, as I have remarked before, an entertaining talker and also an inveterate smoker. His interest in things was, on the other hand, more genuinely keen than I had decided on the morning of my boarding the *Yellow Stone* when, upon introduction, so many questions plied immediately had struck me as coming of a perhaps assumed interest. All this was quite to the contrary.

The Prince ran on and on for an hour or so after Captain Crook, noting the fading daylight, had gone back to his pilothouse. Only when the *Yellow Stone's* engine ceased altogether, and she was tied up to a bank on the edge of a black forest, did we leave our comfortable quarters and learn where we were. The sudden cessation of the machinery began to oppress me strangely.

"We're snug enough here!" said Cameron, peering out into the drizzling darkness.

I was sure that he could not see any more than I, but he appeared to know our landing place.

"La Barge's Point, ten miles below Fort Orleans," he said, with certainty. "She has done well today, considering the weather."

A downpour of rain sent us back under cover, and Mr. Bodmer, excusing himself, went to bed. I was sleepy, too, the weather, the stillness, and my lack of sleep the night before urged me to follow

Mr. Bodmer's example, which I did, leaving Prince Maximilian and Cameron up together.

Entering the saloon where only two lighted candles stood on the dining table, I was more conscious than ever of the oppressive stillness since the boat had tied up, and I instinctively tiptoed to my stateroom so as not to break it. Closing my door, I undressed as though somebody in the little room was sleeping, and afterward lay in my berth with my ears alert and strained for sounds, I knew not what.

I could hear every footstep taken on the boat with frightful intensity, and the pelt of the rain on the deck disturbed me almost as much. I missed the friendly noise of the engine and, for a time, found it as difficult to go to sleep as I had found it on the night before. I thought Mr. Bodmer was stirring in his room, and got up to look out. What pleasure I was beginning to find in his companionship, the kindhearted soul. "Bullets," I whispered to myself, smiling at his aversion to them—"round balls and slugs—Ba!" And the little portrait—how beautiful she was! No wonder he had never married. There was no light in his stateroom, nor in Mrs. Doeffner's, but there was one in Miss Strongford's. I could see it shining out on the rippling water, two windows from mine toward the stern. I had forgotten to see if her window rattled, reflecting, however, that it could not disturb her tonight with the engine still.

I was glad that I thought of the wildflowers, remembering how graciously she had accepted them, and how sweet she had looked in the dark blue gown with the white lace. And her beautiful hair—and her eyes. They were blue like the young girl's in Mr. Bodmer's portrait. They had looked into mine over the blossoms. And there in the saloon beside her stateroom door I had fancied that there was bewilderment in them, yes, and a look of appeal. But out on the deck afterward, I had quickly decided that I had been wrong.

I got back into my bed remembering vividly every detail of Miss Strongford's meeting with Cameron. She loved him, and they had quarreled. How could I ever have thought differently?

I would go to sleep. Miss Strongford was clearly capable of choosing her suitor without my help, and I smiled grimly at my uninvited interest in her affairs. I tried industriously to put them out of my mind, scorning my inability to drop them instantly, and telling myself that it was my dislike and distrust of Angus Cameron which permitted them to linger. I was certain of this until I found

myself seeking compensation (for what I knew I had never possessed) in my newly-found friendship for Mr. Bodmer, my new
position in the fur trade and in the trip itself, and then I would
only fall back upon telling myself over and over again that I had
no real personal interest in Miss Jane Strongford.

Chapter Seven

hen I wakened, the *Yellow Stone* was steaming up the Missouri and bright sunlight was streaming in through my stateroom window. Sleepily I listened to the steady chowwww-chow of the 'scape pipe and the rattle of the tiller lines beneath me, till suddenly the engineer opened up the mud valve. Its unearthly, blubbering roar so thoroughly aroused me that I sprang from my berth in one leap, ashamed of rising so late and, dressing in great haste, went out on deck where I found the whole party already gathered, including the ladies.

I did not look directly at Miss Strongford at first, although I noted that she wore the gray gown of the first morning, and that she was chatting with Mr. Bodmer with her usual vivacity a little way from the wheel. Cameron, who was near the door, told me that we should pass Fort Orleans within an hour. I looked at my watch, nearly seven o'clock. We had been underway since five, and I had heard no sound until a few minutes before.

I walked toward the wheel to greet the ladies, and congratulated Mrs. Doeffner upon her recovery. They were both exceedingly merry and told me they had been first on deck, and that they had enjoyed the sunrise before a man had appeared.

"Ba! So lazy are men!" laughed Mrs. Doeffner, in mimic disgust. Then, "Please put on your hat, Mr. McLeod, you will catch cold," she said kindly. "That is what brought on my trouble," she continued. "I caught a bad cold and it finally resulted in what I feared was chronic asthma. The Prince thought that if I took this trip with him it would leave me—and do you know it has. I am completely free from it. I am so glad I came, so glad, so glad!" The declaration was in the tone of resolve to enjoy the remainder of

69

the journey however distasteful it had seemed to her at the outset. "Ach! There is the breakfast bell—a good thing it is!" she exclaimed, clapping her hands!

"Ja," smiled Mr. Bodmer, whose ears seemed always alert for the bell, "and never before have I been so hungry."

We went gaily into breakfast, Cameron contriving to sit next to Miss Strongford who I saw, with a thrill of pleasure, wore a bunch of my wildflowers at her bodice. I had not seen them out on the deck, but remembered that during our conversation she had leaned over the rail so that the flowers were hidden by her cape falling forward. It was Mrs. Doeffner, however, who entertained us during the meal, telling of her experiences with a pet monkey which her uncle, the Prince, had sent her from Africa, and which she found impossible to give away, even to unsuspicious children. And when, half-indignantly, yet with twinkling eyes, she told us how the monkey had climbed a vine and entered a neighbor's window where he stole and brought home a lady's watch and chain which he hid beneath a sofa cushion in her own house, we were convulsed, especially when in pantomime, she arose and showed us how the watch was discovered an hour or two later by its owner who had called to warn Mrs. Doeffner that burglars were about. "Ach! Such a thief, he was," she exclaimed, panting from her exertion! "But, finally he *did* die," she sighed, so evidently relieved that we fairly shrieked again.

"And, my niece, Mrs. Doeffner, once had a parrot, a beautiful specimen which I sent her from Brazil," suggested the Prince, with a nod inviting Mrs. Doeffner to tell of the parrot.

"Ach! Please! Please, Your Highness, spare me from this ordeal," begged Mrs. Doeffner, clasping her chubby hands appealingly. "Tst—tst—tst—that green blackguard!" she sighed, shaking her head and closing her eyes as though to shut out the bird's image. "It was Spanish he spoke," she burst out in explanation. "And I do not know Spanish. NO!—Not one word. And think of my humiliation when Doctor Wagner, our good minister, a great scholar——" She broke off to cover her face with her hands and to sway. "Oh, such a disgrace he was—that green bird!" she whimpered. "And no wonder; purchased from a Spanish sailor he was, and for me. But," she brightened, looking defiantly at Prince Maximilian, "I gave him away; ja, to my gardener who has no children; only a wife who does not know Spanish."

Mrs. Doeffner's humor set us going happily. She had told the parrot story, all of it, with a few words, her manner supplying hundreds of unspoken sentences, and so vividly that we all understood the parrot's Spanish, too.

"Mrs. Doeffner is a remarkable woman," I said to Mr. Bodmer, hoping he would tell me something about her.

"Yes," he answered, "she is, indeed. You should see her as Das Katchen Von Heilbroun. No one can equal her I am sure." Then he told me that Mrs. Doeffner was a real Bohemian, had traveled widely, was very eccentric, and a great favorite of Prince Maximilian, her uncle. "Her husband, Major Doeffner, was killed in a duel two years ago," he said, guardedly. "The unhappy affair created a great stir, affecting Mrs. Doeffner deeply. It was to get her away for a time that His Highness brought her along on this trip—this and her asthma," he added.

Mrs. Doeffner, I saw now, was a humorous person, and loved life, seeing the comical side of things quickly, and even projecting fun into every circumstance which did not totally forbid it. I thought her near forty. She was plump and short, and would one day be a fat woman, fair-haired, with a large full-lipped mouth whose expression was petulantly kind. I began to like Mrs. Doeffner, and was not so sorry for Miss Strongford in her position as companion as I had been. At first when I saw them together the evident difference in age alone had made me think her position must be irksome. Besides I had thought, from her physical appearance, that Mrs. Doeffner was a phlegmatic person, a woman who while inclined to be listless herself, would insist upon every attention from others, especially from a paid companion. I knew now that Miss Strongford did not look upon Mrs. Doeffner altogether as her employer, but as a friend, and that there was warm personal regard between them. I had seen genuine delight in Miss Strongford's eyes when Mrs. Doeffner had shown us how her neighbor had discovered the stolen watch and chain, and knew that unless she possessed sincere admiration for her she could not have assumed this, since tyranny's wit would not have found appreciation in the eye of its victim. They were friends and I felt glad of it.

Breakfast was most enjoyable, and when the ladies rose to leave the table I thought that Miss Strongford looked very happy, yet she had little opportunity to talk, because Mrs. Doeffner had kept us all too busy for much neighborly conversation.

"Come, my friend, let us look about this ship of ours," proposed Mr. Bodmer when the women had gone. "We–I know nothing about her, and I would learn. Come."

We went first to the engine room where I presented him to Sandy Campbell, an old employee of the Company. Blind in one eye, he was, and always smoking a short, black clay pipe, and damning green cordwood. He had known me all my life and thought my father, next to Mr. Duncan McDougal, Esquire, was the greatest of living men. Sandy's engine, bright and shining, with its heavy flywheel painted vermillion striped with gold, pleased Mr. Bodmer, and immediately engaging the proud old engineer in conversation, he sat down to smoke with him. Seeing the man who had come aboard with Cameron pass the door, I went outside to talk with him and learn what manner of man he was. But it turned out to be I who did the talking. The fellow, whose name, he said, was Hawkins, only answered my questions shortly, or dodged them with uncommon skill, as he pleased, this with no element of rudeness in his manner. He was a man, I concluded, who had been much alone on the plains, and was naturally secretive, though not discourteous. All I learned was that he was "workin' fer Red Cameron a spell." I gave him up and went back to Mr. Bodmer in the engine room.

"We passed Fort Orleans while we were at breakfast," he said, regretfully. "I wished to make a sketch of it from the boat." Then insisting that Sandy Campbell fill his pipe with Turkish tobacco, Mr. Bodmer was ready to move on with me.

Besides Hawkins, the man who had come aboard with Cameron, there were seven white trappers, and four half-bloods–French and *Chippewa*–new engagees of the American Fur Company who were going to Fort Union on the *Yellow Stone*. Mr. Bodmer enjoyed them all, especially Eli Whitney, a white trapper whom he sketched and whom he declared was a philosopher, a man made wise by experience. I still remember how amused he was, and interested, how he laughed when Whitney, after listening to his idealization of the white man's civilization, said with a drawl: "Standin' where *I* be 'tis powerful hard to tell jest how fer the white man, hisse'f is civilized, seein' as how he's the only critter that willfully s'iles his drinkin' water, an' makes whiskey. I reckon civilization's a heap like Christianity. 'Taint rightly understood always, an' nobody's got a patent to it, 'taint likely, Mister."

Eli Whitney bemoaned the fall in the price of beaver skins. "A plus ain't wuth nigh what she uster fetch," he said, regretfully, "An' the price is down to stay, account of somebody's findin' out that silk will make nigh as good a hat as beaver fur."

He, himself, wore a rawhide hat which Mr. Bodmer borrowed to show Prince Maximilian, besides making a careful sketch of it. The hat was a flat piece of buffalo rawhide with a hole cut in it, near one end, the size and shape of a man's head. The edge of the rawhide around the hole was slashed in the form of coarse pinking, the points being turned sharply upward so as to crimp against the head and hold the hat in position. In other words it was little more than an eyeshade, sometimes worn by plainsmen, its main feature being its visor, since the crown of the wearer's head was bare to the elements, so far as the hat, itself, was concerned. Whitney's apparel was that of the regular trapper. He wore leggings of tanned elk skin which left his thighs bare, a breech-clout held in position by a girdle beneath his buckskin shirt open down the front like a coat and reaching to his knees. The shirt, worn over a cotton garment, was caped and fringed, and he wore one-piece moccasins, almost exactly the clothes of the plains Indian.

Indeed the white trapper copied the Indian in many of his ways besides apparel, I learned, and no greater compliment could be paid the old time plainsmen and mountaineers than to mistake them for Indians at first sight. The red man has no beard, no hair on his face, and to be like him many white trappers contrived to keep their own faces shaven clean, especially when in the company of Indians. All this was indisputable admission by white men that the customs of the Indian born to the wilderness were the most practical there, but the adoption of his superstitions by the white trapper, such as carrying a medicine-bundle containing a charm or talisman to keep misfortune at a distance and good luck at hand was something more than acknowledgment. It was the outgrowth of respect for the Indian's powers which the red man attributed to his "medicine." A quick reversion to the primitive by the white man made him superstitious (suspicious) of constant danger in the solitude of unexplored wilderness, where individual cunning and strength so often maintained life. Disaster seemed sometimes to have been narrowly averted by inconsequential warnings coincident to the approach of unseen danger, such as a rolling stone, the rattle of a snake, the voice of a startled magpie or the sight of a running buffalo-herd. Superstition and dread, the hereditary enemies of man, both white and red, have not yet been entirely conquered, and primitive instincts naturally quickened by solitude tend toward the reestablishment of the one in the hope of escaping the other.

Eli Whitney, though wise in many things, wore about his neck a buckskin thong which I knew supported his "medicine" beneath his cotton shirt next to his bare skin, and which to him was potent against misfortune. Upon leaving Whitney I explained "medicine" to Mr. Bodmer, telling him of its deep hold upon the Indians and plainsmen, and that even Eli Whitney was evidently a devotee of its magic powers. He questioned me closely especially concerning the individual selection of "medicine," and was intensely interested in what I told him of "medicine dreams," but I could see he was loath to believe Whitney subservient to superstition and that he was even ready to excuse him if proven guilty, so high was his opinion of the man.

The *Yellow Stone* had, since leaving her night's berth, been making good headway against the current which now did not appear to be any stronger than it had been at the Missouri's mouth, and as Mr. Bodmer and I went back toward the saloon I thought again with misgivings of the liquor in her hold, and the officers at Fort Leavenworth, so soon to be reckoned with. We had passed Fort Orleans, and our last opportunity to unload the liquor was gone. Captain Crook was going to chance seizure and its consequences.

We found Prince Maximilian alone in the saloon, writing in his journal, and learned that Mrs. Doeffner had gone to her stateroom to lie down. He was quickly interested in Eli Whitney's rawhide hat and, while Mr. Bodmer showed his sketches of the white trappers and the half-bloods, made notes of them all. I left them together and stepped outside, wondering if Cameron would set my mind at ease about the liquor if I asked him. He must have planned to meet and defeat the authorities at Fort Leavenworth, and as much as I disliked to do so I determined to invite him to share his scheme with me. It would, at least, lend variety to my torment. My mind made up, I went toward the stern where I found Miss Strongford and Cameron, seated comfortably, in earnest conversation.

Not wishing to intrude I had turned to go back when, seeing me, Miss Strongford asked, "Won't you join us, Mr. McLeod?"

Cameron was slow to add his invitation, and I hesitated, but when Miss Strongford rose as though she, herself, would place a chair for me, he said, grudgingly, "Come, Mr. McLeod, sit wi' us, an' hear o' yer fathers," as if he were speaking to a lad of ten years.

"We have been retelling an old Scotch story," she explained, attempting to cover his rudeness. "But it would bore you, I'm sure, Mr. McLeod, and I am more than glad to change the subject," she added with a quick, dusting glance at Cameron who looked away, his eyes narrow.

"Ay," he agreed not deigning to look at me, "let Mr. McLeod set us agog out o' his wide experiences on land an' sea."

I was nettled, but I pretended not to notice his sarcasm, remembering he had not dared to go so far when we had last been alone. And perhaps it had saved me, too, for now I would not ask him anything about his plans, whatever they were.

"I am sure any subject will please me more than the one we were on," Miss Strongford persisted. I thought she sighed a little.

"Ah, here you are." Mr. Bodmer came around the corner of the cabin, thus saving me from further discomfort. "His Highness would appreciate Mr. Cameron's presence in the saloon," he bowed.

Before he turned to follow Cameron, who so obediently excused himself and left us forthwith, Mr. Bodmer leaned over me. "Rawhide hats, it is, and more bullets maybe, round balls and slugs," he whispered, with a slow wink.

"What fun he is!" said Miss Strongford, looking after him affectionately when he had gone. " I like him so much."

"So do I," I agreed, thinking of the little portrait hidden in his old Spanish trunk.

Cameron had reluctantly placed a chair for me, but upon his leaving I had taken his vacated seat. The chairs were placed so that we nearly faced each other there on the fantail or afterdeck, with only the roofing hurricane deck overhead and the pleasant breeze fanning us and stirring her wonderful hair. Both banks were especially beautiful today and sitting there with all view ahead completely cut off by the cabin, each bit of attractive scenery, every blooming bush and natural park came suddenly to us without an instant's warning, their every feature new and gathering charm from our expectations. Ugly snags, barely cleared, passed us as though hurrying downstream, ducks with broods of downy ducklings that scurried along the banks where our wake was sure to bring terror to their young lives, and now and then a lone blue heron wading in shallow places, unfrightened by our passing, brought exclamations of wonder and delight from Miss Strongford. She was alive to everything, not queer, not living in the past with the old Strongford traditions, but full of gaiety, and ready and waiting for what might come next. I even thought she dared it.

Did she have the half-crest aboard the *Yellow Stone* as my father thought? Would she show it to me if I asked her? I might not have another such opportunity. I would not let it slip away. "I think I know the old Scotch story you spoke of a little while ago, Miss Strongford," I said, bending toward her and modifying my voice so as not to betray my excitement.

She turned sharply in her chair, her cheeks burning. "How could you?" she asked, her blue eyes darting from mine to the corner of the cabin and back again.

"My father has told me the story of Strongford Castle, of old Lord John, the half-crest, and the Moor's shirt," I hastened to assure her, almost running my words together.

"Oh!–How strange it seems that you should know the story," she said, slowly, the flush dying down in her cheeks. "But your father knew my mother," she added, softly, "and I suppose it is natural, after all. You startled me–you–you rather surprised me, though," she laughed, willfully gay again. "The Missouri River is so very far from Strongford Castle, isn't it?"

"Isn't it!" I agreed, thinking suddenly how very pleasant that it was. "And to think you should meet Mr. Cameron here," I said, pursuing my advantage.

"Yes," she said, more to herself than to me, her eyes down the river. "Had you met him before?" she asked without turning.

Was she concerned that I had, that she should keep her eyes thus straight down the river? "I had been introduced to him. That is all. The introduction was two years ago and I did not recognize him when he came aboard the first time," I explained without going into details.

She did not ask for these but dropped Cameron at once and, turning her eyes which would not show the interest she put in voice, she asked, "Are you going to remain at Fort Union?"

"Yes, I am going to be Chief clerk to Mr. Duncan McDougal, Esquire, President of the American Fur Company," I told her proudly.

"There are splendid opportunities here in this beautiful, new land for men who dare a little hardship," she said, her eyes now as full of interest as her voice. "If I were a man I would live here, make my way here where convention is naught, and where only worth can win. I love the way it dares one, Mr. McLeod."

"Did you like living in Germany?" I asked, groping for a way to get back to the half-crest which I was burning to see.

"It was better than living in Strongford Castle (when I left it)" she answered enigmatically. Cameron's voice broke in on us. "They are coming back now," she said, rising. "You will have company, and I must go back to Mrs. Doeffner. Sometime—there are so many things we could talk of—" she suggested, hurriedly, leaving me standing there, pulled a dozen ways at once by conflicting thoughts.

Chapter Eight

One evening, after we had tied up in time to load wood, Mr. Bodmer and I went ashore, both of us glad of the opportunity. He had been quick to notice the changes in the country through which our boat was passing, and here, the wild honeysuckles delighted him. Their blossoms reddened the green tops of the small trees and bushes about which the vines trained themselves, and we saw one of the vines as large as a man's finger embedded in the trunk of a maple tree, so tenaciously had it clung to its right to live as the tree's body had grown. Both the tree and the embedded vine, twisting 'round and 'round the trunk, were alive, although the tree was being strangled to death by the vine shutting off its flow of sap. One day the tree would die and fall and, decaying, leave the vine to seek a new victim that it might climb again to set its color toward the sun. But in the end it, too, would die.

I gathered a large bouquet of the honeysuckles. I had only one purpose in gathering flowers these days. When I saw flowers it seemed to me the natural thing that Miss Jane Strongford should have them, not only because they would relieve the bareness of her stateroom, but because they were like her, full of color, freshness and grace. At least one understood better the wonder of the sun when one saw its light fall on loveliness that did not cheapen in it, but enhanced and gave back a portion of its glory.

On board Miss Strongford was lighting extra candles by which to read aloud to Mrs. Doeffner in her stateroom. She brightened at the sight of the honeysuckles which I handed into her arms, admiring the rich, brilliant color of them and the texture of their waxen green leaves with, what I had not observed when I brought my first wildflowers to her, a real appreciation of them such as Mr. Bodmer and the Prince might have.

Whether the donor of them counted at all, however, I was not able to discern, since her next remark was very general and not what I could in any way take unto myself. "How beautiful are these woods," she said, wonderingly, "and how extensive! One could go on and on and not come to their end, it seems to me."

"They will soon end now," I told her, a little regretfully. "We shall see less and less of timberlands as we journey up the river, till we finally come to the great plains." I watched to see what effect this information might have on her spirits.

"But listen!" she whispered, starting at the deep hooting of a horned owl on the shore, her eyes wide and her lovely head tilted over the honeysuckles. "What is it, Mr. McLeod?"

"Only an owl," I smiled, as the hooting came again from the black forest.

"What a voice for a bird!" she laughed, relieved. "I could easily have believed it a war whoop. Do the Indians ever attack steamboats? I should think they might if they were tied up this way. They seem so very helpless tied to a tree," she said with a playfulness, half pretended, I thought.

I remembered what Cameron had told me of the hostility of the 'Rees. I , myself, dreaded passing their village but, "No," I answered, reassuringly. "They respect a boat of this size, and we are too many for them on the *Yellow Stone*. Besides," I added, wondering if I should mention it, "guards will always be stationed at night when once we reach dangerous territory."

She shifted the honeysuckles, lifting out a blossom here, tucking in a tendril or stem there, with fingers I again noticed were without rings.

"This is such a romantic country, Mr. McLeod, with its unmeasured spaces, its unguessed resources, and with only its wealth of fur being plundered," she said, as though she had thought over the wonder of it. "And if I were a man, I would turn explorer, with piratical tendencies, perhaps, and see it all while it is new. I am keeping a journal, but I am afraid I shall not see enough of the country to write very much in it."

All that we said about the country was interesting enough. It was the sort of conversation I most enjoyed with Mr. Bodmer, but I was always reminded of the half-crest and my own possible relations with Miss Strongford, and we had been talking too generally this evening. It even seemed to me that Miss Strongford had purposely kept it so for some reason—perhaps for fear of return to the topic of the crest inasmuch as I had broached the subject at our last meeting.

"It is as romantic as the voyage of DeSoto and your other American explorers, your journey to Fort Union," Miss Strongford went on.

"Yes," I said, seizing my first opportunity, "and you are the most romantic of all!"

I thought she started just a little, but she laughed, smiling out of her deep blue eyes into mine in the way that from the beginning always made me feel but a lad. "I romantic?" she asked lightly, and a bit playfully.

"Yes, I think you are," I answered seriously. "The half-crest—you must have it with you and—" seeing the merriment suddenly die down in her eyes and leave her almost cold, "you know *it* is romantic."

"So it is," she said, setting down the candle with which she had prepared to depart for her stateroom, and regarding me as though withdrawn to another world. She stood for a moment thus, lost in her thoughts, and I had a swift, fleeting impression of the girl in my father's story turning over stones with Old Duncan Ross, but this was quickly dispelled by a sudden decisive movement of her own.

Laying the flowers down on the table beside the candle, she drew out from the neck of her gray gown a slight gold chain. "Here! Look!" she whispered agitatedly, her fingers nervously loosening the chamois covering of a flat piece of silver not much larger than the half of a silver dollar.

It was a half-shield, the silver on its points, thin and worn, although the engraved lion and the line dividing the lower part were sharp and plain. To touch it was like handling the past, like a glimpse of ancient Strongford Castle itself, its hall filled with armed knights fanatically eager to embark on a crusade in the Holy Land. For the moment as I held the bit of silver in my hand I was transported to the Scottish highlands, to the galleys and to Palestine. Its antiquity and its romantic story cast a spell which was easy to indulge. Vista after vista of Scotch history opened out to me so that I was carried on and away from the *Yellow Stone*, as no doubt Miss Strongford, herself, had been transported in that moment before she drew out the half-crest. Thoughts of Bruce and Wallace and other great Scottish chiefs crowded for recognition in my mind and, remembering them here, I was stirred with the deep pride in my own blood.

> "Armed lions, couchant, twain;
> Gules, proper, vert champagne."

I chanted, softly, glancing at the open saloon door, but still under the spell of the half-crest.

She gently took the half-crest from my hand and, as one answering a challenge to prove membership in some secret clan, she went on with the words of the old verse my father had repeated to me the morning of my departure. How strange to be hearing them now from the lips of Miss Jane Strongford, and how pleasant!

> "And who of brother's blood or mine
> Man or maid of Strongford's line,
> Shall find ye half of Strongford's crest——"

She broke off, tucking the golden chain away again, and gathering up the flowers with an air of dismissing the subject for both of us. "Good night, Mr. McLeod," she said cordially, but in a manner that feared it might have betrayed some customary reserve, and would have it now reestablished. And then having made known her feelings, "I hope you will not dream of Lord John," she said, smiling I thought a little sadly. There were times when Miss Strongford seemed older than myself, although of course she wasn't.

"Permit me, please," I took up the two lighted candles and carried them to the door of Mrs. Doeffner's stateroom, waiting while Miss Strongford went inside to relieve her arms of the honeysuckles. "Good night, Lady Jane," I whispered when she returned for the candles, and feeling myself indeed a knight of old as I made my bow.

"A gude nicht to ye, an' pleasant dreams, Sir Donald," she said, catching the spirit as though it were a game, and curtsying in the doorway. Then two white fingers on her lips, and leaning gracefully forward—"'Tis a secret we ha' between us, ye ken, Sir Donald," she whispered in a playful earnestness, the meaning of which I understood perfectly.

"Ay," I said, turning away that she might close Mrs. Doeffner's door which at once caught my shadowed form cast by the single, flickering candle behind me on the table.

What a wonderful, mysterious girl she was, and so gentle and gracious! I marveled at the unusual in her being so happily combined with the usual sweetness I had been reared to look for in women. At times I almost wondered if she could be real, or if perhaps I had dreamed her, so rare a person she seemed to me. And I had seen the half-crest of old Lord John! Miss Jane Strongford, herself, had shown it to me, and she had called me "Donald," although the prefix "Sir" had left only a little familiarity between us, of course.

I went out of the saloon and stood on the deck, looking into the forest, both hands on the rail. The owl had ceased his hooting, and there were no sounds there except the occasional snap of twig. How often have I wondered at the snapping of twigs in the forest at night! By the sound I know it is the breaking of tiny, dry twigs and limbs of trees, mostly, and not sticks on the ground beneath the tread of prowling beasts. But whether it is the sound of night birds lighting on too brittle perches, or only the sudden change of temperature which darkness always brings and which aids nature to separate the dead from the living, I have never determined.

I let my mind run on at will, thinking mainly of Miss Strongford, though the half-crest and the Moor's shirt, stolen from the castle, Lord John, and troops of Scottish knights were intermingled, crazily, as in a dream.

"Never had there been a more entrancing romance," I thought. And part of it was actually here on the *Yellow Stone*, and in a country undiscovered when old Lord John had quarreled with his kin. The world *was* small after all. Even Cameron was here. The man's remembered green-eyed insolence came between me and my more pleasant thoughts. "What was he to Miss Strongford?" I asked myself in a sudden panic. Did she love him, or was it fear of him she felt? I had a presentiment that Mr. Cameron and I would some day have trouble. I had felt this, in fact, from the moment he had come aboard the *Yellow Stone* with his queer freight, and it had then been unassociated with Miss Strongford. Now, with no reason to offer for it, I felt that she would figure in our affair which I was unable to feel otherwise than inevitable. Instead of spurning the idea, too, I rather courted it as evidencing a just cause. I had disliked Cameron from the beginning, and felt sure it was neither my father's prejudices against him, nor the man's manner towards me which had engendered it, but rather that the feeling was inherent in me, and old as the hills.

To think of the devil is, they say, to summon him, and just now I caught the odor of beaver-musk. As Cameron came out of the dark to lean over the rail beside me, I bristled inwardly.

"A fine night, Mr. McLeod," he said, looking down at the water curling along the boat's white side.

"Yes, sir, it is," I replied, getting out my pipe and tobacco. His sarcasm in Miss Strongford's presence on the afterdeck was still fresh in my mind.

"We've made a good way today," he said, inviting conversation.

I'd furnish him opportunity to display his hatred of the McLeods. "Yes," I replied, "we are one whole day's run nearer the United States officers where the 'protector of firewater' will measure his wits with theirs."

"I'll beat them, you'll see," he said, simply, and I was sorry I had baited him. But I had not forgotten his remarks of the afternoon on the afterdeck.

"Prince Maximilian is mightily interested in American plainsmen, isn't he, Mr. McLeod?" he asked, changing the subject.

Evidently he did not desire to quarrel, and I felt a bit ashamed of my mental attitude toward him. "Yes, he is," I said, "and Mr. Bodmer is the best of company," I volunteered.

"And the lady, Mrs. Doeffner, is she usually as clever as she appeared at breakfast, or have ye met her, so that ye are able to judge?" he asked with an assumed air of half interest.

I had not been with the men since coming from the shore with my honeysuckles more than an hour before. Cameron was endeavoring to learn if I had spent the intervening time in the company of the ladies. "I haven't had the pleasure of meeting her save when you were present," I answered, feeling deep resentment again.

"Hi ho!" he yawned. "'Tis a sleepy spot, this berth we're in, mon. I'll gang alang ta me bed. Good nicht to ye, Mr. McLeod, sir."

He slipped away in the dark as quickly as he had come, the smell of the beaver-musk lingering after him to keep alive my remembrance of the man.

I went toward my stateroom intending to go to bed, but at the door of the saloon I met Mr. Bodmer, evidently seeking me. "Come, my friend," he proposed heartily, "let us drink a glass of wine before retiring."

Softly closing his stateroom door, he unlocked and opened the old Spanish trunk, lifting a bottle and glasses from it with the air of a true host.

"Ach!" he smiled at the yellow wine as it came from the black bottle's mouth. "It is good to have a friend who can speak of other things besides bullets and slugs. So!"

He bowed, handing me the glass. Then bidding me sit down on his only chair Mr. Bodmer seated himself on the berth. "To birds and flowers—and our friendship," he offered, raising his glass and bowing again before he sipped the wine.

Kind Mr. Bodmer! The old Spanish trunk was open, its bundles of dog-eared papers, and tumbled sketch books attesting not only the happy-go-lucky way of its owner, but the genuine industry of the man. Glancing at it I thought of the little portrait, and longed to see it again but hesitated to request the favor until he had poured our second glass of wine. Then I asked him, and was promptly embarrassed by his willingness to show the painting.

CHAPTER NINE

often wonder now how very much I wanted the little portrait. Night after night when I had gone to my bed I thought of it half covetously. How Mr. Bodmer must have loved her to have made her very soul shine out of her eyes with colors! How I suddenly wished that I could paint. Could a man fall in love with a picture, one he could not hope to possess? I did not think so, although Pygmalion had loved Galatea, but Pygmalion had created her as Mr. Bodmer had created the portrait. It was his and, even if he had offered it to me, I would not have taken it from him. I would never again ask to see it.

I wakened at daylight. The *Yellow Stone* was moving out from her berth into the stream, and the rattling of my window again reminded me that I had neglected to see if Miss Strongford's was loose and noisy. I would attend to it today.

Rising, I dressed myself in a new suit of moleskin made expressly for me to wear at Fort Union. It fitted me perfectly, and I thought the color, almost that of lightly smoked buckskin, just right. I had not intended wearing the suit until I had reached my destination, but now I was glad I had made the change, and added a new cravat—a blue one that I thought very attractive. I found Mr. Bodmer already on deck rapturously watching the gray mist rising from the river. He was pacing slowly up and down, hands clasped loosely behind him, and totally unconscious of Cameron who sat straddle of a deck chair, not ten feet away, with his long arms folded on its back.

"Good morning," I bowed to both.

"See, my friend!" said Mr. Bodmer, waving his arm excitedly. "If only the sun would come soon—*now*! What a picture would be here!"

I glanced up the steaming river where among the ragged, cloudlike columns of mist rising from the swirling water, ugly snags threatened the *Yellow Stone*. The sound of the tiller ropes beneath my feet reminded me that the pilot, too, was aware of them. He was even now spinning his wheel to avoid the nearest snag. "It would indeed make a beautiful picture if the sunlight were upon it," I agreed.

Cameron laughed amusedly, and Mr. Bodmer turned upon him. "Ba!" he said, snapping his thumb and finger impatiently.

"Come, my friend, let us look from the hurricane deck," he proposed, leading on.

The *Yellow Stone* began now to carefully pick her way among the snags, the mist which so delighted my companion being, as I had observed, troublesome to the pilot who, like ourselves, was anxious for the sun to rise, and for a more practical reason.

A pair of mallards rose just ahead and with loud quacking quickly disappeared in the mist to circle and fly high over us for safety down the river. A blue heron, with long, trailing legs and widespread wings, flapped lazily across our bows, scarcely missing us, and killdeers, racing along the dim shoreline like little rolling balls striped with white, called, "killdeer, killdeer."

"So! She comes!" said Mr. Bodmer, his hand on my shoulder, as the eastern sky lighted brilliantly with the morning sun. "Ach! But she comes too late—too late," he sighed, glancing at the now fast-fading mists and the clearing channel before the *Yellow Stone*.

"Mr. Cameron—do you like him, yes?" he asked suddenly, all interest in the scene dissipated by the too speedy disappearance of the mist.

"No," I answered, and then thinking at once I should not so readily have admitted my dislike, even to him.

"So—nor do I," he said shortly. "He smells like—like wild animals. Instinctively I avoid him. But His Highness, Ba! Bullets and schlugs!" he shrugged, so comically that I laughed outright.

My persistent dislike for Cameron had troubled my conscience a little. I had no good ground for it, aside for his sarcasm toward me in the presence of Miss Strongford on the afterdeck, for I had been taught to accept apologies, and Cameron had readily offered apology for his earlier rudeness. But now that Mr. Bodmer, whom I already loved and respected, had so emphatically declared his own instinctive dislike for the man, I wondered if it had not been intuition that warned me, too, against him, and if my dislike probably was not justified.

Whether or not it was would be revealed when we reached Fort Leavenworth. That place, I had felt all along, was to be a turning point. I looked towards it with mingled impatience and apprehension. Apprehension gained the upper hand at breakfast, however, when a question from Miss Strongford brought to my mind how rapidly we were approaching the Fort.

"When shall we again see a civilized community, or even a village, Mr. McLeod?" she asked, smiling, when other conversation had lagged.

I saw with pleasure that she wore a bunch of my honeysuckles on her gray dress and had decorated the table with them, as well.

"Fort Leavenworth will be the next, and almost the last settlement we shall seek, Miss Strongford," I replied, glancing at Cameron with tormenting thoughts of the liquor in my mind.

"And we shall reach Fort Leavenworth, when?"

I wished heartily that she would forget Fort Leavenworth, but her pretty manner would invite conversation on any subject she selected, and besides she was apparently ignoring Cameron who knew the river better than I. This last thought gave me pleasure. Could she be purposely ignoring him, I wondered.

"Tomorrow ought to bring us to Fort Leavenworth," I said, and thought Cameron's green eyes grew sullen. Perhaps after all he was a spy set to trap the American Fur Company, and not the secret agent of Mr. Duncan McDougal, Esquire, as he had said.

The day grew uncomfortably warm, and late in the afternoon the sky looked as though we might have an electrical storm by night. Scuds of hot winds shot across the Missouri, whipping the *Yellow Stone's* smoke in every direction, and the quaking aspen leaves kept turning up their silver sides to every passing squall. The Prince was sleeping, or trying to sleep, and I had not seen the ladies since dinnertime. Mr. Bodmer had paced the deck, on the shady side, until he tired of walking and had lain down in his stateroom. Cameron, who I thought had been drinking, sat on the starboard side with his back against the cabin, idly watching the riverbank. Rounding a bend I saw a lone Indian lodge in a cottonwood grove ahead. Cameron saw it too, stood up, and walked to the rail, resting his long arms upon it as he leaned over.

In a little while we had come abreast of the lodge, and there I discovered a man and a saddled horse standing beside it. I knew at a glance the man was not an Indian, but white, and when he waved his hand as though greeting us, Cameron sprang upon the rail, standing straight, his hands holding to a stanchion. In another minute the man had mounted his horse, and was riding pompously up and down the bank before the lodge, holding a curved stick like a sword at "carry."

The pantomime ended as suddenly as it began and the *Yellow Stone* swept majestically on past the scene. Cameron jumped lightly down from the rail, evidently pleased.

"'Tis the brave Captain Burwin I have to deal with at Fort Leavenworth, Mr. McLeod," he said with satisfaction. "I feared 'twould be the preacher-man—an uncommon hard lot is the preacher, too, I can tell you."

"How do you know this?" I asked, remembering that Reverend Mr. Miller had recently been appointed to see that no whisky went up the river.

"Oh," he laughed, "did ye no ken the bra sodger-man march wi' his wee claymore? 'Tis the Captain I have to cheat, ay, 'tis the brave Captain. Had it been the meenister, the gillie on the shore would ha' knelt in silent prayer, na doot."

The man on the bank had given Cameron some message, I was sure, now that he had interpreted it, or pretended an interpretation, but it might be quite a different message, of course, from the one he had transmitted to me. Tomorrow would tell, I thought, rather testily.

"'Twould ha' fretted me sore wi' the preacher ahead," Cameron was saying. "I would ha' been obliged to change me plan, mon, sin' what will easy fool the man-o-war, weel no answer to cheat the man-o'-God."

For the hundredth time I wished heartily that we were safely past Fort Leavenworth. Why could Mr. Duncan McDougal not get along without running such risks? How could Cameron hope to hoodwink the officer? I hadn't the least bit of faith in his plan, whatever it was, nor any doubt that the American Fur Company was running its head into the noose of the United States law.

We had supper a little early and it was not a pleasant meal, perhaps because I was worried. The only bright spot at the table was Miss Strongford's place. She alone looked fresh and cool. The strong wind made it necessary to keep the doors closed so that the saloon was indeed stifling.

Nobody remained after eating, but went out on deck for air. Inky darkness came on almost as soon as we tied up for the night, and by the time the hands had loaded what wood was near, it began to rain pitchforks. Man! How it did pour down, and how the lightning flashed, lighting up the saloon till I could see the honeysuckles on Miss Strongford's gray gown as plain as day, though we had no candles in the room.

It was a terrifying storm, the earsplitting claps of thunder and balls of vivid, hissing fire that went dancing and glancing about the deck and along the shining rails so completely unnerving Mrs. Doeffner that she finally went to her stateroom taking Miss Strongford with her.

At last, though, about ten o'clock, the violence of the storm subsided, and only the rain continued, pattering harmlessly on the deck and running in streams through spouts and scuppers into the river. Relieved of the tension, occasioned by the ripping thunder-clap, the like of which I had never before experienced, the men went off to bed, one by one, I being the last to go.

The air was fresh now and cool, the falling rain, after the crash-ing thunder, conducive of sleep; but tomorrow would not be put away, and for more than an hour it tormented me keeping me awake. We should reach Fort Leavenworth by noon, and nothing had been done with the liquor. It was still there on the cars. I had seen it just before supper. I pictured the arrest of Captain Crook, and myself, as clerk to Mr. Duncan McDougal, Esquire, for break-ing the United States law, and felt the disgrace so keenly that I sat up in bed. What would the Prince and Mr. Bodmer think of the American Fur Company if the *Yellow Stone* was not permitted to proceed up the river? And Miss Jane Strongford? What would she think of my father and me? Cameron! Of course Cameron would go free, even if he were not a spy, which I believed him to be. If Cameron had conspired to turn over the *Yellow Stone* to the offic-ers I would—no, I wouldn't. I'd take my medicine with my father.

CHAPTER TEN

aving fallen asleep, resolved to take my medicine with the Company, I awoke with a mind clear because of my resolve. The morning itself was clear. The *Yellow Stone's* decks, washed clean by the rain were shining wet, and every creek and gully was overflowing its banks with roily water which poured into the Missouri to make it muddier, and I thought a little swifter than before.

But I began to be impatient. I ate my breakfast hurriedly, and I am afraid not very politely. I kept watching Cameron, who seemed cool enough, and immediately as the meal was over I followed him outside, avoiding Mr. Bodmer.

He went down the companionway where, taking Hawkins, who evidently was waiting for him, as well as Eli Whitney and another white trapper, whose name I had learned was Bradshaw, he entered the hold with them. I took a position forward of the smoke-stacks where I could watch the open hatchway, but neither Cameron nor the others came out again. Eleven o'clock came when finally Mr. Bodmer found me in my roost and sat down to talk, complaining of the heat.

"Why do you sit here in the burning sun when there is shade?" he asked, taking off his hat and mopping his head with his handkerchief.

I did not want to tell him that the American Fur Company was violating the United States law, which I would be obliged to do if I explained my long watch in the sun. "I will move with you to any spot you select," I offered. But no sooner were the words said than a rifle-shot rang out on the shore.

"So! Somebody is shooting at us," he said rising and pointing to splashes made by a bullet on the water as it glanced ahead of us–across our bows.

I had sprung to my feet. I heard the tiller-ropes rattle as the pilot hastened to turn the *Yellow Stone's* nose towards the bank. There were two United States Dragoons standing, one dismounted near the water with a musket in his hands, the other, holding his own and his comrade's horse! It had happened–the event I had been dreading for many days.

"Ah ha! Soldiers!" said Mr. Bodmer, shading his eyes. "Are we smugglers, yes?" he asked me with a quizzical look, as though the situation was amusing.

"I suppose they will search the *Yellow Stone* for liquor," I answered. He would learn it later, anyhow. "It is according to a newly enacted law," I added, hoping that the "newly" might excuse the company if, as was certain, the liquor were discovered in the hold.

The open hatch, seeming to invite disaster, held my eyes. Not one of the four who had gone below had shown his head, even when the *Yellow Stone*, swinging obediently in, was tied to the bank.

"Captain, sir, the bank near the Fort caved last night, and my orders were to stop you here where there is a good landing," one of the soldiers, a sergeant, was saying politely.

"I suppose I am to be searched, Sergeant," laughed Captain Crook, going ashore and shaking hands with the bearded soldier. "Are you to perform the task, sir?"

"No, sir. Captain Burwin presents his compliments to Captain Crook, and will, himself, conduct the search after the dinner hour, sir."

Captain Crook looked at his watch. "Sergeant, will you do me the honor of dispatching a messenger to Captain Burwin?" he asked, ingratiatingly.

"Yes, sir."

"Present my compliments to Captain Burwin and say that I request the honor of his presence at dinner onboard the *Yellow Stone* at twelve-thirty. Tell him, please, sir, that I would enjoy presenting him to Maximilian, Prince of Wied, to Mr. Bodmer, a great Swiss artist, to the ladies of the party, and to the son of Mr. Kenneth McLeod, Secretary and Treasurer of the American Fur Company, who are my passengers."

The sergeant, after giving some low-spoken orders to the soldier who promptly took a position nearer the boat, rode away.

It was half-past eleven. We were trapped, with no chance to unload the liquor now, and I marveled at the sang-froid manner of Captain Crook who, after returning on board, told the ladies of the coming dinner guest, explaining that he was a dashing officer of Dragoons who, following orders, was obliged to make a formal search of the boat. "Simply a form, ladies," he laughed, easily, "and as distasteful to the Captain, himself, as it is to me. But I am desirous of robbing the disagreeable service of its sting, since I admire Captain Burwin," he added, "and I shall feel deeply grateful if you will help me entertain him at dinner."

"Ach!" Mrs. Doeffner, delighted, clasped her chubby hands beneath her chin, and beamed at Captain Crook. Her eyes pretending thanks for promised diversion, were brimming with mischievous fun. "Why, Captain! You brave man! You have saved our lives. We were perishing! A strange gentleman—an officer of the Army? We shall be delighted. Yes, yes, indeed, and I think I understand," she smiled knowingly, "you would make an impression on this soldier, the Captain. Ach! We will do our best—and see! We have only an hour!" she cried, in mock despair. "Come," she said to Miss Strongford who, I thought was a little excited, too, over the coming dinner. "Come, Jane, my dear, let us wear our prettiest clothes! Himmel, in an hour!" They ran merrily to Mrs. Doeffner's stateroom, and its door slammed suggestively. Then what an opening and shutting of trunks! What excited conversation in German!—with an occasional "Ach, Himmel!" from Mrs. Doeffner. I could have believed them preparing for a presentation at court at least.

Prince Maximilian and Mr. Bodmer were apparently as glad of the coming diversion as the ladies though I think Mr. Bodmer was wiser than he pretended, and noticed particularly the absence of Mr. Cameron, which he must have thought very strange.

Promptly at half-past twelve Captain Burwin, with the Sergeant and escort of four dragoons, appeared on the bank, resplendent in full-dress uniform, his tight-fitting, long-tailed blue coat, and a high, gold-braided collar, cocaded chapeau, spotless white trousers and sash giving him a rather stiff look, although he was gracious enough when Captain Crook presented him to Prince Maximilian, the ladies, Mr. Bodmer and me.

"I feel in thus accepting your hospitality, sir," he bowed to Captain Crook after a pleasant remark to each of us as presented, "I am acting like the unprincipled highwayman who borrowed his victim's pistol and then took the poor fellow's life with the weapon."

The ladies laughed, delighted.

"Nonsense, Captain! If you find a store of liquor aboard my boat, I hope you will be gracious and divide it with me. That is all. Come. Dinner is served."

As we moved towards the dining room, talking and laughing, Captain Crook stopped and leaned over the rail. "Below there!" he called to a deck-hand. "Go to the engine-room and tell Mr. Campbell to come ahead with his engine just enough to take the strain off that for'ad line." Then, turning to Captain Burwin, he said, "The current is swifter today, Captain."

"Yes, sir. The rain last night was a torrent here, and it has increased the flow of water considerably. It caved the bank near the Fort early this morning, so that I could not have you land there as I wished."

The engine began turning now and, although slowly as ordered, there was a noticeable vibration and a little noise in the cabin as we sat down at the tables which I noticed had a wineglass at each plate.

Captain Burwin was captivated by Mrs. Doeffner, who was especially lively and who kept him in the merriest of moods from the beginning. As though feeling herself a conspirator, too, and enjoying the role immensely, she saw to it that Captain Burwin's glass was kept full of wine, served by Hans, the Prince's man, who spoke little English, and who was constantly at hand. She looked very much a lady of accomplishments, which indeed she was. In her pretty dinner gown of pale blue, and with her hair done much more becomingly than usual, she was even handsome. But I thought Miss Jane Strongford was so sweet in her blue dress with the white lace that I forgot our troubles for a while in looking at her across the table. She appeared relieved, jollier than common, and I knew it could not be the wine, because she drank but a sip, shaking her head at Hans who passed her by after the first serving. Was it because Cameron was not present, I wondered. The thought pleased me mightily, although I couldn't be sure of it, of course. When I could, I engaged her in conversation.

I then became so engrossed with her that I forgot the others entirely, hearing only bits of their conversation and laughter brought out by some sally of Mrs. Doeffner's, as though from a world removed from ours. The party had been easily taken over by our elders and, for myself, I was content that it should be so, scarcely able to believe my good fortune of seeming to feast alone with Miss Strongford.

Captain Burwin had seen considerable active service in Indian campaigns, and Prince Maximilian, pressing him, drew out many of their incidents which, as usual, interested him, especially those dealing with the Indian's hardihood against fatigue. There was nothing of the braggart in the Captain who was eminently fair in his estimate of the red man, and he gave freely of credit where he believed it was due.

Whenever she could do so, Mrs. Doeffner adroitly took the Captain to herself, and until the Prince had fashioned another question which would lead the guest on in recounting his experiences, kept him pleasantly engaged. Then the conversation among the others took sudden turns, and the Captain and Mrs. Doeffner were, for the time, left out.

"I cannot believe it, truly!" Mrs. Doeffner was saying incredulously when the coffee was served.

"What is it that you cannot believe?" asked the Prince, smiling at his niece.

"That Captain Burwin is forty–so young and gallant he looks!"

The officer's face, a little flushed now, was beaming. "Madam, I assure you that I am nearly forty-one, and that I am, therefore, a connoisseur of both good company and mellow wine. Both are here in the excellence," he bowed to Mrs. Doeffner, and to us all.

Captain Crook, who had taken little part in the conversation, now arose solemnly, and looking into our faces said slowly, "Ladies and gentlemen, it is with sharp regret that I feel obliged to mention business at a table with so many distinguished guests–a table where, in the name of the American Fur Company, I am the honored host. But it is two o'clock, and if Captain Burwin is to complete a thorough search of my cargo in time for the *Yellow Stone* to find a desirable berth for the night, I must speak. Therefore, permit me to offer a toast to our guest and the United States Army."

Prince Maximilian spoke softly to Hans, and the glasses were quickly replenished. We stood up–"To our guest and the United States Army," offered Captain Crook. And we drank the toast, which I knew was the curtain for the next act, whatever it would be.

Bowing his farewell, the good Captain left the diningroom with Captain Crook and excusing myself, I followed at once, taking up the same position I had occupied in the morning. I saw them enter the hold through the open hatch, Captain Crook assisting Captain Burwin who I thought staggered a little. Were they going to bribe him, I wondered, or−. I felt a cold thrill as I thought of foul play, and then quickly put it out of my mind as unworthy of place. They turned down the starboard side of the hold, Captain Crook with a lighted candle in his hand, and the soldier following.

In a few minutes more my suspense would be over. Drunk or sober any man could see the barrels of liquor on the cars. The boat's engine, still turning over, kept her easy with the current, and its noise prevented my hearing anything below. The open hatchway was tantalizing. Did I imagine it, or was everybody on board keyed up to the snapping point? Not a soul was in sight. What was going on in the hold?

Minutes passed ever so slowly, and I was about to go down into the hold to have done with it when, to my surprise, a car with two barrels upon it passed the hatch, then another, and another, until all four cars with their barrels had come into sight on the track and disappeared again, all going slowly in precisely the direction the Captains had taken. They were literally following the unsuspecting officer with the whiskey!−actually pushing it along at his heels!

The cars made not the slightest sound on the tracks, the buffalo hide which I had seen on each of their wheels, and which I had thought was vagary, completely silencing them as they traveled. Besides the *Yellow Stone's* engine would drown any ordinary noise below deck, and the hold was very dark.

"Clever," I was obliged to whisper, as Captain Burwin's cocaded chapeau appeared in the hatchway, coming under it from the port side. I understood it all now. They had gone completely around the hold from stem to stern. The padded cars had started traveling up the port side of the partition as the Captains proceeded down the starboard hold. And then, when the officer, carefully examining whatever he chose and talking with Captain Crook, had turned into the port hold to come back toward the boat's bow, the soft-rolling cars had begun their trip down the starboard side to stop where they had stood when the inspection began. They had literally followed Captain Burwin over every inch of the track, Cameron and his rascals pushing them along from stern to stem, and then from stem to stern. "Clever," I thought again, enormously relieved.

"I am delighted to give you a clean bill, Captain Crook," Captain Burwin was saying, happily, when I reached them on the deck. "I had information which led me to believe that you had a quantity of liquor on board, sir. I am convinced that perniciousness dispatched the messenger who brought it, and I regret the delay I have caused you."

"Nonsense, Captain!" laughed Crook, probably more relieved than myself. "We enjoyed your company famously, sir, and I hope you will honor us again."

"I shall be glad, indeed. Goodbye, sir, and good luck to you and your crew."

Captain Burwin, as though anxious to allow us to proceed, hurried ashore where, doffing his chapeau and waving gallantly to the ladies on the deck, he watched the *Yellow Stone* steam away, feeling mortified at his supposedly unwarranted interference with her voyage.

CHAPTER ELEVEN

ameron did not come to the diningroom for his supper, and I did not see him until we had tied up for the night a long way above Fort Leavenworth, and on the other side of the river. Captain Crook's selection of the night's berth might not have been influenced by fear that Captain Burwin would decide upon another search of our cargo, but I thought it had, and was glad the great river was between us and the officer even if he should follow to try again.

Now that we were past the Fort with the liquor aboard I felt not only relieved, but a little jubilant, a feeling which neither my reason nor conscience justified, since I sincerely disliked the idea of breaking law, especially Federal law, and because I knew that this success in hoodwinking Captain Burwin might easily lead later on to the company's destruction. But on the other hand I had been trained by masters of the fur-trade whose motto was "win at all hazards." Besides my blood was young, and always in the veins of youth there is a strain of admiration for daring, even for lawbreaking, sometimes, so that I was willing now to admit Cameron's loyalty to Mr. Duncan McDougal and his cleverness as well.

There was a cool night breeze, and I was sitting alone on the afterdeck, Mr. Bodmer having left me to go to his bed, when I saw Cameron. He came up to see me.

"'Tis a bra nicht the nicht, Meester McLeod," he greeted, seating himself on the chair Mr. Bodmer had vacated.

"Fine, indeed," I replied. I wanted him to know that I gave him credit for cheating the officer, and telling him of it would relieve my conscience. I had believed him a spy, you remember, so I said, "You fooled Captain Burwin very handily, Mr. Cameron, and I

97

have been anxious to learn what you would have done if Mr. Miller, the minister, instead of Captain Burwin, the soldier, had searched the *Yellow Stone* for liquor."

"Ay, I suppose you *are* curious. But a trick once used is a trick sold to the world at the price of its one success. I'll keep the lid tight on my box of unused devices, by your leave," he answered, curtly.

If I had asked an impertinent question, I had done it idly—to make talk—and I felt that he might have avoided an answer in a more gracious manner. However, I could not find fault with his *reason* for not exposing his schemes, if indeed he was the company's professional smuggler, as he seemed.

"As you please, Mr. Cameron," I said, good naturedly.

He threw one leg over his knee and, tilting his deck chair back against the cabin asked, "Did Crook tell you that Captain Burwin had warned him against the 'Rees?"

"No."

"Well, he says they are bad. They have lately killed three more trappers, men of Sarpy's outfit, damn them, and will likely pepper us as we sail merrily by."

I thought of the long nights in the *Arickara* country when the *Yellow Stone*, tied up and helpless, might be attacked. "We shall soon have to put out guards," I suggested, thinking that the measure, if employed, would disturb the ladies.

"Ay, but not for ten days yet," he agreed. And then as though struck with a sudden thought or determination, he leaned forward, his chair's legs striking the deck sharply. "And there's one gillie aboard this boat who can't be trusted," he whispered, his face close to mine.

The beaver-musk on his shirt was strong in my nostrils and my thoughts went kiting back to his first night on board. Did he desire now to make a confidant of me?

"Is his identity a secret?" I asked, not willing to invite rebuff a second time by enquiring the name of the person outright.

"Not between *us*," he whispered, readily enough. "Maybe you've noticed a Breed aboard—a pock-marked half-*Chippewa* with a cataract over one eye and big rings in his ears?"

"I have," I answered, remembering the man's deeply scarred visage, especially the nose which had been disfigured by a blow—the kick of a horse, perhaps.

"He's a rotten egg, that gillie, and will bear watching if the *Rees are* bad."

"Why not have him put ashore?" I suggested.

"No, no!" he whispered emphatically. "He knows too much. He would make us trouble if we put him ashore. Leave him ta me, and say not a word about this ta anybody until I give ye permission. Crook would bungle and put him ashore in a second if he knew, and the gillie would go hot-foot to Burwin and upset our kettle, mon!"

"As you like," I said, "but you ought to speak of this to Captain Crook, I think."

"Not now—not now, not so near to Leavenworth. I'll keep my eye on the devil, though, and if my suspicions are proven to me, I'll tell Crook fast enough. Then we'll drop him ashore so far from Fort Leavenworth that he won't care to go back, even for revenge. I thought I'd tell you, so that you might smell around a bit. I mean size the gillie up. There's time enough yet—and I might be wrong, you know, Mr. McLeod."

Like a partially quenched fire that smoulders, my instinctive suspicion of Cameron, after having been somewhat allayed by the Burwin episode, now rose up again. I could not believe his reasoning sound. Captain Crook would not have put the half-blood ashore where there was the slightest danger that the fellow would go back to Fort Leavenworth with the tale of the ruse practiced upon the Army officer.

Then why had Cameron told me, made me his confidant, instead of Captain Crook? Perhaps his distrust of the half-blood was only a growing suspicion which, for fear of confirmation, he did not care to impart to the Captain who had enough to think about. This might be his reason for confiding in me, of course. Yes, I thought it might. I knew that in his place I should want to share my suspicion with another. Perhaps I was permitting my dislike for Cameron to carry me too far. But there was his man, Hawkins, and Eli Whitney. Surely together they could take care of the miserable half-blood, even without annoying Captain Crook. How did I know that Cameron had not told Hawkins and Eli Whitney? But if he had, why had he come to me? "Smell around a bit." Indeed I would.

Tribal alliances were not uncommon. While the *Chippewa* and the *Rees*, widely separated, were not fast friends, the suspected half-blood might, through marriage, or some overt act which had made him a *Chippewa* outlaw, have become associated with the *Arickara* tribe. I knew that his paternal blood would not count in our favor, and that in thought, sympathy and habits, the fellow, like all the offspring of the white adventurers who had associated themselves with the people of the plains, was an Indian. They could not possibly have been otherwise, since environment, and the evident preference of their fathers for the life and ways of their mother's people precluded pride of white kinship, and made every tribal characteristic and cause their own. Even their fathers, expatriates whom wilderness had weaned away and made more red than white, were often partisan tribesmen, so that Cameron's suspicion of this particular half-blood might easily be sound.

I began to speculate. What could the half-blood do that would count against us? Hardly more than desert the *Yellow Stone* and, by cutting across the country, carry information regarding our number and whereabouts to the *'Rees*, knowledge which their own scouts would already possess if the tribe was at war, and intended attack. Petty theft would be the utmost of his accomplishment before his going. I could see no great loss in his taking himself off, if he wanted to go, but nevertheless my interest was whetted keen.

After breakfast in the morning I walked out forward of the stacks where I could see most of the forward hold-deck, and almost the first person I saw there was the half-blood. He and another of his kind, kneeling on a buffalo robe spread upon the deck, were intently gaming. I have forgotten the name of the game they were playing, but a number of the small bones of the feet of antelope strung on sinew string are tossed and caught on a thin skewer of bone or hardwood. The score was counted according to the position of the skewer when the string is caught upon its point. Neither noticed my appearance on the deck above them, and I had a good look at my man.

If his face had not been so scarred it would have been rather finely cut, almost effeminate, and he was a runt beside the burly fellow before him. Although I could not see his eyes, altogether he appeared too insignificant to occasion a second thought. "But I'll go down and engage him in conversation just the same," I decided.

He must have sensed my gaze, my very thoughts. As though a goad had pricked him, his eyes, one white and blighted, the other wild as a frightened deer's, flashed up, met mine and fell again. My interest came back to me. Something *was* wrong with the fellow.

I turned and walked leisurely to the companionway and down to the hold-deck. When I got there my man was gone. His erstwhile companion, sitting alone on the robe, was filling his pipe. I decided to sit with him, thinking perhaps my man would return. But just when I had reached the robe somebody called and the fellow, nodding pleasantly to me, picked up his robe and went aft.

I sat down on a coil of rope, my back to the woodpile, as though I had not observed anything unusual in my man's running away, feeling sure that he was watching me. "The poor fellow is crazed," I thought, "and might run amuck. Queer that nobody except Cameron had noticed the man's condition." Perhaps Sandy Campbell had. I would ask him.

A blue heron flying down the river and rising, passed over the *Yellow Stone*. I turned slowly around, my head bent backward as though my gaze were following the bird, when dropping my eyes I beheld the man's scarred face peering at me round the corner of the woodpile. I was very careful not to let my eyes linger an instant, and he drew back out of sight again at once. It was disconcerting. There was no telling what he might do, poor devil.

Nobody happened to be in sight, except the two in the pilot house, and they were watching the river, not the deck below them. I could hear singing farther aft where the big half-blood had gone, and an Indian drum was beating time to a song. Perhaps Cameron would be there. I'd see. Standing up I stretched as though bored and then strolled along the woodpile, glancing through the apertures between the loosely piled sticks, until suddenly I found myself looking squarely into the man's good eye. He stared a second, and was gone, and I heard him running away.

Whenever the eye of a watcher meets the eye of the watched, both instantly know it, whether both be men, or one a human and the other a beast, and whichever is more afraid, that one's fear is betrayed in a flash. I knew the ways of these people. The half-blood was deathly afraid of me. Why? I could not guess.

To seek him out and question him would be futile too, I decided. Superstitious beyond belief, and suspicious of any save his own kind, the man had evidently been made afraid of me by some agency in which he had confidence, and only the greatest tact could now dispel his fear, I well knew. Walking on past the woodpile as though nothing had disturbed me I suddenly became aware of Cameron coming along the deck, and stepped into the engine-room to avoid talking to him just then. But he had not seen me, and after a minute or two, I came out again and now discovered Cameron and the one-eyed half-blood in close conversation by the woodpile. The half-blood did not look up as I passed, but Cameron winked, cunningly. He was "smelling about" himself, evidently, and I wondered what he would tell me later on.

There was no opportunity to push my investigation further now and, satisfied that Cameron would have something to report, I went up the companionway to the boiler-deck where I found the whole of the Prince's party in the shade of the cabin.

Excepting Miss Strongford, who was sewing busily, all were intent at reading, and these only bowed politely as I walked toward two vacant chairs farther down the deck. But Miss Strongford, her needle poised over her work looked up to smile so cheerily that upon reaching the chairs I moved them into deeper shade, and there, with a great show of industry pretended to dust one of them with my handkerchief, bowing politely to her as though she had set me at the task of preparing a seat for herself. My mood pleased her and, nodding a ready acceptance of my implied invitation, she gathered her work and came smilingly to the chair.

"Where has Sir Donald kept himself hidden, lately?" she asked, spreading the white linen in her lap.

"He has been lax in his bounden duty to Lady Strongford and, if she will permit him, he will repair on the instant to her state-room and there mend her noisy window sash."

She bent over the white linen in her lap. "Sir Donald is indeed mindful," she remarked. "It does drum a frightful tattoo whenever the engine runs."

"May I go now?" I asked, rising.

"Yes, let's stop the tattoo at once," she laughed. "The door is unlocked."

Faintly perfumed, her stateroom was neat as a pin, and it was with a feeling of intrusion that I entered it. The blue dress with the white lace hung on the wall beside a gown of buff color which I had not seen her wear. "It would match her hair beautifully," I thought, while I tried not to spy about. The tiny chamber had taken on an air of its occupant, which I felt. Perfect competency was as apparent as happiness, and reserve was in its orderly neatness. Somehow the dresses, and a white handkerchief with a lace border freshly ironed and folded on the bureau made me think of the little portrait in Mr. Bodmer's old Spanish trunk.

I went directly at my task, and with some tacks and leather, already secured from Sandy Campbell, it was the work of only a minute to make the sash tight–too tight, I found when I attempted to let it down. I shaved the leather with my knife, and tried the sash again, moving it up and down until it worked smoothly and yet would not rattle. When I was satisfied that I could not improve what I had done, I opened the window to leave it as I had found it, and looking out I beheld Cameron watching me, intently, his mean, accusing green eyes so suddenly firing my anger that my blood leaped in me and burned. The baseness of his soul was in his eyes and, before their light could change, my own had discerned it there.

I knew he sensed my anger, but without a sign of resentment he bowed, pleasantly, and walked leisurely down the deck. Was there ever, before him, such a man as Angus Cameron? I shut my jackknife and returned it to my pocket, looking at, yet only half seeing, the blue dress with the white lace on the wall. Would Cameron, even in a humorous vein, speak insinuatingly of my presence in her stateroom to Miss Strongford? I dared him to do this; but I must go out on deck, and there must be no trace of my anger in my face.

"'Tis done, Lady Jane," I said, taking up our playful way of talking, and at the same time sitting down in the chair beside her. "There will be no more tattoo."

"Thank you, Sir Donald. I shall miss it, although I prefer some other amusement. There was such a perfect cadence to that window's rattle that it often trifled with my imagination. It was quite wonderful. Why, if there could have been Scotch pipes playing I might have danced to their tunes. And the window seemed to prefer 'The Campbells are Comin'.' I tried many, but 'The Campbells' was best. It was this way"–She hummed the lively Scotch air, cleverly keeping time in imitation of the window's rattling, her thimble tapping her chair and her toe the deck.

She was in a merry mood. If in her heart there was anything but joy, she defied the world to find it there. "Did you like Captain Burwin?" she asked, laying aside her work with the evident intention of visiting with me. "I thought him charming, perhaps toward the last a bit in his cups, but withal, I thought his frankness out of the ordinary. Didn't you?"

I did not answer this. Cameron was coming with a chair. Without invitation, he placed it near mine.

"'Tis the on'y place on the whole ship," he grinned, "where gab is footloose, and work defied. On wi' the fest! I'll tak a hand wi' ye, and ye will."

Miss Strongford unfolded the white linen, and her needle flashed into the cloth.

"Hi Ho! Life is on'y a snare an' a delusion, after a'," Cameron smiled, watching the needle a moment. Then turning to me, "Where have you kept yourself this afternoon?" he asked, quite genially.

If there was any hidden malice, any taunt, in his words I could not detect it, but there might be such, I well knew.

"Here, there, and everywhere," I answered, purposely giving him a chance to emphasize it if he would.

But we fell to talking of the fur trade, and after listening for a while over her work, Miss Strongford went to her stateroom, and Cameron and I went on exchanging experiences.

Cameron had willfully spoiled my afternoon, but I had two reasons for being agreeable to him. He had not mentioned my visit to Miss Strongford's stateroom; and I hoped he would tell me something about his conversation with the half-blood. But he didn't, and I would not ask him.

CHAPTER TWELVE

ameron continued affable, and even when two weeks had passed and we were following the Missouri's winding course through the plains, he had not once shown his meaner self, although at times I thought he might be spying upon Jane Strongford and myself. Whenever he could find excuse, even a flimsy one, he intruded rudely upon our company, and often I wished heartily that he was anywhere but aboard the *Yellow Stone*. On the other hand I couldn't blame him altogether for this, since he had outworn every one of the saloon passengers, even Prince Maximilian having at last tired of him. The novelty of acquaintance with a plainsman, which had so interested His Highness at first, had become an old story and now, like Mr. Bodmer, the Prince fled whenever Cameron approached, so that aside from Mrs. Doeffner, who occasionally engaged him in short conversation and who I think found fun in quizzing him, he was *de trop* with the passengers of the *Yellow Stone*.

I had hoped that Miss Strongford would speak to me of Cameron, and once, after a particularly rude intrusion on his part, I had purposely led her to an opportunity which she passed over although I well knew that she had recognized not only the opening to discuss her countryman, but my curiosity as well. I confess I was piqued a trifle, too, in what I thought her lack of confidence in me. But this much I now knew—she did not love Cameron, and it had been surprise and terror, almost childlike, which she had quickly veiled with her woman's eyes the morning she had first seen him on the hurricane deck of the *Yellow Stone*. But these had seemed lately to have lost their power over her for some reason unknown to me, and I thought that now distrust akin to loathing of

Cameron had taken their place. Still she would not give me her confidence, if indeed there was anything to confide, and I thought there was.

One night, long after we were tied up to the bank edging a grove of giant cottonwood, and, when good Mr. Bodmer, after giving us a glass of his now scanty supply of wine, had gone to his bed, Cameron came to me on the afterdeck where I was sitting alone with my rifle. I had been thinking of him, and curiously of the half-blood whose behavior so puzzled me. I had no taste for thoughts of Cameron and tried to put them away, because whenever I permitted my mind to dwell on him, he was sure to appear. He came now, and like a small boy who believes in signs I blamed myself for his coming.

We were in the *Arickara* country, and for nearly a week had put out guards at night, every man keeping his rifle close at hand at all times. No lights were permitted aboard, no loud talking might be indulged in, and always as soon as the pilot could see, the *Yellow Stone* moved on. No Indians had been seen, but instead of considering this a good sign, we were fearful that their absence meant mischief later on—that the 'Rees must have congregated for war.

Cameron sat down beside me, his rifle across his knees. "I think I have been entirely wrong in my suspicions concerning that half-blood," he said, as though we had lately been discussing him. "He's a bit loony, mayhap, but that is all," he added, removing his black head-silk and fanning his face with it, the beaver-musk thick as a fog.

I waited to reply. I had been trying to discover ground for Cameron's expressed distrust of the fellow, and was no nearer an understanding of it than of his very evident fear of me.

"He may be a bit off—crazy a wee bit, you know," Cameron said again, "but he's harmless as a pet rabbit."

I believed that Cameron must surely know of the half-blood's groundless fear of me and, if he did know of it, it was strange that he failed to mention it now—to offer it as proof of the fellow's unbalanced mind.

"I did not tell Crook of my suspicions, and now I'm mighty glad that I didn't. Did *you*?" Cameron ceased fanning himself and laid the head-silk on his rifle.

"No," I replied, at the same time determining not to speak of the half-blood's strange fear of me.

"Damn the mosquitoes!" The black head-silk flirted spitefully about his face and mine. Then he said, "I'm glad that you didn't. It would only have worried Crook. I think I shall use the little gillie once in a while after this—put him out on guard with *you* or *me*, so that even if he is not right we can handle him. I can't use everybody every night, you know, and these foreigners (meaning the Prince and Mr. Bodmer) are no good *whatever.*"

"As you like," I said, but seeing no good in his plan.

Cameron, because of his experience and cleverness, had been given charge of our guarding the *Yellow Stone* against a surprise attack, and each night six men were stationed on shore by him at points of his own selection. These men were relieved every two hours, so that aside from Prince Maximilian and Mr. Bodmer who, although they readily offered their services, were not used, nobody now had a whole night's sleep. Cameron himself was tireless, always going out with the relief guard and returning with the relieved men. Sometimes on the last guard before daylight when attack by Indians is most to be expected, he stood guard himself. He could only catnap, if he slept at all during the nights, and only after the boat was on her way again could he really rest undisturbed.

"Well, then," he said, "if you are willing, I will put the half-blood out with you, or where you can keep an eye on him tomorrow night, and we'll see how he acts. This will give Eli Whitney a chance to rest up. I've used him a good deal. Can't keep Crook or the pilots, or Sandy Campbell up all night when they have to work all day."

"I'm satisfied," I told him. At this he put on his black head-silk and went to waken the relief. I watched him in the moonlight, going down the gangplank to the grove with the six men.

The next day, after a sound sleep until noon, I went with Mr. Bodmer to visit Sandy Campbell, for whom the artist had formed a genuine attachment, and in rounding the woodpile came suddenly upon the half-blood.

His terror of me I found had not in the least abated and, seeing me, he dodged behind the wood again like a frightened coyote, leaving on the deck, where he had been sitting, a small rawhide pouch painted and decorated with tattered bird-feathers. This was his medicine-bundle, I knew, and he had been engaged in invoking its aid, probably in his coming guard duty, when I appeared.

Mr. Bodmer stooped to pick up the pouch, but I restrained him, and we went on to the engine room, where I left my companion to go back to the woodpile. I had determined to engage the half-blood in conversation, and learn why he feared me.

Walking back, I saw at once that the medicine pouch was gone and, after circling the woodpile, that the half-blood had gone away from it. I began whistling idly, heading for the other pile of wood. I'd follow him now, and if I could, without driving him overboard, talk with him. Arriving at the objective woodpile I leaned against it and filled my pipe, lighting it with my flint and steel, as leisurely as I could. "Why will you not speak to me, brother?" I asked, gently, in good *Sioux.*

There was no answer—not a sound behind the wood, although I was sure the fellow was there.

"I am a friend," I continued speaking ever so softly. "I would smoke with you. See, my pipe is lighted, and I am alone."

Still no answer, and as I returned my pipe to my mouth the fellow slipped around the far corner of the woodpile and was out of sight behind the cabin in a twinkling.

There was no use in trying to be friendly with him now. I should be obliged to wait. What wild notion was in his head? I could not even guess.

I returned to the engine room and for a moment hoped that Sandy Campbell could tell me why the half-blood's actions were so peculiar.

"Ay, mon," he said. "He's a wee beet afrighted o' you an' Red Cameron, but most of a' o yerse'l'."

"Why?" I asked with high hopes.

Sandy shrugged his shoulders. "If yerse'l' don't know, mon, how can I? They're a queer lot with their feerfu' supersteetions an' their crotchets; the de'il tak em' a'."

Mr. Bodmer had long since settled himself to smoke comfortably with Sandy, and so I excused myself. I went out and up to the boiler-deck where I found Miss Strongford and Mrs. Doeffner sitting in the shade. Mrs. Doeffner had not yet accepted as serious the danger from Indians, and when I came up she asked, lightly, "How goes the war with the Savages?"

A shot, and a jingle of broken glass answered her.

Both ladies fled into the saloon, Mrs. Doeffner, in her haste upsetting her chair. Discovering a wisp of powder-smoke rising from a clump of willows, I fired into the bushes, but saw no result of my shot.

Men were now running to the boat's rail, rifles in hand, and Cameron, wakened by my shot, came tearing up the companionway.

"What the devil's this?" he demanded, as reloading, I rammed home a ball.

I pointed to the broken glass in the open saloon door.

"Wheew!" he whistled, looking in at the ladies who now were crouched under the table there, Mrs. Doeffner, frightened at last, and Miss Strongford looking as though it were a game of some sort which she had half a mind to enjoy instead of fear.

"Better stay inside," advised Cameron, seriously, his hand on the door-casing.

"Ach!" returned Mrs. Doeffner, glancing first at Cameron and then at the broken glass on the deck. "Do you imagine us fools enough to sit out there to be—to be—?"

"Eaten alive by mosquitoes?" laughed Miss Strongford, settling herself in a more comfortable position. "Shall I read to you, Mrs. Doeffner?" she asked, glancing humorously at that lady.

Just then Prince Maximilian, who had been sleeping, came into the saloon, rifle in hand. "What is the matter?" he asked, curiously, seeing the ladies under the table.

"We are playing toads. This table is our toad's stool, and it is pouring rain, Your Highness," Miss Strongford answered, her eyes dancing.

"We have been fired upon—only one shot," supplemented Cameron. "Nobody hurt." Then turning to me, "Did you get him, do you think?"

"I am sure I don't know."

Hearing this, the Prince went outside and took a stand on the afterdeck, as plainly anxious for an opportunity to try a shot as any man could be. An hour passed peacefully, however, then Mr. Bodmer appeared, pipe in mouth. He came slowly up the companionway. He had no weapon and, leaning over the rail by my side, enquired about the ladies, turned to inspect the broken glass, and then sat down, his face a little troubled.

"I suppose now I must forever carry a gun about with me—a gun with bullets and slugs, if I would be in style," he said with humorous discontent.

Miss Strongford laughed merrily, and rising, Mr. Bodmer looked curiously into the saloon.

"So," he grinned, pointing with his long pipe-stem at the two women, "is it also now stylish to sit on the floor?"

"Indeed it is," said Mrs. Doeffner, a little testily, "and you should get a gun like the others."

"Yes, Herr Bodmer," Miss Strongford urged, "gentlemen should carry rifles when ladies are obliged to sit for safety beneath dining tables. Don't you think so? Why, Mr. McLeod fired at the savage who shattered the glass in our door—perhaps he killed him!"

"Ja, and so quickly he shot!" exclaimed Mrs. Doeffner with a complimentary glance at me.

Mr. Bodmer drew away from the door and sat down. He was hurt by their banter, and I could see that his sensitiveness had betrayed him to the belief that even I might think him cowardly.

"I was in the engine room with your Mr. Campbell," he said in explanation of his absence when the shot was fired. "But now I will not go there again. I shall stay on the deck with you, my friend, and I will carry a gun, ja."

Then as though anxious to show his own appreciation for my promptness in returning the Indian's shot, he said, "Come, drink a glass of wine with me before there is more shooting to make us forget that there are other things besides bullets—round balls and slugs."

I followed him into his stateroom where for more than an hour we talked together over a single glass of wine. Then, reaching into the old Spanish trunk he handed me the little portrait, unasked.

"So," he said, as I took the picture almost reverently from his hand. His spoken "so" was as though he, good man, had not only given me his confidence, but had shared with me his only treasure.

CHAPTER THIRTEEN

he shot which shattered the glass of the saloon door had warned us that the half-expected trouble ahead was likely to be real, and of course the farther we ascended the river the nearer we drew to the *Arickara* village, the seat of our danger.

After supper, which was had early that evening, Mrs. Doeffner repaired to her stateroom before there was need for lights, which were not allowed, and the Prince and Mr. Bodmer went out on the deck. Miss Strongford and I had more than two hours together in the saloon before the *Yellow Stone* swung in toward the bank. It was already dark, and the boat was very carefully feeling her way to her berth for the night when I suddenly remembered that, as yet, I did not know at what hour I was to go on guard duty. I must, at once, report to Cameron and learn, since if I were given a late assignment I must get some sleep beforehand. The suspense of the night after what had happened in the day had already drawn us more closely together and now rising, regretfully, I ventured to be more bold than ever before.

"I am obliged to leave you," I said, "perhaps only to return in a few minutes. Will you wait for me? I may be back."

"I will wait," she agreed, clasping her hands, nervously, I thought, "but if you go out there, be careful, Sir Donald." She tried to cover her solicitude with a little added lightness.

"Yes, of course," I answered her, feeling suddenly happy at her anxiety.

"There will be no trouble," I assured her. "If I do not come back within fifteen minutes go to bed and sleep soundly." I bent in the dark to smile into her eyes.

"I'll try, but I am afraid to be left alone," she said, turning away

111

from me. And somehow I felt that she was not thinking of that one night alone, and not alone of Indians, either.

"You sha'nt be left!" I replied passionately.

"McLeod!" Cameron's voice was not loud, but close to us there in the doorway. Miss Strongford drew back quickly into the saloon.

"Yes," I answered, stepping out with my rifle.

"First guard. Come on."

I followed him down the companionway and on down the gangplank with five others, one of whom I saw was the half-blood who kept the others carefully between himself and me.

Cameron placed us one by one, first leading us up the river a quarter of a mile where he left a man, then traveling back in a semicircle to a point about a quarter of a mile below the *Yellow Stone*. He stationed men at well-chosen places until the sixth was left on duty by the river below the steamboat. Mine was the third post assigned, nearly a quarter of a mile straight away from the river, abreast of the boat, and just where the extensive grove began thinning toward the plains. "I'll be back, shortly," Cameron told me, quietly, as he went on to station the remaining men, one of whom was the half-blood.

I was beside a giant cottonwood tree. It was at least four feet in diameter and not very tall. Not a breath of air was stirring in the grove, and the mosquitoes rose in clouds whenever I moved. It was yet early, and the men were not all stationed. I began clearing away the ground about the tree so that I might not, in moving, step on and break noisily the dry sticks lying about. I had spent a long time at this, and was leaning against the cottonwood, wet with perspiration and thinking I had never before experienced a night so close and sultry, when Cameron came back as he had promised.

"Mind that damned half-blood," he whispered, his hand on the tree. "I put him close to you. He's right across that bit of swale there," pointing in the darkness to an opening in the grove, a swampy spot, perhaps. "If he should show up nasty, don't wait, man. Let him have it." He mopped his face with a dark handkerchief that smelled strongly of beaver-musk. "Whew," he panted, fanning himself with the scented cloth, "it's hot as merry hell. But the blood's all right, a bit daft, but right enough," he broke off, as though an afterthought to reassure me. "See now," he pointed again, "he's behind that bush yonder—that lone one, right across from us here, see?"

The bush, a small quaking aspen, hardly tall enough to hide a man, I thought, was not seventy-five yards away, but with the background of dark trees and other bushes was only discernible at all because of its position.

"Yes," I said, thinking that Cameron had indeed stationed him close enough.

"Well, I'll be going back," he whispered, his hand brushing away the swarms of mosquitoes that hummed about our heads. "Good luck to ye, Mister McLeod."

Cameron gone, I settled down to watch and listen and wait. No man who has not stood guard at night in the Indian country can ever know the things one seems to see and hear at such a time, even when perfectly self-possessed and cool. One's senses, quickened by danger, are so keened that they turn fanciful. I searched the whole grove and, beginning systematically at a point on either hand, skipping nothing until suddenly remembering the bush across the swale behind which the half-blood had been posted, I would turn in a flash to stare at it in weird fascination.

Last night Cameron had told me that his suspicions concerning the half-blood were not justified. Tonight he had distrusted him again. Why use him at all under the circumstances? What good was he? Five of us would have done the work as well. What harm could he do even if he were treacherous? Questions like these came to me, staring at the bush.

The moon would soon be up. She was even now rising, and the bush was constantly growing plainer to my sight. I began to see farther and farther through the cottonwood grove, but after a thorough search of every other thing within the range of my vision, my eyes, as though glad of my permission, always lighted at last upon the bush across the swale.

And how persistently the mosquitoes made me suffer. The air, full of them, seemed itself to hum monotonously, and tortured, I fought them quietly, breathing them into my throat and lungs, sometimes. "Two hours of this," I thought, my face and hands bleeding and smarting. No other night had been like this, and I knew that not more than an hour had passed.

At length the moonlight fell upon the swale, upon the bush itself, but nothing seemed to stir there, not even a leaf was rustled by the least perceptible night breeze. I could see through the top of it now, and anybody standing behind it would certainly have shown us his head, but I saw no head, made out no form. There was nobody there! Could it be possible that the half-blood, a traitor, or a coward, had sneaked from behind the bush, unseen. Well, if he was gone, he was gone.

I forced my eyes to go the rounds of the grove once more, holding them steadfastly to their task of scanning every outline to perfect recognition before I allowed them to rest again on the bush.

There was nobody there. Where could the half-blood have gone? *How* could he have gone? Had Cameron known that he would slip away without my seeing him? Had he, perhaps, thought to make me appear ridiculous as a guard by this?

Brushing away clouds of mosquitoes, hardly moving, in order that I might see, I strained my eyes until they ached. But there was nobody there.

Dripping with perspiration I tore my eyes away from the tormenting bush and resolved to consider it no more than other bushes. And now, strange enough under circumstances so trying, my thoughts turned gladly to Jane Strongford. She had asked me to be careful tonight. She was afraid on her own account, too. Jane Strongford afraid and needing me! I marveled. How sweet and beautiful she was! I thought I would like to see her wear the buff-colored dress which I had seen in her stateroom. It would exactly suit her hair. And what beautiful hair it was! I'd tell her so. I'd tell her tomorrow. And I'd ask her to wear the buff-colored dress, too. Perhaps Mr. Bodmer would paint her portrait in the dress, if I asked him. How I would love to own a little portrait of Miss Jane Strongford! I'd rather have it than even the little portrait in Mr. Bodmer's trunk. I had never known a person so gay as Miss Strongford—or so cheerful. She seemed always to be lighthearted and without a care. And yet I wondered if she really was, or if deep down, if there was not some secret trouble which she kept to herself. Why did I always feel the presence of something hidden, if it were not really there to be felt. The Camerons held Strongford lands, of course, but what real power had Angus Cameron over Jane Strongford. He had, though. It was all a terrible mystery to me. I had made up my mind a dozen times that she did not love him, and tonight she had said she was afraid, and I had known it was of Cameron, and yet why would she not tell me about it and let me challenge him so that she would be free from him. She seemed to care for me somewhat. What was his power over her?

I held my eyes away from the bush for ages, it seemed to me, and now a breeze was stirring the leaves over my head. I looked over at the bush. Its top was swaying in the bright moonlight, but I was still certain there was nobody there.

"Must be getting along toward relief time," I thought, again turning my eyes to searching the grove. The breeze was blowing stronger now, helping with the mosquitoes, and it was from straight across the swale.

Suddenly I straightened my body, and then bent forward. I had caught the odor of beaver-musk, faint but unmistakable. "Relief time," I thought, thankfully. Cameron must be coming. He would pass the half-blood's post, discover that he was not there, and I would tell him that the fellow had not been there since the moon came.

And then the breeze parted the top of the bush; somebody *was* there, after all! I saw him. And at the same time a flash of fire.

As though struck with a heavy iron bar, I pitched forward upon my face, a numb, burning sensation in my left shoulder which spread to my breast and arm instantly. "I'm shot," I thought, rolling over and staggering to my feet just as another shot flashed across the swale. I saw the flash of it—heard it, and stooped for my rifle. But I was dizzy and sick now, and I sank down against the tree, pulling my rifle to me. I tried to look—to see across the swale, but the bush swayed crazily, and my strength was gone. "I'm shot," I thought, resignedly, my ears ringing like sleigh bells.

"Are you hit, man?" It was Cameron. My temples were thumping, and I could no longer see.

"I've done for him, damn him! He tried to murder you, man," he said, savagely, his voice sounding far off and dulled by tumultuous noises.

I think I must have fainted then, for I remember nothing more until I heard Miss Strongford's frightened voice saying, "Please go away now, Angus, and send Sandy Campbell to me."

I opened my eyes but could not bear the light of the candle which somebody was holding close to my face.

"So, my friend, could you drink a sip of wine, yes?"

Good Mr. Bodmer's face was sad, and his eyes were wet with

tears. "I shall be all right," I said. But I had lost much blood, and went off again before Sandy came.

There was sunshine when, half conscious, I again opened my eyes. The familiar "chowww-chow" of the 'scape pipe was pleasant to hear, besides a cool breeze fanned my face. But my thoughts were muddled—wild, and I didn't like the candle so near my face. Why did they hold it there? Where was the swale—the bush? I was ill, that was it. Beaver-musk had sickened me. Cameron's dark handkerchief had spread contagion. In the interest of Miss Strongford I would go to Captain Crook about that handkerchief.

Then a flash of vivid memory came. "Chowww-chow." The *Yellow Stone* was traveling. It was not candle-light, but sunshine. "I'm shot," I thought, without caring whether I got well, or died.

It was Prince Maximilian and Sandy Campbell who dressed my wound which was in my left shoulder just over the lung. The bullet had not lodged, fortunately, and I was strong and healthy, so that within ten days I was up and about a little, very stiff and sore, but thankful to be alive.

We had passed the *Arickara* village without trouble and were looking for none now, although each night Cameron put out his guard when the *Yellow Stone* tied up. The shot which shattered the glass of the saloon door had no doubt been fired by some renegade 'Ree who, unable to incite his tribe to open warfare with the American Fur Company, had sought to make war alone.

I was sorry that I had missed seeing the 'Ree village, because nobody ever told of going up or down the river without mentioning this troublesome spot. But I well remember the day we steamed by it. They had removed the door of my stateroom, so that even when alone there, if I spoke or made a noise, somebody would come to learn if I required anything. Miss Strongford and Mr. Bodmer were always coming or going, and often Miss Strongford read aloud to me. But this day—the day we passed the 'Ree village, Miss Jane and Mr. Bodmer were in my room together when Cameron came to enquire how I was getting along.

Miss Jane had been reading when Mr. Bodmer came in with a sketch of a badger, and after showing it to me, he had begun a story of a dog and badger fight which he had once read, when Cameron's coming stopped the tale almost between syllables. Then, as though at last determined to satisfy his conscience which until now he had deliberately suppressed, Mr. Bodmer laid the sketch face-downward on the berth, and turned squarely, thrusting his hands into his coat pockets, said, "Tell me, how did this shooting occur, Mr. Cameron?" He spoke quietly, but abruptly, his eyes looking straight into Cameron's, as though by watching he might catch a lie there.

My blood leaped to my temples. I saw Miss Strongford start, and her fingers pinch the book till her nails were whitened.

Cameron's green eyes narrowed, but did not waver. He must, of course, have told the story many times before, yet now he could not repress a sneer, and looking into Mr. Bodmer's eyes through his own narrowed lids, he spoke patronizingly, as though to a questioning child who had enquired into affairs beyond its power of comprehension.

"Oh, 'tis not much of a tale, and need rob no healthy man o' sleep. We were a bit suspicious of the blood, Mr. McLeod and I, though I thought to use him to prevent the savages from breaking your rest, do ye see? I put him on guard where Mr. McLeod could watch him, thinking if the gillie were treacherous he'd catch him at his didoes. After a bit of thinking, I decided I'd go back and take a look myself. And 'tis well I did. Ay, 'tis well, the dirty beast!"

Then as though he would condescend no further, he turned to me, his back to Mr. Bodmer.

"I thought he'd killed ye, man," he said, gravely. "To my last breath I'll never understand why ye didn't plug him when he raised his rifle. 'Twas almost bright as day in the moonlight. The devil's luck it was that I didn't get there a minute sooner. Ay, half a minute would a-done it. Why, man, he'd no more than fired when I let him have it, himself, the cowardly whelp! An' ye did na' see the gillie raise his rifle, man?" he asked, incredulous.

I shook my head.

"Mr. McLeod would hardly shoot a man down for raising his rifle, Angus," Miss Strongford reproved. And Mr. Bodmer, as though he would question further, asked, "But why set a watcher to watch a watcher?"

Cameron laughed, amusedly. "'Tis the holy inquseetion moved to the Missouri. I was a fool to use the blood. Ay a blithering fool, an' I'll admit it. But admission will na mend McLeod, more's the peety. I'll come again. Good day to ye."

Mr. Bodmer, puzzlement in his kindly eyes, stood for a moment staring at the open doorway. Then clasping his hands behind him, and muttering in German, he went softly out of my state-room.

When he had gone, Miss Jane, as though she had been waiting, dipped a linen cloth in cool water, wrung it, and sat down on the berth beside me. "Who was it that shot you, Sir Donald?" she whispered, with a swift glance at the open doorway. "Tell me," she demanded, gravely, laying the cool cloth on my forehead and smoothing my pillow.

I closed my eyes so that she would not see confirmation of her own suspicion there. She had not felt that she could give me *her* confidence, and this thought still rankled a little. Besides, I could only guess who shot me.

"I do not know," I answered.

"Look at me, and say that, Donald," she pleaded.

I only shook my head. Sighing, she rose and walked to the open window where she stood staring out at nothing until Mr. Bodmer came back with a glass of wine.

"Buffaloes! Herds of them—thousands!" he said, enthusiastically. "I have long waited, and now they are here. How much I wish that you, my friend, could come on deck and see them—thousands of them."

Miss Jane took the glass of wine and slipped her arm beneath my head. "Drink a little, if you can," she said, brightly.

Sipping the wine, I looked at good Mr. Bodmer, who was nervous from a burning desire to further see the buffalo herd. "Please go," I urged him. "Do not lose this opportunity on my account."

And like a small boy suddenly relieved of duty to play at a favorite game he went outside, almost running in his eagerness to sketch the herd.

Miss Jane laughed so merrily at his eagerness that I laughed with her in spite of the pain in my shoulder. Laughter was a good way, I thought, to end a rather trying day.

CHAPTER FOURTEEN

 had never before been seriously ill, although when I was eleven I had contracted a mild case of small-pox through a forbidden visit to a newly arrived mackinaw where another boy assured me he had seen a two-headed buffalo calf alive. The boat was from the 'Ree country where there had been a scourge of smallpox, and my father had warned me to keep away. But a two-headed buffalo calf, alive, had proven too great a temptation, and although the calf proved a hoax, I caught the disease.

Now, feverish and weak as a kitten, and I knew, sometimes a little flighty, I spent hours, nights, thinking of the half-blood and Cameron. They obsessed me, and even when I slept I dreamed of them. Now I could never learn the secret of the half-blood's fear of me, but believed it came from the same source as the bullet which took his life—Cameron. Had the half-blood shot me? *Could* he have shot me?

Over and over, without variation, I thought back to the night on guard, to the bush in the "swale," the evident absence of the half-blood from his station, the breeze which brought the odor of beaver-musk and my thoughts of Cameron, the sudden appearance of what I felt certain had been a human form behind the bush, the flash of the rifle, and afterward the sensation of being wounded, followed by the second shot which had killed the half-blood. I had heard that second shot distinctly, and not ten seconds after I had been wounded by the *first.*

One can sometimes ponder so long and intently over a situation that his wits are benumbed by the repetition of what he believes is all the argument which can be brought to bear. My thoughts, too sluggish, could find nothing new, until one morning when I awoke after a fitful sleep with a startling question in my mind. "How could Cameron have fired the second shot so quickly? How could he?"

I remember that I sat up in bed. It was not yet daylight. The boat was still tied up to the bank, and I could hear somebody snoring dismally. Cameron could not have fired both shots–not from the same gun. He could not have shot *me* and, then, loaded his rifle and killed the half-blood in the space of time elapsing between the shots, as measured by me.

As one, obliged by stubborn reason, relinquishes a long established belief, I began to see that, after all, the half-blood *might* have shot me–that he *must* have shot me.

This admission finally made, I settled back on my pillows, ashamed of a persisting suspicion of Cameron which my reason could not cure, and burying my ears in them to shut out the snoring, I counted the matched boards in the ceiling dozens of times in the growing light before I at last heard the guard come aboard. Soon after that, the bell jingled noisily, and the willing *Yellow Stone* began her day's work, her first "Choww–chow" putting a stop to the snoring, for which I felt spitefully glad. I had always liked to hear the sound of the 'scape pipe, but this morning I discovered its monotony annoyed me nearly as much as the snoring, and thus I knew that, if being cross and out of sorts were good omens, I was getting well.

Two miserable hours dragged by before a soul stirred in the saloon. At last when they began setting the breakfast table I heard Miss Strongford's step outside my door.

I do not remember that I had any definite plan in mind when I reached out and pushed a book from a chair near my berth to the floor but, as I anticipated, the noise of the falling book brought Miss Strongford into my stateroom.

"Top of the morning to you, Sir Donald," she laughed, brightly, putting her cool hand on my forehead. "Oh, you are so much better. And what would you like for breakfast? Now please don't say 'eggs' or you'll break my heart."

"Oh a juicy buffalo-steak, well done, with potatoes boiled with their jackets on," I laughed, "but please, Lady Jane, first get Sandy Campbell to dress my shoulder. I want to get out of here," I said, sitting up and feeling my beard which was an inch long now. And then the idea that had been back in my mind, I suppose, when I knocked the book off the chair, shaped itself into definite resolve. I asked her to lend me her hand mirror.

"Oh, your whiskers aren't so unbecoming," she protested, smiling at what she thought was my vanity. "But Mr. Bodmer will shave you; and please let *me* dress your wound this time. I'll be quite as careful as Sandy Campbell."

I hesitated. The task could not be a pleasant one; but my idea was crowding me. I wanted her hand mirror.

"Say yes," she urged, her eyes still smiling, "and I'll get the bandages at once, and we'll have it done before the others are about."

"Yes," I said, "and *please* remember the hand mirror."

She was back in a moment, and first handing me the mirror, which I laid carefully on the bed beside me, she went directly at dressing my shoulder, her fingers like feathers compared with Sandy's.

"Why, it's almost well!" she exclaimed happily when, gently, she had removed the clinging linen over the wound, thus baring it.

"Let me see," I said, picking up the hand mirror and holding it so that I could see the wound—the bullet's hole in my flesh.

But, "Quick, Donald!" she urged as though she were speaking to a child, the fresh linen ready in her hands. "It must not be left exposed. Come, that's enough! It's almost healed."

But still I looked, and with a feeling akin to gladness I saw plainly that no trade-ball had made the wound. The half-blood's weapon, a gun traded to all Indians by the American Fur Company, was known among trappers and plainsmen as a "fuke," and shot an ounce ball—sixteen to the pound. The wound had been made by a much smaller ball. I thought about thirty to the pound. And Cameron's rifle used just thirty balls to the pound.

"Donald, I shall scold in another minute," she said with pretended severity.

Satisfied now, I laid the mirror aside. "I'll be good," I promised, feeling that she knew some problem had been solved by her hand mirror.

"Who shot you, Sir Donald?" she asked once more, as she put the cool linen over the wound.

I heard her, but did not answer. I was still puzzling. It must have been that the half-blood had *never been* behind the bush across the "swale," but behind another close to it. That was the way of it.

Cameron had crept up, shot me from behind the bush he had so carefully pointed out as the half-blood's, and then, knowing exactly where the half-blood was located he had sprung upon him and shot him with his own gun. He had been cunning as a coyote, since if he failed to kill me in the uncertain light, I would know that the shot came from the bush he had designated as the half-blood's position.

"Who shot you, Donald?" Miss Strongford's voice was tenderly persistent, and her eyes were near my own.

I think I would have told her that Cameron had fired the shot if only she had been willing that time to confide in me all she, herself, knew about him. What did I now know of her relation to him? But I would not ask her again, and she hadn't volunteered any information. "I don't know, exactly," I answered, feeling a little ashamed, nevertheless.

"You will have to be very, very careful now, Sir Donald," she whispered, as though I had answered her quite differently. "There! Have I not done as well as Sandy Campbell?" she asked, gathering up the old bandages and the hand mirror, no trace whatever of vexation in her manner.

An hour later, shaved clean, I was out on deck, and how good it seemed to be again in the sunshine. The *Yellow Stone*, steaming past ever-changing breaks and badlands, seemed to be sailing in Paradise. Everywhere was wilderness without a human being in sight, white man or red. Even the camps of the wood-hawks (men engaged by the Company to cut cordwood for the steamboats) had long, long ago been left behind, for this was Indian country now, and no camp was safe from attack by war parties wandering over the plains. Every other day Captain Crook was obliged to tie up and set the men chopping dry wood in the groves, so that the *Yellow Stone* was thus retarded, and while Prince Maximilian seized upon these delays to kill deer in the river bottoms, furnishing us fresh meat, the rest of us were beginning to feel the tedium of the journey.

Toward three o'clock, when the sun was blistering hot and the air so dead still that one was glad of the motion of the boat which seemed to furnish him needed breath, we came suddenly to a low gap in the bluffs. Through half-closed eyes I saw it come into view as the boat swung around a bend of the glassy stream, and I caught the glimpse of the parched plains it afforded, saw the heat shimmer and dance over the grass already cured by the sun. Simultaneously I heard the signal bell for more headway.

There was nothing in sight to warrant a spurt of speed. Lazily, I arose and went around to the starboard rail to look. A herd of buffalo was pouring through the gap into the river, and Captain Crook intended to pass before it reached the channel. Responding promptly to the bell, the engine began to set the boat vibrating. *Here* was excitement. Could the *Yellow Stone* make it? It would be nip and tuck. Begrudging the moment required, yet determined to share the thrill, I ran back. "Mr. Bodmer! Everybody! Come quick!" I called, and raced again to the starboard rail where, just as I arrived, I heard Cameron's voice call into the engine room below, "Open her wide, Sandy, man. Give her fits!"

"Goodness!" gasped Mrs. Doeffner, shading her eyes with a hand that trembled, perhaps because the *Yellow Stone*, herself was now trembling violently under extraordinary speed. "Ach!, Himmel! They will climb over us! Why does he not stop the boat?" she cried, so excited that she began speaking rapidly in German, though to nobody in particular.

The Prince and Mr. Bodmer were held entranced and speechless by the sight. Miss Strongford, slipping her arm under Mrs. Doeffner's and reassuring her as though she were a child, was unmistakably enjoying the excitement of the event, herself, for her cheeks were flushed and her eyes bright as she talked quite freely with the Prince, her usual reserve with him all but forgotten.

I could only glance away from the river. My deepest interest was with the herd's leaders, now far out in the water, some already swimming. Others, hundreds, plunged after them, their legs at first churning the water into foam, until reaching the deep water, they at length sank down to swim, their heads and humps a moving mass of brown and black toward which the *Yellow Stone* was forging rapidly. Seeing nothing but the objective bank, though pushed toward us by the current, the leaders, now hundreds, were halfway across when I saw that the herd on the shore had widened and was plunging in far below the gap. The *Yellow Stone* could not possibly pass the leaders, I thought, and the thousands of buffalo now entering the water below the gap would soon be abreast of us—even behind us. I glanced up at the pilothouse just as Captain Crook reached for the bell rope. Then a cloud of dust borne by a gentle breeze through the gap floated over us, and hid the banks.

The bell jingled, and instantly the engine stopped. The current took hold of us and we drifted back, back, but too late. The water all about, ahead, on both sides, and behind us was black with buffalo. The *Yellow Stone* appeared to be on a sea of black heads, black, sharp horns, and round staring eyes. And the noise! The engine still, the air was filled with wild snorting, sad blowing and bumping of horns. The odor itself was disconcerting.

Captain Crook dared not start the engine lest he break the paddle wheels against the sturdy bodies of the swimming buffalo that, unseeing, bumped against the *Yellow Stone's* sides, milled in the current, pushing and crowding until getting their bearings they went on around us. The boat was powerless, being shoved about like a chip by the surging mass of bodies, and we expected every minute to go upon a bar, since the channel might as well have been in Jericho for all the good it could do us now. Once, when far out of the channel and in imminent danger, Captain Crook rang for steam, but no sooner had the wheels begun turning than there was a crash, and the engine stopped.

I heard a little startled cry from Miss Strongford and turned quickly. Her arms were about Mrs. Doeffner, who had fainted, and would have fallen but for her. Prince Maximilian and Mr. Bodmer carried the lady into her stateroom where Miss Strongford bade all us go away and leave them, which we were glad enough to do.

A buffalo calf had been caught by the paddles and lifted into the housing where it jammed, breaking the starboard wheel, badly. Again we were drifting, and only luck could save us from the dangerous sandbars. This situation, added to shouts, and few shots fired by Prince Maximilian and Eli Whitney who killed two fat cows for meat, so excited us all, even the old hands lost their calmness by its unusualness. When, at length the *Yellow Stone* drifted free, I felt that we had been Providentially delivered from peril. With great difficulty, yet skillfully, the crippled steamboat was worked to a berth against a cut bank and tied up.

Everybody felt the situation keenly, especially Mrs. Doeffner who, when told that for several days the *Yellow Stone* would be unable to proceed, became humorously indignant, although I thought her fun covered much of genuine disgust, and that she was in reality tired of the voyage. But the Prince, now interested in the carcasses of the two buffalo which, after considerable trouble, had been hoisted aboard, was having the time of his life, and to the amusement of Mr. Bodmer, who, resigned, made many sketches of the herd which was still crossing the Missouri not far above us when darkness came.

The guards were put out as usual that night, and there was some real apprehension felt, since Indians are always apt to be near great buffalo herds. But nothing happened to disturb us on board the *Yellow Stone*, except that the wolves, following the great herd, howled dismally throughout the night, often coming very near us, so near that Mrs. Doeffner was glad to have the company of Miss Strongford in her stateroom, I heard her say.

CHAPTER FIFTEEN

hen morning came we learned that Cameron and his man, Hawkins, had gone on foot to Fort Union. Captain Crook said that by cutting across the country they should reach it in four days. The Captain had deemed this move advisable since the river was falling rapidly and this, after considering the delay occasioned by the repairing of the broken wheel, made the date of the *Yellow Stone's* arrival at the Fort very uncertain. The boat, in good water, could not accomplish this distance in less than ten days, and it might be a week before she could set out again, so that he had dispatched a letter by Cameron to Mr. Duncan McDougal acquainting him with our situation.

I was heartily glad to have Cameron gone. To be near him had lately irked me because I felt he already guessed that I suspected him of shooting me, and although I recognized the folly of such a course, I had ached to face him with the charge. His absence I knew only postponed this, since I had determined upon it, and it had been the presence of Miss Strongford, more than my physical condition, which had kept me from it. My pride, which every minute had goaded me since the morning I had seen my wound in Jane Strongford's hand mirror, was salved only for the time being by Cameron's absence. I could not act now, of course, and in the meantime I would get well–get into condition to satisfy it. And moreover, since he would no longer be interrupting us, I thought I could win Jane's confidence.

Out on deck, as far as possible from the hammering and sawing (for the men had already begun the work of repairing the broken wheel) we sat in the cool of the morning with the sun not yet shining upon the river, the ladies, Mr. Bodmer and I, speculating on the probable time the workmen would require, and devising means to baffle the pestiferous mosquitoes which found unusual opportunity to torture us, tied as we were to the bank. Prince Maximilian and Eli Whitney had gone to hunt deer in the bottoms immediately after breakfast and would not be back until late in the afternoon.

The noise of the workmen echoed in the badlands, the blows of sledge or hammer bounding from cliff to cliff in a bewildering fashion until one could imagine an army at work destroying a captured city.

Mr. Bodmer had moved a folding easel to the deck and, a little removed, was sketching a scene above the *Yellow Stone* where the breaks were especially colorful and strange in form. I moved my chair near his and watched with the same interest I always felt whenever he worked with brush or pencil.

"So! He is gone," he said, with a look up the stream. And while his pencil swiftly traced lines upon the canvas, "It is as though our good ship had been washed clean," he added, almost inaudibly.

I knew he referred to Cameron's departure, but somehow I did not wish to discuss him even with Mr. Bodmer. Cameron was now a personal matter with me. I held my peace.

"My friend, I feared that you would be foolish." Mr. Bodmer went on, again looking up the river where now the sun's rays were just dusting a red clay cliff above the green top of a giant cottonwood tree. The brightening colors held him entranced a moment before he turned back to his canvas. "Be wise," he said, seriously, his pencil busy, "and when you act, first shoot him dead, and then explain."

"Fill my pipe, will you please, Mr. Bodmer?" I asked, handing him my tobacco pouch.

With his pencil lengthwise between his teeth, he filled the pipe. "Dot man is vose as a shnake," he said, the obstruction of pencil seeming to prevent the use of his usual good English.

Just then Mrs. Doeffner got up and went into the saloon, and my attention was diverted from Mr. Bodmer. I watched to see if her absence might be but temporary, and as she did not return, I glanced at Mr. Bodmer. I hesitated to leave my friend so abruptly, and was about to speak when, with a smile, he turned to his canvas. "So," he said, and there was not only permission, but counsel in his very tone. If he had said, "Yes, by all means, go. Do not mind me in the least. I can see you almost anytime," he could not have spoken more plainly.

Walking along the deck, therefore, I took Mrs. Doeffner's chair. Jane Strongford nodded, without looking up from her needle.

"Who, in your opinion, stole the Moor's shirt from Strongford castle, Lady Jane," I asked, and without premeditation.

"How queer!" she exclaimed, her thimble stroking the linen in her lap. "I was thinking of the Moor's shirt, that very thing, and even as you sat down."

"Then you should have an answer ready," I suggested, smiling encouragingly at her.

"Oh, how many stories I have made about the Moor's shirt," she said, looking dreamily down the river. "But they're all stories," she sighed, returning to her work with a little shrug that was not coquetry in the least, but a characteristic dismissal of the subject. "Charles Strongford took it, of course. My mother believed that he was killed in the foreign wars, and she was probably right. He would not have dared to remain in Scotland. Even in England or France the Moor's shirt would have come to light if Charles had lost his life in battle there, since the shirt was famed afar."

"Where did she think he died, then?" I asked.

"Perhaps in America," she said, flushing a little, no doubt with the thought of such a denouncement. "It was at the time of the Spanish conquest of Mexico that the shirt was stolen from Strongford castle."

"Was the half-crest with the shirt?" I pursued.

"We thought so," she answered, looking steadily at me.

I pondered over the ideal picture of the Moor's shirt and the half-crest in America. My thoughts were captivated with it. Who, indeed, might today be their owner in some old Mexican village, with doubtless never a thought for what they might mean to their rightful owner?

"Tell me, Lady Jane," I said, earnestly, "if the Moor's shirt were found what good would come to you?"

"None whatever, Sir Donald. But if the half-crest could be found, the House of Cameron would pay ten thousand pounds to the finder, even now, although quiet title to the old Strongford fief has long rested with the Cameron," she sighed, her eyes down the river again.

My father had told me this. How well I remembered. "But a

counterfeit–could not some clever silversmith fashion a mate for
the missing half?"

She laughed amusedly. "How could he when there is no pattern save the half that is with me?"

"No, he could not," I agreed. "But Angus Cameron, tell me of
him, Jane," I begged.

A flush burned upon her face and vanished, leaving her white.
She stood up.

"Not now," she said with an ominous calm.

Why I did not more considerately observe her change of mood
I do not know. I had also risen. I seemed determined to have my
say. "Is he–do you love him?" I asked, relentlessly.

She twisted the bit of linen upon which she had been sewing as
if it had been a dishrag. "No! No!" she cried. "I hate him! I am
afraid of him," and she burst into tears, dropping the bit of linen at
my feet, and fled toward her stateroom.

Without knowing what I did, I followed, my very soul ashamed.
"Jane," I called, but the door of her stateroom closed behind her
and I stopped in my tracks to stare. And as though to give me
more of deserved punishment the clang of the workmen's ham-
mers suddenly ceased, and I heard Miss Strongford sobbing on
her berth. How could I face Mr. Bodmer? What would he think of
me? Determined to explain what he must have witnessed I went
out to the deck, and picking up the bit of white linen I laid it upon
a chair before approaching him.

"See, my friend," he said, eagerly, pointing to a swimming beaver just above the *Yellow Stone.* "There is another, a very large one.
Watch! See? There he is–a pair, mates." And for an hour good Mr.
Bodmer talked so continuously of the river and animal life that I
found no opportunity to explain. He did not intend that I should,
for without saying so he told me that he had witnessed nothing–
that nothing had happened to worry anybody–even me.

Chapter Sixteen

On the morning of the fifth of June, the *Yellow Stone's* broken wheel having been repaired within the space of four days, we had set out again, and ten days later we had come to Fort Union. I can only attempt to describe my feelings when we passed the mouth of the Yellowstone River, which I knew was only six and a half miles below the Fort. I had been anxious to reach my destination, and I had dreamed of my new work and of succeeding in the business which was my father's. But now that the Fort was at hand, my heart was heavy with thoughts of parting with Jane Strongford. I realized now that the hour was approaching when I must let her go, that my feeling towards her had developed into a passion, and the knowledge that she did not share this emotion had driven me to despair for days. I had watched her with, I doubt not, a distasteful hunger in my eyes. And whenever she chanced to look at me I felt myself to be a beast. There had been a great change in Jane Strongford since the day I had asked her if she loved Cameron. She was no longer gay, except perhaps momentarily, and then I thought her fine courage had probably been tested to the limit. Something terrible and inevitable was on her mind, and my question had strangely seemed to bring her face to face with it. I had thought before that I knew all of the crest story, but now I knew there was more to it than my father had told me, something of later development than his story took into account, and it concerned the Cameron connection with the affair I felt sure.

She had declared passionately that she did not love Angus Cameron, an open question that had stood in my way all along. Yet when I was convinced that she cared for me a little, that her feeling was something more than friendly, she put me off, sadly, but firmly, and I was thrown back upon puzzling over what tragedy had transpired in Jane Strongford's life that my father did not know of, and which must seem to her hopeless. I thought of the times I had asked her to tell me the Moor's shirt story and the difficulty there had always seemed to be between us whenever I mentioned it. Something *had* happened in Jane Strongford's life, something that was more than travel and Strongford tradition and the girl's natural courage and poise. Her gaiety was sometimes determined gaiety, and it was covering some unhappiness, that lately had become inescapable, which hopelessness weighed heavily upon her now.

She was beside me on the deck as we approached the Fort. A score of mounted Indians were on the north bank of the river waving buffalo robes, firing guns and yelling a wild welcome. I strained my eyes for a glimpse of the Fort, at the same time longing to put off the moment of seeing it. At last I beheld its flag waving lazily in the hot breeze from the top of a tall pole—a large American flag which had once flown from the mizzen peak of an American man-o-war. At another time it must have thrilled me to see it so far from saltwater. There were the bastions, tall and white as snow, with red, pointed roofs, portholes and embrasures, the two weathercocks of which I had so often heard, one a buffalo bull, the other an eagle, both fashioned of copper and both pointing down the stream as though in welcome. Fort Union was indeed good to look upon. Its tall palisades, twenty feet high of heavy cottonwood logs hewn and fitted tightly together appeared to shelter a city—a walled city in the wilderness, so extensive, so well ordered and strong did they seem to me from the deck of the *Yellow Stone.* And yet with all its warlike front, its armed bastions and its tall stockades, there was an air of homely hospitality about it that I could feel.

As we gazed there came a spurt of smoke, a flash, and a deafening report from a porthole in the northeast bastion. Then a shot rang out from the bastion in the southwest corner near the river, and the great folding gate in the palisade fronting the Missouri opened wide. The *Yellow Stone's* whistle answered these salutes, and out of the open gate of the fort there marched sixty armed men, with Mr. Duncan McDougal, Esquire, clad in chain armor at their head.

How often had I heard of his chain armor. Purchased, by his order, in England, Mr. Duncan McDougal wore it for protection when he visited Indian villages, and on occasions of state for effect upon visiting chiefs and the Fort's engagees, some of whom were mixed bloods. He wore it now, and how foreign it seemed here in America where I felt sure it had no counterpart.

I turned to Jane Strongford in my excitement. Her hand trembled on the boat's rail, and she smiled at me through tears. It was a moment of strange, mixed feelings for us both.

The *Yellow Stone* came into the bank where her lines were made fast, and the armed men on shore, forming lines on each side of the way leading up to the fort's gate, Mr. Duncan McDougal walked proudly down between them to greet Prince Maximilian and Captain Crook. It was all like a picture from life in the feudal days of Europe. I thought of old Lord John, and the shirt of the Moor, the half-crest, and Charles Strongford's dagger sticking in the breast of the manikin in Strongford Castle, and I wondered if I could be dreaming.

In a moment, however, life bestirred itself in the usual way. Jane Strongford was gone with Mr. Duncan McDougal, the Prince, Mr. Bodmer and Mrs. Doeffner, and I was left to follow dazedly at my will. Mr. Duncan McDougal had shaken my hand—"Report to me in an hour," he had said, shortly, and his curtness had made me feel that I was somehow not in high favor.

I had packed my clothes, and now I went into my stateroom for them, thoughts of Cameron in my mind. When I came out again he was on the deck below overseeing the unloading of the strange freight and the bags of corn, but he pretended not to see me. Having nearly an hour at my disposal I left my bags on the deck, and went ashore with the halfhearted intention of inspecting the famous painting of the peace treaty with the Indians which had been done by Mr. Moncrevier, Esquire, on the large gate. My father had also told me of this in mentioning the interesting sights I should see on my journey.

The gate being open, I was obliged to swing it a little so that I might have a view of the picture, and so intent was I that I did not notice an Indian seated with his back against the palisade close to the gate until he had risen and moved away. He was slight and undersize, but straight and lithe, a man nearing fifty, I thought. Knowing that first impressions are not easily overcome among Indians I did not want to begin my sojourn at the fort with a feeling of offishness between its people and me.

"Do not go away," I said in *Sioux*. "I am a friend. What is your name?"

He stopped and faced me. I thought I had never seen an Indian like him, but somehow I could not tell what it was that inspired the thought. He wore a breechcloth and leggings—the conventional apparel—and aside from a medicine sack suspended from his neck, wore no ornaments, not even rings, to in any way distinguish him from other Indians.

"My name is Medicine-coat," he answered, apparently surprised at my use of *Sioux*. "What is *your* name?" he asked, stepping backward, as though he did not want me nearer.

"Antelope," I told him, swinging the gate a little that I might see the picture on it. My back turned, he walked silently past me going toward a lodge down the river. As I caught his glance measuring me, I knew now his strangeness was in his eyes. They were *blue*.

I watched him enter the lodge by the river and when I turned to look at the *Yellow Stone* there was Cameron watching us from the forward deck, his strange freight piled about him.

How could I settle my account with him, now that I felt myself to be in ill favor with Mr. Duncan McDougal? I knew that Cameron was responsible for my superior's attitude toward me, and I feared it would be more manifestly disagreeable when we met again. I would first have to win Mr. Duncan McDougal's respect, or the least resentment shown by me toward Cameron would be set against me in favor of Cameron's charge, whatever it was. I would have to wait—or return to St. Louis on the *Yellow Stone*, leaving my quarrel behind me. But I dismissed this consideration almost at once, remembering that Miss Strongford knew about my quarrel and I should seem a poor coward. She had begged me to be careful, but running away was a different matter, and besides there was my father's pride and my own.

It was with a feeling of resentment that I entered the stockade. But when I beheld its orderly enclosure my pride in the Company wiped it out. Fort Union was spick and span, a great credit to the American Fur Company and Mr. Duncan McDougal, Esquire. Even the two brass cannons near the flagpole, polished and shining like gold in the blazing sun, were testimonials of my superior's efficiency and worth. The house of the Bourgeois was splendid, with large windows, green blinds and a wide veranda extending its whole length, but I only glanced at it in passing. I heard a blacksmith's hammer at work, and walked toward the sound of his ringing anvil, pridefully mindful as I passed of the neat, white houses with their bright, red roofs. Men standing in doorways or squatted in the shade of buildings or the palisades, knowing well who I was, bowed pleasantly, and some stared, curiously, of course.

I was watching the blacksmith temper a trap spring when Cameron's strange freight began to be stored in a new house, evidently built to receive it. Finally after the last piece, carried by two men, was inside, Cameron entered the building and closed the door. There were two small windows without glass, and they were high up, so that nothing on the inside could be seen from the ground, but I could hear Cameron and the men unpacking the freight.

The time for my reporting to Mr. Duncan McDougal had now come, and I went straight into the office in the house of the Bourgeois from which a clear view of all that passed within the fort was afforded. In a moment my superior entered, and with only a nod sat down at a desk which he opened.

"Check this freight, Mr. McLeod," he said, handing me a sheaf of papers. "See that every pound of it is aboard the *Yellow Stone*, beginning at once. The water is low, and every hour is precious. By the way, those are your quarters," he said, pointing to a room opening off the office. "Have your dunnage brought."

He stood up. He was in haste to join his company, but resting his hands on the desk he looked searchingly into my eyes. "Take any and all men for the loading, except Mr. Cameron, who is otherwise engaged. You'll find Mr. Donaldson in the warehouse. He will know where to lay his hands on everything listed. I shall be engaged this day, but supper will be at sundown, and you will sup in the mess room with my guests and me," he bowed stiffly.

I gave him my father's letter which, after a glance at the envelope, he held in his hand. It appeared to soften him a little, I thought, but as though determined not to permit sentiment to figure in our affairs, he said, bitterly, "I am fearful that your father will be disappointed in you, Mr. McLeod."

"Why, sir?" I asked, stung by his prejudiced attitude toward me.

"I wonder oft times at the sons of men I have known," he said half to himself, his tall, powerful form straightening, his hairy hand at his belt wherein two pistols stuck. "Ay, I've marveled that a mouse could come o' good, red blood. But we shall see what we shall see," he finished aloud and, with another stiff nod, he strode from the room leaving me dumb with resentment.

A coward! Mr. Duncan McDougal believed that I was a coward! And Cameron–what excuse–what ground could he have taken for this? How could he have fashioned his story so that it had convinced Mr. Duncan McDougal–condemned me, unheard? I would find Cameron!–have it out with him! My arm was yet too stiff to use my rifle. I would go to the *Yellow Stone*, get my pistol–then find Cameron! I tossed the sheaf of papers upon the desk and turned.

"Oh, here you are, Sir Donald! What a lovely room!"

Jane Strongford stood in the doorway, one little hand resting against the casing. She had the air of having said those words for the benefit of whoever might hear them, but not for me. To me she said, in a low voice, "Donald! What is the matter?"

"I'm to load the old *Yellow Stone*, and do not know where to find a pound of freight," I answered with an attempt at gaiety that was not wholly successful.

She stepped inside and faced me, her lovely cheek very pale. "No, Donald, you are not troubled about freight," she said. "It is Angus Cameron again! I want to ask you one thing before I go. I want you to promise me to wait until–until you are well before you, you quarrel...."

She broke off and turned toward the door, looking hurriedly both ways along the veranda. Then she came very close to me, clasping her hands tensely in her anxiety. "Go back to St. Louis, Donald!" she whispered. "Come back with me!"

My blood rushed to my face for very joy. I longed to take her in my arms, but dared not.

"No, Jane, no, not until I have finished here," I said tensely. "But will you wait for me in St. Louis, until I come? Will you, Jane?" I begged, taking her hand, gently.

"If you will promise me to wait two whole months before you–you quarrel, I will wait in St. Louis until I can say goodbye to you there–if I can stay so long."

"It will not be long! And you shall not say goodbye to me. I *love* you! I want you to be my wife. Will you?" I drew her toward me, but she put her hand against my breast.

"Oh, you don't know what you are saying," she cried, turning away her head, and she would have burst into tears, but a shadow fell on the veranda and she stepped around the desk just as Cameron filled the doorway.

"I beg an ounce of your pardon," he bowed. The beaver-musk pervaded the room. "I was in search of Mr. Donaldson," he explained.

Hearing voices in the next room, he walked along the veranda to its open door, and Mr. Duncan McDougal came out to talk to him, stopping directly in front of the office door.

Jane Strongford turned to walk down the hall leading to her apartment, and picking up the sheaf of papers I followed.

"Then you will wait for me," I whispered, catching up.

"Yes," she answered. I passed her on my way to an open door that led into the Fort's enclosure at the back of the Bourgeois house.

CHAPTER SEVENTEEN

whole month had passed since the *Yellow Stone*, laden so heavily that there had been grave doubt about her being able to make the trip in the shallow water, with Miss Strongford and Mrs. Doeffner aboard, had departed for St. Louis.

Not once in that time had Cameron been in my company. He appeared to avoid me except at mess table, where he sat fourth from the Bourgeois, Mr. Duncan McDougal. I, as chief clerk, sat on his right, so that even there we were separated by two men which did not easily allow conversation.

I had long since learned the nature of Cameron's strange freight. There was no secret about it now. It was a still for the unlawful manufacture of whisky and high-wines for the fur trade. Mr. Duncan McDougal, in determination not to be circumvented by Federal law, had purchased the still, and immediately upon his arrival at Fort Union Cameron had begun to convert the corn we had brought up the river into trade-drink. And in addition to the corn, the country abounds with wild plums. When ripened sufficiently Indian women had been engaged to gather them, and Cameron, in his retreat, cunningly converted the plums into firey liquor. And so, in spite of the law, the Fort was now well supplied with strong drink for the Indian trade. I was sure this condition of affairs could not long continue. The Company had too many enemies and, through them, complaint was sure to reach Washington where Senator Benton, who had sought always to befriend it, would experience difficulty in even tempering Federal wrath against it. In the meantime, as chief clerk to Mr. Duncan McDougal, I was being taken little by little into his confidence, and I acted always under his orders, asking no explanations whatever. I was kept so busy that

137

not once since we arrived had I been able to join in hunting, although many a day I longed to take a hand.

The buffalo-horses, which my Superior kept, were the finest in the whole country. They were beautiful as models. Whenever Mr. McDougal heard of a famous buffalo-horse among the tribes he would not rest until the animal was brought to Fort Union. If it measured up to expectations, it was sure to remain, even though his Indian owner might drive a hard bargain. There were twenty choice horses now in the string at Fort Union, every one of them dying to run.

The horses were closely herded on the sweetest grass by day, and at night driven into the stockade where in severe winter weather they were fed a ration of chopped cottonwood bark stripped from smooth, young trees. My superior's beauties were continually prancing because of their high spirits. This feeding was not all waste, since the cottonwood trees were first cut into cord sticks and, when peeled, dried quickly for use on the Company's steamboats. We called the stuff "horse wood," and there was always a quantity on hand at the Fort.

I did not blame my superior. I could never keep my eyes from his horses prancing into the stockade at sundown nor, furthermore, could the visiting Indians. The Indians fairly worshiped these horses, so fleet and of every color. I think, however, a strawberry roan, with a Roman nose and one white hoof, was king of them all. What a horse he was, that roan! I've seen a group of Indians stand for hours talking as much to the horses as to their own companions. Indeed more than once in Fort Union have I watched a naked *Sioux* admiring a buffalo-pony which may once have been his own, and which he someday hoped to steal, I suppose.

The hunt was almost a daily pleasure and, as large quantities of meat were required, the sport was encouraged by Mr. Duncan McDougal, who never lost an opportunity to use his horses. Mr. Bodmer went only once "to get the atmosphere" and, "once was enough!" he also confided. When shaken by racing over the plains, he had returned to the fort. In his usual quiet and peculiar way, nevertheless, I found that Mr. Bodmer was already making the most of his new surroundings.

One day, late in September, the Prince, Eli Whitney and Cameron, having gone with Mr. Duncan McDougal to run buffalo on the plains above Fort Union, and being unable to find Mr.

Bodmer, I determined to take a bath in the river. The day was clear and warm, the sky as blue as a robin's egg, and there was not a breath of air stirring. Even the Indian dogs were asleep in the shade of the tall palisades. All the fort was still as death, its doors wide open. Old Sooty, the blacksmith whose hammer began at daylight, was napping outside his shop, a grimy hand over his eyes to shade them from the bright sunlight. Tallow, his dog, not much larger than a house cat, crouched close to his side and, jealous of everything that might disturb Sooty, she bristled and showed her sharp, little teeth to everybody who passed. And the two guards walking lazily along the balcony, or chevaux-de-frise, evidently would also have liked to be napping. For if they so much as glanced across the palisades, it was only at long intervals, since they were not expecting enemies or even trade at this time of day.

With soap and a towel I started for my swim. I opened the gate and left it ajar so that I could reenter the fort without calling the guard. I turned down the stream, intending to go below Medicine-coat's lodge to a favorite beach. I had seen Medicine-coat many times since I first met him at the gate, and had tried constantly to engage him in conversation, but each time without success. My interest in him was considerable from the first. He had blue eyes. Moreover, I thought him inordinately proud, even for a *Sioux*. I had watched him when he thought himself alone and shall never forget one morning when I had gone early for a swim and came upon him standing by the river. He had neither seen nor heard me, for his thoughts were far away; and what a picture he made! Erect as a bronze statue, with arms folded across his breast and his eyes fixed upon the brightening horizon where the rising sun was bringing the miracle of light, I thought him the proudest man I had ever seen. And once afterward, when down by the river in the evening, I had heard him singing to his drum. Creeping closer I had seen him seated alone on the ground, his face shining with pride in his song. I knew that both these occasions had been ceremonial, yet in neither case had he worn any finery, nothing which I thought had been donned especially for them, unless it was an elkskin shirt without fringe or other adornment, and which I had not seen him wear at any other time.

Another reason for my curiosity was the fact that he would not permit me to come near him. His persistence in avoiding me had reminded me of the half-blood, but somehow I knew in this case it was not fear of me, but some other reason that made Medicine-coat hold himself aloof. I noticed that it was not only me whom he kept clear of, but that he never permitted any white man to approach him. I had also wondered if they had been aware of his attitude of withdrawal. I determined to get acquainted with him and thus discuss the motive for his behavior. It might be his medicine, or a vow he had taken, of course. It was his blue eyes, however, an unheard of feature in an Indian, which made him and his peculiarity intensely interesting to me.

His family talked with me frequently enough, or I mean his woman did, for he had no children, and I had given her a red head-silk for Medicine-coat which he sometimes wore. Still, although he accepted my present, whenever I attempted to engage him in conversation he always walked away.

At a point below his lodge in a little grove of trees this afternoon I undressed and took my bath. I was nearly dressed again when I heard laughter farther down in the grove and, hurrying to complete my toilet, I slipped along the riverbank to discover who was so happy. You cannot know my surprise when I came upon Medicine-coat and Mr. Bodmer sitting side by side.

I hid to watch them for a moment. There they sat. Mr. Bodmer could not speak a word of *Sioux* and the Indian could not utter a syllable of either French, German or English, but both could laugh, and both were laughing at Mr. Bodmer's sketches. Scarcely breathing I crept as close as I dared. Mr. Bodmer's pencil danced on the paper while the Indian looked on, entranced, and when the pencil stopped Medicine-coat laughed as before, and so heartily that the white man now joined in with him. And their combined laughter was so contagious that I was unable to repress my own.

But what a change mine wrought! Springing to his feet Medicine-coat vanished, as he had always done at my approach, and good Mr. Bodmer, his face reddened by embarrassment, could only stare while I stammered an apology for my rudeness.

"Surely to laugh demands no apology, my friend," he said, picking up his scattered sketches and crumpling them in his hand, his embarrassment all gone. "I was entertaining a savage lover of art and—and a savage with blue eyes. Did you ever before hear of an American savage, an Indian with blue eyes?" he asked, the student of primitive life, as nearly always, uppermost in his mind.

"No," I answered. "But tell me how you got into Medicine-coat's confidence. I have tried in vain to win him. He will not permit *me* to come near him."

"So. Three days now I have come here to sketch, and twice this Indian has hovered near. Yesterday I made a hurried sketch, comic thing, and tossed it to him. It was a wolf-dog running off with a steaming kettle, and an irate woman following in mad chase. He came near enough to hand it back to me. Then I gave him the sketch, which pleased him. Today he saw me come here again and followed. I sketched for his amusement, and we became interested in each other—he in my sketches, I in his eyes which are blue as my own. I cannot forget them. They puzzle me. How do you account for this man's blue eyes?"

"I haven't accounted for them."

"I have seen here horses, white horses and spotted horses, with blue eyes, even white eyes, or eyes that were nearly white, like glass. How do they come, my friend. Do you know?"

"No," I answered again, remembering many such eyes among Indian horses. I had even owned a pinto pony with blue eyes, myself.

"The blue eye in horses is not natural, I am sure," he said, musingly, "any more than blue eyes are natural in this Indian whom you call Medicine-coat. Perhaps if the mystery of one could be solved, its explanation might help us with the mystery of the other."

I looked to see if he was laughing, but he was in earnest. And he had given me a thought. "Both the blue eye and the horse came from Europe," I said, remembering that not in the language of any Indian tribe I knew, except the *Crow*, was there a *single* word for "*horse.*" All the other tribes with which I was at all acquainted used some hyphenated designation for that valuable animal, such as "elk-dog," to distinguish the animal from their earlier beasts of burden, the dogs. Even the exception, "Echeeta," the *Crow* word meaning horse translated literally meant "*something with which to hunt,*" or "*a thing to search with,*" I had been told. "Of course," I said, seriously, "I thought at once of white blood in connection with Medicine-coat's blue eyes. But blood of the white man does not seem to answer for Medicine-coat's blue eyes, as the eye of the Indian mother is known to be given to her child, even though its father be a blue-eyed white man. I have never before known a blue-eyed half-blood, and only one quarter-blood who had blue eyes, and she, besides, had nearly red hair. I can discover no trace or trait of the white man in Medicine-coat. The man seems to be a full-blooded Indian."

"The albino appears in all races, even among the lower animals," reflected Bodmer, puffing his pipe, "but this man's skin and hair are not of the albino type, at all. So!" he broke off, pointing up the river with his crooked pipestem, "We have visitors."

A dugout was landing at the fort. In it were a white man and an Indian woman. The man, shouldering a bale of robes, went up the roadway to the gate, and I saw the guard let him in. The woman, after watching him enter, laid herself down in the canoe so that she was out of sight. Knowing that my place was now within the palisades, if there was to be trading, I left Mr. Bodmer and hurried into the fort.

When I reached the store I saw that the man was already trading. I first noticed that his robes were last fall's kill. Some were even dressed and painted, and I recognized them as 'Ree robes from below. I also noticed that the man's face was covered with a short, black growth of beard. When he came nearer to me and put his hand on a bale of blankets on the counter, I saw to my horror the reason for the beard. The man had recently recovered from smallpox. My heart leaped at the wanton wickedness of the fellow.

"Get out! Take your robes and leave the fort!" I ordered, at the same time kicking the robes out of doors. The fellow bolted after, as though he were a part of them.

I might easily have stopped him after this, but I did not want to, God knows. Instead I waved the guard to let him pass, running after him to see that he got into his canoe and off. My mouth was dry. Good God!

I ran back to the store heaping the robes and the blanket—everything the scoundrel had touched—on the ground outside. I burned them, the smell of the scorching leather making me sick with fear. I berated the amazed trader for his lack of care and then quickly repented of my show of temper, remembering that the scoundrel might not have given him an opportunity to see his hands. The trader had naturally no cause for suspicion, while I had the advantage of having been made suspicious by the fellow's behavior down by the river. At least the woman's lying down in the canoe had at the time looked peculiar to me.

Smallpox had ravaged many a camp, and I had been taught to be on my guard against it, and especially to suspect used or painted robes. The disease had even been employed in times past as an ally to defeat rivals in the fur trade, or at least I had been told that such had been the case and, now that I had collected my wits, I believed this man was a messenger of spite.

I took every precaution I could, burning a quantity of sulphur in the store and charging everybody now in the secret to guard his tongue from wagging. A quiet gloom nonetheless soon settled upon us which I feared foreboded disaster. And with many misgivings I waited the return of Mr. Duncan McDougal.

He came at last and heard me out alone in his office, uttering not a word until I had finished. Then he filled and lit his pipe and, as he paced up and down the room, his long, light hair, streaked with gray falling about his broad shoulders. His gray eyes, as cold as winter's daybreak, looked straight ahead as though already searching out a way to vengeance. I could not keep my eyes from his face, nor my mind from repeating the words of my father, "He is a dour, gude, mon."

Suddenly, as though forced by smothering passion, Duncan McDougal stopped by the desk and it cracked with a blow from his hairy fist. "'Tis the work of ——, damn him!" he husked. (I have not named the man because to this day I do not know if the charge was true.) "You did well, McLeod, to burn the robes. No man could ha' done better. W'll ha' no talk o' this, mind. And we'll bide a time. Ay, and ye shall see what we shall see."

With this he went out of the room leaving me with my thoughts. How glad I was that he laid no blame at my door. I had felt a little guilty about being down at the river when the fellow came, although it was my right, of course, to go and come at will. Until long after candlelight I sat there looking out toward the main gate of Fort Union and brooding.

I, myself, was immune from smallpox, having had the disease, but I had grave fears for the Indians if a case should break out in the fort. Whole tribes had been wiped out by the disease, and the havoc it wrought among them was always so swift and terrible that I would have given anything now to have been assured no scourge would come.

I could not sleep. Even a dog gnawing a bone outside fretted me. I got up and lit my candle. I knew that no letter could reach Miss Strongford in St. Louis. There was no established connection between the Fort and St. Louis, and not until the *Yellow Stone* should return next Spring could we even hear from our friends in the city. But nevertheless, I wrote a long, diary-like letter to Miss Jane every night telling her in detail each happening of interest since she sailed, especially of Medicine-coat and his blue eyes, his queer manner, and of Mr. Bodmer's success in making friends with him when I had failed. I withheld, of course, the cause of my sleeplessness. I did not even remind her that the promised two months of waiting was nearly up. Instead I told her again and again of my love which tonight seemed painfully sweet and unattainable because of my mood. Indeed, at the end of my writing I had worked upon myself so that I even wondered if the life of adventure was after all the life for me and resented having lost an opportunity of winning Jane Strongford amid the comforts of my home city.

This mood, however, was quickly dissipated as I recalled my duty to my father, to whom, after all, I owed my position, and for whose name I meant to succeed. As for Jane I felt sure that she loved me, and that I could win her for my bride.

CHAPTER EIGHTEEN

 plunged into my work with increased energy. Fort Union, exactly four years old, was yet new to me, and my pride in its splendid appointments grew each day. They constantly reminded me of duty and my own station as Chief Clerk, which position had been bestowed upon me by ultra conservatives—men who, believing in my father's name had, for once, waived youth and inexperience. Cultivating this sentiment for my own contentment I never passed the portals of Fort Union without mentally extolling its builder, my superior, and marveling at the enclosure's neatness of plan.

There is always romance in entering the folding gate on the river front. It is twelve feet wide and fourteen feet tall, bearing upon it the picture of the peace treaty I have already mentioned. Passing the outer gate one finds himself in a tall, closely picketed enclosure. This forbids communication with the Fort, itself, but on the left, will admit one to a reception hall where war parties, or trading Indians of doubtful temper, are met. It is separated from a store by a heavy, loop-holed log partition in which a shuttered window enables trading with hostile patrons. These establishments occupy a strong building one hundred fifty feet long by twenty-one feet wide, and as high as the stockade.

Passing the inner gate of this enclosure, and looking north beyond the flagpole, itself sixty-three feet tall and encircled by an octagon, a paneled railing is seen that encloses a garden twelve feet in diameter. One's eyes then fall on the House of the Bourgeois, a fine structure occupying seventy-eight by twenty-four feet of ground. Its spotless exterior, its inviting, shady veranda, plentiful glass windows, green blinds and graceful dormer windows fairly

145

proclaim order and well-being. Behind it is the kitchen, so close (six feet, indeed) that the cooks can easily serve the mess in the House of the Bourgeois without having their cookery cooled in transit.

On the right of the river gate near the east palisade is a building which covers one hundred and twenty-seven by twenty-five feet of space. Here are several large rooms, all like the others and smoothly planked inside. Beginning on the north end they are used as follows: first, a warehouse where merchandise is stored; second, the general store where whites buy and sell goods; third, the wholesale warehouse in which are kept many fine furs and much dried meat; and last, on the South, is the press room where all furs and robes are pressed into bales and sometimes stored. It's not sealed overhead, and it has accommodated three thousand bales of buffalo robes at one time.

Across the Fort's enclosure near the palisade on the west is another large building, one hundred and nineteen by twenty-one feet. In it are six apartments of almost equal size, two being for clerks, one for resident hunters, and the others given over to the Fort's engagees. The only artisan not quartered here was the tailor, whose apartment is in the House of the Bourgeois, next to my own.

North of this long building and in line with it is the ice house, twenty-four by twenty-one feet, where fresh meat is constantly kept for the Fort's company. Still farther north is the powder magazine, twenty-five by eighteen, built securely of stone to the thickness of six feet, tinned and shingled against dampness. Nearly opposite, on the east side, is a well-founded blacksmith's shop where Sooty plies his trade.

Besides these, under the balconies, are many comfortable, small houses. Along the north palisade are ten good stables, and at other points pens and stalls where cows are kept, and where buffalo calves, often brought in by the hunters, are raised by the Fort's engagees. Then there are the chicken coops and pig pens—all completely out of the way under the balconies. One is conscious of plenty of unused room for other small buildings which would in no way hamper the enclosure.

But, of all the structures, the bastions in the northeast and southwest corners of the stockade are the most sturdy and imposing, being built of stone to the thickness of three feet. Each covers a space twenty-four feet square and is more than thirty feet high. Iron-railed balconies surround their second stories, and upon these guards are constantly kept to avoid surprise by Indians and to watch for approaching visitors. On each bastion's roof, which is pointed and steeply pitched, there is a staff supporting a waving American flag. Within are cannons, kept charged and with their mouths close to the portholes. In the northeast bastion are *two* cannons, an iron three-pounder and a brass swivel, while in the other there is but *one* cannon, a brass swivel. In both are six loaded muskets, besides plenty of powder and balls for instant use. These handsome stone towers, like every other building within the Fort, are painted snow white with bright, red roofs, so that a visitor is at once struck with admiration for the order and neatness of this formidable quadrangle fronting the wide Missouri and enclosing two hundred twenty by two hundred forty feet of ground.

Its palisades, hewn cottonwood logs set tightly together into a framework, stand twenty feet above the ground and forbid attack by any enemy possessing no artillery. The balconies, eight feet wide and fifteen feet high, set upon the tops of the X's forming the framework supporting the palisades, render the unseen approach of Indian war parties an impossibility.

With all its buildings—all its establishments, there is left unhampered a parade ground (I call it) of one hundred eighty-nine by one hundred ninety-one feet—excepting the brass cannons and the flagpole in its center.

And this is Fort Union, set gracefully upon a level prairie, two miles long and more than a mile wide, that slopes gently to the sandstone and clay slate bluffs on the north. Beyond them, every way, stretch the endless rolling plains often dotted with herds of buffalo and antelope. The vistas from the bluffs, especially the higher ones, are entrancing. A never ending variety of views present themselves. The courses of two great rivers are plainly traceable for leagues, both lined with green trees and both flowing through richest wilderness. Even the mouth of the Yellowstone, six and a half miles below Fort Union, is plainly visible from the bluffs, and one sees to advantage the countless groves of timber across the river, above and below the Fort on both sides, containing ash, cottonwood and elm standing in underbrush so thick and tangled that traveling there is indeed difficult. The Fort, itself, the hay corral just below it in which each fall are stored one hundred fifty cartloads of hay from the plains, the Fort's garden which supplies our vegetables are all spread like a picture before one who stands upon the bluffs to look about him and admire. Even Indian burial trees, with many dark, wrapped forms lashed to their branches, are in sight from the bluffs. Always upon going there I look first to learn if the oft-counted dead are yet in the trees, since the winds sometimes blow fiercely, and then the battling trees are apt to lose their burdens to the hungry buffalo wolves. And always by the river, above and below the Fort, are skin-lodges of the living people of the plains, their pony bands scattered over the bluffs under the eyes of Indian herders. They come out of the vastness surrounding us and go wherever their owners' fancy leads and their prowess as warriors permit. Some lodges are large and fancifully painted; others are small and plain, but each tells its own story of tribal importance, success or failure in war and hunting. Just now there were few of any kind, and of this I was glad.

During the bright, wonderful days which so invigorated me that I felt equal to any task, great preparations were made for the late fall trade. To augment the season's harvest of furs, the Company's trappers had been outfitted and sent away to their winter quarters even before the *Yellow Stone's* arrival. The destination of these trappers was only generally known at Fort Union, since "beaver sign" and the proximity of the hostile Blackfeet determined their final locations. But all were westward, toward the great Rocky Mountains nearly five hundred miles across the plains, and all were in dangerous territory over which a capricious winter season was soon to set its rigors against their early return to the fort. Each year the pitiless plains, with their natural inhabitants, took toll from these parties composed of fearless men schooled to every hardship, and while most of them finally returned successful, some were never again heard of. Many a time had I listened to my father and Mr. Duncan McDougal speak of lost parties of trappers when relics of battle, bits of property among the Indians which had once belonged to some missing man, embellished conjecture which could not possibly have been wilder than the truth itself, if it were known. I shall never forget the departure of Eli Whitney from Fort Union, nor how these tales presented themselves to me when, with only one horse and a few necessities, he set out alone to find a party of three trappers with whom he had previously promised to cast his lot for the season. He seemed to me then to be romantic reality setting forth to keep an appointment with a myth. And how forcibly, a few days later, was I brought to realize that the great plains were peopled, and that anywhere on his journey Eli Whitney might meet his end.

The day was perfect, with a tang of fall about it that made one know that perfection had been reached, and that it could not long maintain itself, but would decline. I was watching Sooty's little dog, Tallow, worry Anderson's tomcat near the flagpole when I heard a guard call, "'Tenshun! Visitors from the North!"

Roused, I sprang from the veranda so suddenly that Anderson's cat thought I had sided with Tallow against him and, to save himself, he climbed the flagpole beneath which Tallow began to dance and yelp as though she had won a great victory. Climbing to the balcony I looked the way the guard pointed. Indians were coming toward the fort, twenty of them behind a warrior mounted on a snow-white horse.

In a moment Mr. Duncan McDougal was beside me and, leveling his telescope, he looked at the approaching visitors. "Good!" he exclaimed, closing the telescope with a blow of his hand. "Mr. Cameron!" he called, loudly, "Turn out the guard in form!"

Mr. McDougal hurried to his apartments. By the time I had found Mr. Bodmer, a guard of thirty men was formed in two lines inside the gate, each man wearing a military hat which gave him a smart appearance.

A cannon belched smoke and detonated loudly from the northeast bastion, and Mr. Duncan McDougal, wearing his shirt of chainmail, a long sword in a silver scabbard and a plumed chapeau, walked toward the gate with the staff of an American flag in his hand.

"Strikes-the-enemy is coming," he said as he passed Mr. Bodmer and me, and I saw that he was greatly pleased. He spoke sharply to the guard who stiffened into a more soldierly attitude, and then the gate opened to receive the party.

The Indians had not been obliged to even alter the leisurely gait of their horses, and looking straight ahead they rode proudly into the enclosure. Strikes-the-enemy, with the tinkling of a hundred hawksbells on his finery, wearing a marvelous headdress of eagle feathers, and holding an ornate, many-feathered coup-stick with accustomed dignity, looked every inch a capable man. His horse was richly adorned with the furs of otters and white weasels,

with eagle feathers in both mane and tail, and striped with red
paint to show beholders the numerous wounds his rider had sus-
tained in battle. Pawing the ground impatiently to set the hawksbells
jingling, he neighed to show his own mettle and the savage worth
of his rider to the assembled whites.

Mr. Bodmer was deeply impressed. "What is his name, again?"
he whispered, eagerly. But without waiting for my reply he walked
busily around the adorned horse, his eyes full of amazed interest.

Not a man of the visiting party deigned to even notice him or
anybody else until, with the guard presenting arms, Mr. Duncan
McDougal stepped forward and formally welcomed Strikes-the-
enemy to Fort Union.

The Indian loves ceremony and, possessing natural dignity, he
excels in ceremonials, especially wherein feature parade is para-
mount. He delights to meet pomp with pomp, and never have I
seen him fail to hold his dignity above reproach, nor shrink before
a presence backed by habitat and power. He is formal, an ambas-
sador, and his speech and bearing never cheapen the cause he
represents. As a messenger, after saying exactly what he was sent
to say, and meeting one eye to eye, he will listen to arguments and
even threats, and deliver back its kernels, good and bad, without a
hint of his own opinion.

Strikes-the-enemy, a *Gros Ventre* chief with whom Mr. Duncan
McDougal had long been acquainted, was feasted, and for four
days and nights the fort was merry. The fifth morning at sunrise,
laden with gifts and leaving behind a fine buffalo-horse which the
Chief had presented to Mr. McDougal with his promises of continued good will and much trade, our visitors left us. The closing
of the gate threw the fort's company back into the rut of waiting to
exchange its goods for robes and furs, and for days the place was
dead.

The weather, which had been ideal with spotless blue skies by
day and starry nights, now turned suddenly cloudy with high winds.
Rain came, and then sleet, and finally snow driven with a force of
wind unhindered over a thousand miles of plains. For nearly a
week nobody left the stockade except the horse guard. The equi-
noctial storms, violent and with almost the cold of winter, had
come exactly on time, and everybody at Fort Union knew that as
soon as they were over trading would commence. But the sudden
change from summer to winter was depressing, and whenever a

man left his own shelter he scurried to that of another without delay. Those among us who, on moonlit nights, had frequented the balconies to shoot wolves, of course forsook the sport and played chess or checkers instead. Beneath the wet snow was gumbo, and within the palisades it was slippery as grease. A moccasined foot set upon it was likely to land one anywhere. Withal the fort was a dreary place now. The skin lodges of the Indians, seven in number, looked wet and forlorn and, save the smoke coming out of their tops, showed no sign of life. However, at night the fires inside glowed with softened blurs of shadows that suddenly cut them off when an Indian intruded his form between the fire and the lodge walls. Every night, too, the wolves howled above the shriek of the wind.

When the storm began, its sudden coming interested me, but still the evenings were apt to drag, and by the second night, after playing chess with Mr. Bodmer, I spent hours writing a letter to Jane Strongford in St. Louis. I delighted in this task, looking anxiously forward to the hours I might spend with her in this way and writing long, detailed letters which were really a diary of life and affairs at Fort Union.

Sometimes I wrote to her as though I knew she often talked with my father and he now knew the gay, self possessed and glorious young person Miss Jane Strongford really was instead of the "queer lot" which had been his preconceived impression of her. This was a source of deep satisfaction to me. It was as though I confided in somebody who could understand all the wonder of her which eased my feelings considerably, making her seem less a character in some romantic story and thus almost unattainable, and more a person of everyday life. She would always be romantic, I thought.

And sometimes my letters took up the tale of the Strongfords, themselves, as told me by my father, and I wrote as an old, trusted retainer, going ever so far on imaginary trails in search of the half-crest and the Moor's shirt, even to Mexico, to serve Lady Jane. And once I even ventured to discuss with her Angus Cameron, but found I could not go very far with this, and destroyed the letter, to sit and ponder afterward till nearly day. What was her secret? I had been sure for a long time that she had a secret.

I was glad she was in St. Louis, not here. It was too lonely here with the rain and sleet driving against the windowpanes, but at the same time I ached with a longing to see her. Sometimes it seemed hard to realize that I had actually seen her, that we had talked intimately on the boat for days at a time. When, in my berth, I dreamed of her, we were always on board the *Yellow Stone* all right, but something always kept us from getting together, which is of course, not as it had been at all–but a way with dreams.

The fourth night of the storm, while finishing a game of chess with Mr. Bodmer, before writing a letter to Miss Jane Strongford, the wind unfastened one of the office window shutters so that it was blown back with a startling bang. I hurried out to secure it and, to my surprise, nearly fell over an Indian woman crouched in the doorway.

"Who are you?" I asked in *Sioux*, shutting the door to save the candlelight within, as I spoke to her.

"Mary," she answered in English, folding her blanket closer about her face. "Me, Joe Finlay's 'oomans. Joe, he's bad seek. Me I'm comin' tell you now."

There was something foreboding and terrible about the woman's being there and what she told me, though I did not stop to reason the matter out. Finlay was a half-blood, and one of the lodges near the flagpole was his.

"Wait," I said, going into the office for my hat, having decided to visit Joe Finlay at once.

"I'll be back in a moment," I told Mr. Bodmer, and I followed Mary to the lodge where one glance at Joe seemed to explain all my feeling of apprehension and my hurried, unreasoned decision to go to see him. He had smallpox.

Cautioning Mary and her four children not to leave the lodge nor to permit visitors until I came again, I went directly to acquaint Mr. Duncan McDougal with the situation.

He promptly had Prince Maximilian and Mr. Bodmer moved upstairs where, above the office, large dormer windows made very decent quarters of the spacious half story. Then he sent for Cameron, spending an hour or more closeted with him, and I have been certain since then that subsequent action, taken by Mr. Duncan McDougal for safeguarding the Company's interest in the fall trade at Fort Union, was hatched in the mind of Angus Cameron that night.

The Plains Indian, whenever ill, repairs to a tiny sweat lodge fashioned in a bowl shape with a framework of willows covered tightly with buffalo robes, placed on the bank of a stream. His attendant, having heated stones white hot, rolls them into the sweat lodge where the naked sick man sprinkles water upon them. The result is a vapor bath of unbelievable severity. The pores of the skin are opened by the steam rising from the watered stones, and when the perspiration is pouring from his body and he feels himself dizzily weakened by the enervating vapor he rushes from the sweat lodge and plunges headlong into the icy river. In cases of smallpox such treatment nearly always resulted in death on the instant. Knowing this, every precaution was taken to prevent the sick man, Joe Finlay, from following the custom of the Plains people. But in spite of our watching and our advice, poor Joe, in the worst stage of his disease, was secretly sweated, dipped in the river, and later carried to "*the cliffs*."

Before all this happened every Indian in the Fort had been inoculated from the pustules on Joe Finlay's body by Angus Cameron, under orders from Mr. Duncan McDougal. "To have it over with before the trade comes," was the only explanation given. Further authority was assumed over the situation in the interest of the fur trade when, to prevent the spread of the scourge to the Plains (truly a mercy) and at the same time to keep secret the plague at the Fort, the Indians were prevented from leaving. Even the lodge of Medicine-coat was forcibly moved, set up within the palisades and carefully guarded with the rest.

There was not an Indian who survived the pestilence. The horror of it chilled my blood. Leads-the-wolf, a handsome warrior of thirty-five, terrified by the loathsome appearance of Red-moon, his stricken son, threw himself into a shallow grave dug by his woman and stabbed a knife into his heart. Each night the wailing of the women, especially terrible to me because I believed the inoculation ill-advised, now grew fainter, and each day *the cliffs* received more dead, decked with personal finery and hurriedly wrapped in buffalo robes, until the last was gone.

As fast as they died their lodges and every scrap of property which had belonged to the unfortunates were burned. Even their dogs, half wild and uncared for, were killed so that within a day after it was all over, every visible thing which might remind us of the scourge was wiped away. Nobody was now to visit *the cliffs* on pain of death.

This order had been given to the engagees, assembled by Mr. Duncan McDougal who knew that the painted robes and trinkets might attract some of our people and that anything filched from *the cliffs* might, of course, bring the plague back to the Fort. "If any one of you goes to *the cliffs* I will have him shot down like a dog," he had told us. And everybody knew that he would keep his word. Nobody, I am certain, feared the order so much as I, or felt that the penalty of violation was as likely to come to himself.

Throughout the scourge I had done whatever I could, visiting the sick and even attending the dead to *the cliffs*. But from the first a hopelessness had laid hold of the Indians. The inoculation had not only produced the disease, but also a mortal terror, which did more to carry them off than the malady itself, so that they seemed already downed by a deep melancholy that invaded every lodge before its members were actually stricken.

I have intentionally passed hurriedly over most of these scenes, touching only (and lightly) the essential points of this most harrowing experience, but now I must tell of the sickness and death of Medicine-coat, whose passing, at last, brought about a reckoning between Angus Cameron and me.

Misery, dogging misery, weakens the proudest spirit and, together with fear, will finally break it. No man's spirit can long withstand the pair, but of the two, fear is worst, and persistence in its recognition is the spirit's mortal wound.

Last to die, Medicine-coat, I believe, might have lived. But when his woman was carried to *the cliffs*, despair, which seemed the major part of the disease, settled upon him, as it had done with so many others, and his proud spirit broke. He had not yet taken to his bed. He had even gone with his woman that day to *the cliffs*, and yet when that same night I visited his lodge, I found him decked out in all his finery with his face painted and wearing his blackened elkskin shirt. He had laid himself down to die, and upon my entering the lodge he spoke to me pleasantly, telling me that his spirit was soon going to the *shadow hills*, and that he was content to have it so. To my assurances that he need not go if only he would not give up, he offered no argument, and even when, hoping to arouse his pride, I protested rather hotly against his lack of pluck in his adversity, he only smiled grimly, as though he did not expect me, a white man, to be able to understand.

"Your heart is good," he said, feeling with his slender fingers the medicine packet about his neck as though to assure himself that it was there.

"Your heart is on the ground," he said again, "and I have not been your friend."

His blue eyes swept the painted lodge from which nearly all save the robes upon which he was lying had been stripped and burned, and then turning upon his side he faced me across the tiny fire. On the ground beside him were his fuke, his lance, and his bow and quiver of arrows, while beneath his head I saw his buffalo-neck shield, which was painted handsomely, although I could not make out in the firelight anything of the design it bore.

I thought he noticed that my interest had been directed to the shield because he shifted it and then, as though the act had at last determined him he began to speak slowly, measuring each word.

"Listen, Antelope," he said, "I would speak to you as none of my blood before me have spoken. I am the last of those of the blue eyes. They will come no more. No children are mine. I have had four women. None were mothers, and all are now gone to the *shadow hills* where the men of the blue eyes have welcomed them. "The *medicine coat*," he faltered, and his hand stroked the blackened elkskin shirt, "which only those of the blue eyes knew, or might wear—the *medicine coat* which has defied the arrows of our enemies since he, *The First Blue Eyes*, brought it to this world from some other—will go with me to *the cliffs.*"

A wild thought came to me. "What other world, Medicine-coat?" I asked, creeping around the fire to his side. Could the blackened elkskin, by any chance, cover chain mail? "What other world? Tell me," I urged, curbing well my excitement.

"I know not," he answered. "My grandfather told me that his grandfather had said that he, *The First Blue Eyes*, came out of the South and brought the *medicine coat* from his world—another world than this, and there he had seen much war—much of hard fighting. This, and the story of his capture alive by our people, is all I know— all that my grandfather knew.

"Our people could not kill him. They surrounded him by the big medicine wheel toward the west, and starved him until he fell from weakness. But they could not kill him. No, because he could not be killed with weapons. Our people carried him to our village. When he grew strong again they made him chief. He took a woman of our people. Always, to each father's line, only one son was born with blue eyes to wear the *medicine coat* since *The First Blue Eyes* came to this world. Now there is no son," he sighed. "They of the Blue Eyes shall come no more."

The mystery of *why* Medicine-coat had blue eyes was solved. It was either a *strange happening of nature* or, perhaps, the "*powerful medicine*" the Indians believed *The First Blue Eyes* possessed that had produced, in each generation, only one son with blue eyes to wear the *medicine coat.*

I tried to keep excitement from my voice. "Did *The First Blue Eyes* bring no other thing to this world save the *medicine coat?*" I asked, looking at him tenderly for he seemed to me very pathetic, lying there, the last of his line.

I saw a change in his eyes like a shadow, and he hesitated, his hand groping at his throat where the rawhide packet hung.

"His *medicine,*" he answered. "The *medicine* which has never failed his sons of the blue eyes, till now.

"See, Antelope," he panted now, pulling the shield from beneath his head and handing it to me. "It is not that—but like...."

"What are you doing here, Mr. Cameron?" The voice, just outside the lodge wall, was that of Mr. Duncan McDougal.

"I thought I heard two Indians talking in this lodge, sir, and I stopped to listen. But I guess 'tis only young Mr. McLeod that's with Medicine-coat who's about due for lifting. I was rather hoping to have done with the work o' cleanin' up, sir, and stopped to see if the savage was dead," he explained.

Angus Cameron had heard—how much? Perhaps *all!* Would his conclusions match my own? Would he believe, as I now believed, that *The First Blue Eyes* had, in Scotland, borne the name of Charles Strongford? Of course he would, I thought heavily. What trick of fate had fetched him to the lodge? How many times had he appeared when any other presence would have been more welcome, even the devil's own.

I turned the shield to the firelight. On it, dimmed, but yet discernible was unmistakably a half-shield with what might well have been intended for a "couchant lion" by the savage artist who could have no other pattern than the *missing half of the Strongford crest.*

My heart was thumping now with excitement. What news I had for Jane Strongford! I would somehow take from the man's neck the medicine packet—the half-crest (there was no doubt in my mind that it contained the half-crest) and hand it over to *her.*

My excitement and wonder and all that the finding of it made me strong with courage and resolve. In this moment I recognized no obstacles. There were none in my elation. Somehow I would take and hide the blackened elkskin shirt, the Moor's shirt, and someday it should pass again to its rightful owner. Had Cameron seen the shield? I was sure he had not. But it did not matter. I would hide it. Lifting the edge of the robes upon which Medicine-coat was lying I slid the shield underneath them.

A second later Angus Cameron entered the lodge and sat down to light his pipe.

CHAPTER NINETEEN

The dawn came, and at last fate, which had seemed to hesitate in breaking the tradition of "those of the blue eyes," permitted Medicine-coat's spirit to pass to the *shadow hills* where he believed those of his blood waited to receive it. He had spoken no word since Cameron came. He had only turned to lie on his back and wait for death that was self-summoned, while we, Cameron and I watched like a pair of wolves to plunder.

The offensive odor of burning buffalo robes and lodges came to me with the change of morning's breeze from the far side of the flagpole where the smouldering ashes of the destroyed property of the dead were being fanned to new life. I could not contrive to take the medicine packet from the dead man's neck, and to secure the blackened elkskin shirt was equally hopeless with Cameron there. Bitter was my position indeed. I dared not leave, and I knew that he would not. However I had made up my mind that I could prevent the coveted things from falling into his hands here in the lodge, and that much I was determined to do. Then, in spite of the order of Mr. Duncan McDougal, I would get them somehow. Meantime I must keep the shield from Cameron's eyes.

"He's dead," I said at length. They were the first words between us since, unasked, he had entered the lodge.

"Ay, and the lodge and all must be burned, Mr. McLeod," he answered, his cunning, green eyes mere slits. "I'll take care of it," he added, rising.

"Take down the lodge," I told him, beginning to wrap Medicine-coat in the topmost robe, while I knelt on those that hid the shield.

I could almost have believed he thought that I had not heard the story, or that Medicine-coat's tale carried nothing of importance to me, for with seeming alacrity he went outside, whistling. But I soon discovered that instead of pulling the ground pegs, the first and most logical step, Cameron had pulled the skewers which held the lodge-skin together so that it instantly fell away from the poles with a great swishing sound exposing the interior and me on my knees beside Medicine-coat. I had not time to take the medicine packet. Besides, like a green parrot, his whistling stopped, and he kept up a flow of questions which, in decency, I answered, and these served to keep my mind diverted from the quick action I had intended when he went outside. Nevertheless, as the lodge-skin came down, fanning a swirl of white ashes from the dead fire over Medicine-coat, I managed to roll the shield in two robes which had been under him and, leaving the body securely wrapped, especially about the head, I carried the roll to the fire by the flagpole now fully fanned to consuming life, and pitched it into the hottest spot. The roll landed fairly, and as I turned to go back, I met Cameron with the lodge-skin in his arms. With this on the fire the shield was safe enough, and in a few minutes the lodge poles had followed, so that only Medicine-coat's body was left on the ground where his lodge had stood.

A creaking cart, high-wheeled and crude—the cart of the plains, was now brought to the spot at Cameron's summons, and together with a pock-marked Frenchman, Cameron and I lifted the body of Medicine-coat into its box.

"Pete," he said to the Frenchman, "fire this spot. Burn the hell out of it." Then turning to me, the pony's lead rope in his hand, "Ye'd better go to yer quarters, Mr. McLeod. Ye've had a nicht of it, mon, an' there are plenty here to do the dirty work."

Did he think me a fool? "No, Mr. Cameron," I said, shouldering my rifle, "I need the walk."

"As ye will, mon, of course," he smiled, determined, as was I, that Medicine-coat's body should go unrobed to *the cliffs* where, no doubt, he hoped I would not dare to venture again.

"Ay, as ye will." He turned to the Frenchman who was already gathering material for firing the site of the lodge, ordering: "Leave off the burning till we come back. Three of us will go. Come!"

Off he started, his long rifle over his shoulder, and one hand leading the pony. Pete, the Frenchman and I, trudging behind, had just passed out of the North gate when Cameron began to sing lustily:

"Oh, why the deuce should I repine
An' be an ill-foreboder?
I'm twenty-three an' five feet nine,
I'll go an' be a sodger."

And thus he sang all the way to *the cliffs* where we deposited Medicine-coat's body among the other dead, I marking well the spot where we laid it down.

And so to the Fort we returned, Cameron leading the pony and singing merrily above the whining of the cart wheels, his stride obliging the pony to trot if he would keep up. His lilting song, so heartless, pitched me into a confusion of thoughts as I walked rapidly with the Frenchman toward the open gate of Fort Union, through at last with the plague, thank God.

I had found the half-crest and the Moor's shirt! But how could I manage to visit *the cliffs*, even at night, with Cameron's green eyes forever watching me? I meant to possess myself of the medicine packet and the blackened shirt of Medicine-coat at all hazards. Did Cameron have like intentions? I would watch him like a hawk, and I would somehow outwit him. I even thought of laying the whole matter before Mr. Duncan McDougal, but cast this thought aside when I remembered that, even with the best story, I could tell Angus Cameron would have a better right to the property of Medicine-coat than I, in the eyes of such a judge, at least. If Cameron had accompanied me alone to *the cliffs* I might have had it out with him then and there. I confess I had hoped he would do this, but when he added the Frenchman to the burial party my chance to accuse him of shooting me, and then fight him, was gone. I could not confide even in Mr. Bodmer. My story was too impossible of belief. He would advise against my going to *the cliffs*, and secretly expressed determination to do so would make him an unwilling accomplice and sorely fret him.

There was nothing I could do but wait for an opportunity to go at night to *the cliffs*, while I kept my eyes well on Cameron. But judge of my surprise—my overjoy when, within two hours after returning to the Fort I learned that Cameron was going up the Yellowstone River with a supply of trade goods brought to the Fort by our boat, together with a barrel of high wines of his own making.

We were at dinner when Mr. Duncan McDougal spoke first of the expedition and, Cameron readily agreeing to attempt the trip,

I was directed to attend the loading of the designated freight into a mackinaw. This, to me, was a joyous task which by sundown was completed. Cameron, with nine men, set out at daybreak on the following morning for the mouth of the Big Horn River, on the Yellowstone River, where a small party of our men had established a temporary post in order to handily trade with the *Crows*. Several establishments of this sort had earlier been set up at the mouth of the Big Horn, but fortune had not favored them, and now Mr. Duncan McDougal was endeavoring to hold the *Crow* trade by well-timed expeditions into their country, hoping thus to finally draw them to Fort Union.

With Cameron gone, I began that very night to plan a visit to *the cliffs*. How was I to get out, and then back into the Fort, unseen? Any guard would readily permit me to pass out or in at will, but a prolonged stay outside the palisades at night would occasion talk—demand an explanation, perhaps. Besides there would be a bright moon, and the guards on the balcony, could see me far away—so far that I should not dare go directly to *the cliffs*, but instead should have to go first down the river to a point opposite *the cliffs*, cutting across from there to them. And of course I should have to return by the same route. *The cliffs* were two miles from the Fort, and a half-mile from the river, so that even if I traveled as directly as the winding stream permitted the trip would cover at least four miles and, considering the route and the task intended, would require a good two hours of time.

Though realizing the risk of being caught I had determined upon this plan. My plans had, however, been unnecessary, as fortune decreed another and more natural means of approaching the desired spot. Just after dinner the next day Prince Maximilian asked me to accompany him to run buffalo, a herd of which animals had been reported some six miles down the river, and out on the plains. I accepted eagerly. I had long wanted the experience of a buffalo hunt, and I now wondered, with a thrill, if Mr. Duncan McDougal would let me take the Roman-nosed roan. I made bold to seek his permission, not only to go with the Prince, but to use the horse of my choice, and was delighted with his evident pleasure when, after granting me leave to go, I asked for the roan. His gray eyes lighted. "Ay, take him, McLeod," he said. "And mind, do not let him run to hurt himself. He'd do it, man, he'd do it, with a fool on his back."

We rode out of the Fort at about two o'clock, each leading, besides, his choice of buffalo runners for the chase. Mine was the roan. I could scarcely wait to straddle him.

We located the buffalo herd, a large one, and "getting the wind" drew as close as we dared where, staking our saddle horses by their forefeet, we mounted our buffalo runners, and the chase was on. This was my first actual experience and, used as I had been all my life to tales of buffalo running, I was so fired by the excitement, so blinded by the dust and deafened by the thundering hoofs that I forgot the Prince, forgot myself, and the world. I had shot six fat cows when, my horse slowing quite noticeably, I pulled up and waited for the remaining herd to race past me, killing one more cow near the end. Perspiration was dripping from my forehead, and I was caked with dust. The roan was lathered where the bridle reins chafed his neck, and his sleek sides were panting painfully. Yet he pawed the ground and neighed, anxious to race on until he dropped in his tracks from exhaustion. I got down and led him out of the dust, the rumble of the running herd yet in my ears causing me to feel bewildered. Nobody—nothing was in sight besides the dust cloud raised by the frightened buffalo herd disappearing toward the North. Listening I could hear no shots from there. Could the Prince be running his mount to such a length, I wondered. I turned back, still leading my roan and twice passing dead buffalo, but whether the Prince's or mine, I was unable to tell. I could now see several other dead buffalo on the plains, lying in almost a straight line toward the river several miles away. "The carts and the butchers from the Fort ought soon to be in sight," I thought—and with this thought came another that set my blood tingling.

Mounting the roan I set out for the river, flying straight for a point about seven miles below Fort Union. Once at the breaks I was out of possible sight of the butchers, or the Prince. Here I dismounted to walk, leading the roan to give him rest. It was near sundown already. Four hours' time was all I needed, and I should be back at the Fort.

CHAPTER TWENTY

hen at last I thought the evening dark enough to be safe I started up the river among the breaks, working steadily outward toward *the cliffs*, which I knew were a little north of the river's course. By the time the full darkness of night had come I was out of the breaks and could ride again, which I did, since it was important that I beat the moon's coming.

The early night was starlit and warm, as in the months of summer, and the going comparatively easy. At last when I thought I ought to see *the cliffs* the wind brought me proof that I was indeed near them, and then determination alone kept me going.

In a moment more, however, I was among the dead, and in another I had found Medicine-coat. Working rapidly I cut away the thong which held the medicine packet. Then with less difficulty than I had anticipated I stripped the blackened elkskin shirt, which opened its full length from his form, and quickly ripped away the elkskin covering of what were unmistakably the remnants of a shirt of fine, chain mail, broken and dropping to pieces with its great age.

Rolling the iron shirt into a bundle not larger than one of fine cotton would make, I started to leave when my toe struck against a copper kettle which had been brought from the Fort with its dead owner. With a half-formed notion of what I should do with it, I picked it up and carried it to a point where I might breathe a breath of fresh air.

Instead of going to the Fort I now went to the river. There I filled my kettle with water and, kindling a fire in a thick grove, I thoroughly boiled the crumbling iron shirt. Anxious to be through and be off I took time to cut away the rawhide from the medicine-

163

packet and, bending near my fire, beheld with almost reverent thankfulness in my own hands the lost half of the Strongford crest–the mate to the half Miss Jane Strongford wore about her white neck. I remembered how white it was against her bright hair, and my passion made me almost drunk with joy at the next thought. The half-crest was *mine*–mine to give her, Jane Strongford of my father's story, wonderful and beautiful–the woman I loved.

"Oh, Jane, wonderful girl, I've found it! I have it!" I whispered, fairly dancing around my boiling kettle. Then sobering with thoughts of the necessity of a strategic entrance into the Fort and of a straightforward tale of getting lost, I dropped the half-crest into the boiling water that it, too, might be freed from centuries of contamination.

Spilling out the water from the kettle, I recovered my treasure, hot and cleansed, which I slipped safely into my pocket. I then burned the bits of rawhide which had covered it, and with my kettle brought water once more and quenched my fire, afterward throwing the kettle far out into the stream.

I shall never forget how the roan horse snorted and pulled back when I poured the water on my fire thus bringing sudden, black darkness to the thick grove, nor how, when dropping my kettle to quiet him, I was struck with the notion of letting him break away and go, and of making my way afoot to the Fort. I knew it would strengthen my story of getting lost, but the roan was too valuable. He might be stolen. I dared not take this chance, and quickly decided to ride in, which I did with an amazing absence of difficulty, and with the *iron shirt* securely hidden within the waist of my own. My explanations, too, were easily made and readily accepted. My coup had succeeded. I had beaten Angus Cameron.

Now I must hide my find. I felt self-conscious with the *iron shirt* beneath my own and, being obliged immediately to discuss the hunt with the Prince, Mr. Bodmer and Mr. Duncan McDougal, I excused myself in the beginning, going to my quarters to tuck the *iron shirt* beneath the blankets of my bed where I believed it would be safe until I could make better disposition of it.

I was not very tidy after the chase and, not only to make a more respectable appearance but to feel fresher, I washed my hands and face and, before leaving the room, attended to my fingernails. I put my hand into my pocket and with a quick thrill felt the half-crest. What, though, if by some mistake, some carelessness, I should let it be seen. I was not willing to take any chances now. The half-crest was *mine*, and I meant to keep it in spite of fate. I wouldn't carry it. There was no need to have it in my pocket. I'd hide it, as well, for tonight, in my bed with the *iron shirt*. I put it there, carefully smoothing over the bedding before I went out to the mess room where, seated about the table with their toddies, were Prince Maximilian, Mr. Duncan McDougal and good Mr. Bodmer, all waiting to hear me tell of my experiences—of how I became separated from my hunting companion, and how far I had followed the herd.

Oh, there was much to talk about. There has always been much to tell among hunters. I was no longer a novice, but an initiate now, and told of my kill and of the wonderful qualities of the Roman-nosed roan while they sipped their toddies. I made no great tale of my success, even telling to their amusement of my awkwardness in reloading my gun on the flying horse, and I think it was my praise of the roan that brought a kindly light to the eyes of Mr. Duncan McDougal.

"You tell it well—like an old hand, Mr. McLeod," he said, chuckling over his glass, "and not at all like the young friend of old Davey Duff who killed the elk."

"Ja, tell us of this young man who killed the elk, please," begged Mr. Bodmer, who was always ready for a story.

"Oh, the young man went hunting one morning," said Mr. Duncan McDougal, stirring his toddy, "and when he returned to camp at night old Davey Duff was sitting by the campfire broiling meat.

"'I killed an elk, Mr. Duff,' says the young one, sticking out his bloody hands for Duff's inspection.

"'Good,' says Davey, turning his meat.

, "'Yes sir, Mr. Duff,' says the young one, squaring himself for spinning his yarn. 'I went up that big coulee this morning, and I hadn't gone very far when I saw something that I thought might be an elk.'

"Davey grunted.

"'I was just going to shoot when it moved—and by George, Mr. Duff, it *was* an elk, a bull—a great big one—and I followed him a long ways.'

"Old Davey turned his meat again.

"'Up near the head of the coulee,' runs on the young one, 'I saw something that I thought maybe was him, and I was just going to shoot when he walked off again. You bet I knew what I'd do now. I'd climb up the hill, and look on the other side. That is what I did, and when I got up there, there he was again–and I pulled up my gun and was....'

"'Shoot! Shoot, man in the name o' God, an' let us have meat– ay an' peace,' says old Davey."

This story brought others, and midnight came before I realized it.

I was sitting facing an open window then, and the office clock was striking the hour of twelve when it seemed to me I caught the odor of beaver-musk on the draught which flickered the candles on the table before me.

I glanced apprehensively at Mr. Bodmer, my thoughts unreasoningly of Cameron (who of course was by now far from the Fort) but Mr. Bodmer was engaged, pouring liquor into his glass. He had not caught the odor so suggestive of Cameron, and I reflected that I no doubt was just now over-sensitive, anyway, of my enemy's favorite perfume. Others besides Cameron used it, though they were generally Indians or mixed-bloods. I tried vainly to recall someone among the whites, besides Cameron, who fancied beaver-musk, but was not able to recall a single one. Anyhow the odor was gone. Perhaps I had imagined it. I had caught only a breath of it through the open window as though somebody whose clothes were scented had passed outside. Probably it was an Indian. Cameron was gone, and even if he had returned to the Fort he could not know of my ruse. It had not been planned, but had come to me out on the plains, and I had carried it to conclusion. It had been almost as though some super-power had aided me to what had gentled fate and turned me toward success. I knew by the clearness of the scheme as it unfolded to me, and by the ease with which I had carried it out that all was well. Therefore I dismissed Cameron from my thoughts, and turned them back to Mr. Duncan McDougal, who was telling stories of the days when he and my father were young.

I can see him even now as he sat there that night in the candle-light, a large, bony man with cold gray eyes and tonight, wearing his shirt of chain mail, as though he feared some shadow might creep upon him from behind. God knows 'twould have been a bold one to have come at him face to face, for there was that in the

McDougal's eyes which must have come straight from the devil. And his arms! Man, they were long, and as hairy as an ape's, too. But I think, withal, he had a fine head, the head of a master of whatever he might set out to do. Besides, when he was not goaded by anger, Mr. Duncan McDougal had a voice that would win him a vantage point among men anywhere. Once won, his head would know how to keep it against odds and by almost any means. I admired him, but could not love him. He, because of Cameron I felt sure, had little affection for me, although I believed I had won his respect.

He was attracted to the Prince, and largely through mutual interests, especially of hunting, listened, with Mr. Bodmer and me, until after two o'clock to tales of the Prince's hunting in Brazil, a country that had given him many thrills, and the passengers of the *Yellow Stone* so many entertaining stories.

I was very tired, and felt glad when Mr. Duncan McDougal spoke of the lateness of the hour and we parted, each going to his bed directly. I carried a lighted candle from the table to my quarters, and no sooner had I opened the door than I smelled beaver-musk, as though betraying a visitor no longer present. It sent the blood throbbing to my temples.

Dropping the candlestick upon the table near my bed at once I threw back the blankets. The half-crest and the iron shirt were gone!

 s though Cameron's green eyes were feasting themselves upon my confoundment I hastily curtained the window and sat down on the bed, fairly dizzy with anger and chagrin. Then unable to believe, I again examined the bedding, this time removing all the blankets. Gone! The iron shirt and the silver half-crest were not there! The beaver-musk had warned me, and perhaps in time had I but believed in the warning. Cameron had stolen the half-crest and the iron shirt for which I had risked my life–and upon which my whole happiness seemed to hang. Springing to my feet I seized my rifle. Cameron must be in the Fort. I would find him, charge him with attempting to murder me, and then kill him! I opened the door and stepped out into the dark hall, only to dodge back again. Somebody was coming slowly toward me with a lighted candle. I closed my door, softly, and waited.

"Tap, tap, tap." I opened the door to Mr. Bodmer, who, with a bottle partly full of wine and two glasses, came softly inside. "So–," he said, sitting down on the tumbled bed without apparent notice of its condition.

"This is the last," he smiled, holding the bottle to the light, regretfully. "You killed two more buffaloes than His Highness, and we will finish the wine, my friend. So!"

He poured the two glasses which emptied the bottle, carefully attending to the drops, and dividing them between us. Then glancing around the room, as though the disarranged bed had aroused some suspicion, his eyes fell upon my rifle which I had left leaning against the door casing. His shaggy brows puckered questioningly.

Impulsively I poured forth the whole story, withholding nothing, not even my burning love for Jane Strongford, while he sat there spellbound, his kindly eyes growing owl-like with wonder. "Oh, why—why didn't I kill him before tonight!" I ended, my fingers clutching his arm and my mouth dry, so feverishly anxious was I to have him understand the hopelessness of the situation.

"So! So, my friend. But you must not kill him *now*," he said, solemnly sipping his wine.

"Kill him? Of course I shall kill him!"

"So? So? And forever lose the half-crest? No, no! First find the silver thing, and then, ja, kill him, of course my friend.

"Listen! You are excited. Drink your wine. You have not thought enough of what you propose. To kill the duck that has stolen her nest is to lose the eggs altogether. No, no, my friend, it is not a good way. Watch the duck and thus find the nest, ja. Mr. Cameron has the half-crest, or he has hidden it safely. He dare not speak of your visit to *the cliffs* while he has it in his possession. On the other hand, you dare not complain of the theft lest you incur the penalty for visiting the burial place of Medicine-coat. No, no. This is no time for Mr. Cameron to talk, nor for you to shoot. So, drink your wine.

He took a sip from his own glass. "Now here, my friend, is romance which defies the painter's brush," he said, his friendly presence calming me. "One picture, a dozen, a hundred could not tell the story. *The First Blue Eyes*, I might paint him, perhaps, ja, and even Medicine-coat, I might easily paint *him*. But what a tale stretches between these two, a Scotch knight and a red Indian! Think of the adventure of those who have worn the iron shirt since it was stolen from the Strongford castle. My mind is too full of racing pictures of Sacacens, Christians, knights and Indians, to have thoughts of Mr. Cameron."

"This shield of Medicine-coat's bore a crude replica of the half-crest, you say?" he asked, only to turn me farther from my anger.

"Yes, and Cameron did not even see it," I told him, thinking how I'd beaten him there.

"So! The world—we make of it a queer place," he mused aloud. "And go where we will we find customs which we think belong not there. It is as though mankind had a common beginning," he said more thoughtfully, "for not only are its customs disseminated, but its truths as well, ja, and its excellence, too. I am convinced that each race of men excels in some particular attainment, and that each possesses truths, quite common to its own masses, that these are unknown, except to the masters among the others. Truth, all of it, is in the world, but it is shattered into bits and scattered. Did a race of men in some remote age of the world once possess it all, and through some great catastrophe lose it?" He smoked a moment in silence.

"This might have been," he went on looking steadily at my rifle by the door. "Truth, customs, excellence, possessed by such a race might easily have been carried away in bits by survivors fleeing from whatever disaster that overwhelmed it. Why, my friend, if suddenly our civilization is no more, and this company here at Fort Union should be cut off forever, who besides your Mr. Sooty would know how steel is tempered? This remnant of our race, possessing only morsels of its truths, would be obliged to start all over again and with a few puny truths drag itself up. Our civilization is truly great, but individually we know so little. And truth does not thrust itself upon us. One must remain among strange peoples to learn their truths, for these are imparted by mind to mind after acquaintance has established confidence between him and them. It is not so with their customs. These are not often guarded, and the universality of some of them points to a common origin.

"Here, the lance, and shield bearing a device peculiar to its owner, the war parties made up of restless, adventurous spirits wandering through the wilderness in search of excitement and gain, the warfare, flaring up between the tribes, the vows you speak of, taken voluntarily and in secret by individuals, the Back-fats, the Owls, the Wolf-men, the Foxes, secret orders into which the favored and select are initiated and whose vows are inviolable, the Chiefs, the Councils, the Medicine men, the charms, medicine or talisman, my friend, have you ever thought seriously of these? Here, in America, there being no more Holy Wars in the old world, dwell the knights errant. The iron shirt, and the half-crest, outlasting their time over there, have come here only to be with those who understand them."

He relit his pipe with the candle. "How quickly he has learned the Indian," I thought, and caught by his mood I let him run on.

"So." He puffed rapidly, as though his thoughts were hurrying him. "It is not so long, my friend," he smiled, "not so very long since your ancestors and mine, if by good fortune they were knights and not serfs, were wearing iron shirts, and with butcher knives lashed to long poles rode about the land looking for trouble—quarrels with weaker neighbors who possessed something they coveted. Ja, and they were thieves and cutthroats by profession, like these red fellows on your plains. I have measured them, one with the other, and we have not much to boast about on our side, my friend. The scalping—ja, I have thought of that, considered that, too. At first I believed that we had a little of the best of it there but then I remembered that our knightly ancestors, instead of taking a small patch of an enemy's scalp to remember him by, cut off his whole head, and as a souvenir set it on a pike—a spear, to adorn their castle walls. So! Now we are through with such nonsense over there. Instead we now have bullets, round balls and slugs. Ba! We are improving, not rapidly, but—Come," he broke off, "go now to your bed, and sleep." His kind face was smiling as he knocked the ashes from his pipe into his cupped hand and put them thoughtfully into his coat pocket. He would never throw them on the floor, waiting always until he was out of doors, when he carefully cleaned the pocket.

In spite of my previous excitement, I had seen that his logic in regard to killing Cameron was sound, and being now relaxed by his dissertation on the Indian as knight errant, I was glad when, after putting away his pipe he began questioning me of all I knew concerning the strange story of the crest.

He quizzed me about my last conversation with Miss Jane Strongford when I had asked her to be my wife, and she had answered so strangely that I did not know what I was saying. This last he turned over and over in his mind, his eyes far away, and his hand stroking his mustache and twisting its ends with his fingers, which was a habit of his whenever he was thinking deeply.

He got up from the bed to leave me. "Ja, my friend," he muttered finally, more to himself than to me, "Kill dot man. But first find the half-crest. And now, sleep. Goodnight."

I had not to wait long for daylight. Morning came quickly after our talk, and with the dawn people began to stir about. I went out of the house and to the river gate. Nobody had seen Mr. Cameron. He had not been back since the mackinaw had gone down toward the mouth of the Yellowstone the morning before. Of course I knew better, but to this day I do not know how Angus Cameron managed to enter Fort Union and leave it again, unseen. Nor did I ever learn how he could have known that I had visited *the cliffs*. I believe, however, that with his cunning mind he only guessed the truth and that he acted upon his guessing, having first tricked me into believing that his own mission forbade his interference with mine.

CHAPTER TWENTY-TWO

At ten o'clock a guard on the balcony near the river gate called "'Tenshun! Across the river a white man is coming toward the fort!"

The call electrified us. Tallow, Sooty's little dog, filled with sudden excitement, began to caper and bark, racing after several men who bolted for the balcony, frantically nipping their moccasined heels to help them up beside the guard to look. But one man, exasperated, turned and with a vicious kick sent her ki-yiing back to Sooty who, fired with fury, met her in the door of the blacksmith's shop and shook his grimy fist at the wide world before he took her in his arms. The gate was opened, and a half dozen men went down to the river where a canoe was sent across to fetch the visitor who proved to be one of Cameron's men.

Mr. Cameron had been cut off from his party. He had taken a small canoe from the fleet at the Fort and, preceding the mackinaw with its crew, had not been seen since he turned up the Yellowstone which, of course, he could ascend more easily than the heavy mackinaw. The party, following Cameron's canoe, had journeyed until near two o'clock when, hearing several shots, the men had hidden the mackinaw and sent out a scouting party which had searched the banks and groves farther than Cameron could have gone—much farther than the point where the shots had been fired. Why had they waited so long before sending a messenger? Because the scouting party had been very thorough, and had not returned to the mackinaw until after daylight? No, they had found no trace of Mr. Cameron, or the canoe.

There was a great bustle now. Mr. Duncan McDougal and twenty men hurried into a mackinaw and left forthwith, while the

Fort's gates were closed, and a double guard set.

But I went straight to bid Mr. Bodmer a secret farewell, feeling heavy-hearted and sad in spite of my great excitement. Tears filled good Mr. Bodmer's eyes and ran unheeded down his cheeks, as he clasped my two hands in his, and bade me over and over his *aufwiederschen.*

Gathering up a pair of heavy blankets, some dried meat and whatever of other food I needed, I waited only long enough after this for the rescuing party to be well out of sight and then, with my outfit in a light canoe, set out to follow—or so I told the guards at the gate.

Cameron had tricked the others, but this time, not me. He was on his way down the river—to St. Louis—to Scotland, with the half-crest and the iron shirt! Would he find Jane Strongford? Would he show her the half-crest? Could it, in his hands, make any difference in the relations existing between them? What had she meant when she had said that I did not know what I was saying? Mr. Bodmer had been puzzled by this. Could it be that she—My God! A thought came—a thought that sickened me, and I heard my paddle crack with the strain of the stroke I gave it. Oh, I'd follow him! I'd follow! I would not stop to eat or sleep until I overtook him.

I gave not a thought to the dangers of the trip, but sent the light canoe bounding down the river at a gait. I knew that Angus Cameron, believing himself safe from pursuit, would never keep the pace. And I fell into an even, powerful stroke, making use of the swifter water which carried the canoe along at an amazing speed, passing the mouth of the Yellowstone River dangerously close to the rescuing party in the mackinaw, and laughing at their gullibility—forgetting my own. On the blanket, handy before me, I had laid my rifle. My pistol was in my belt, and I wore my powder horn and bullet pouch so that I was ready for trouble with hostile Indians or Angus Cameron. And never was my heart so light.

At sundown, letting the canoe drift, I ate a lunch, drank of the river and, humming a song, I picked up my old, strong stroke which I did not lessen until nearly daylight. Angus Cameron had not more than twelve hours the start of me, and presently I must be careful. I must see him before he discovered *me.*

Kneeling in a canoe is grilling work to one unused to it, and although I had been a canoe-man since early boyhood I was glad to stretch my legs on shore after a while, where I built a fire with some dry alder twigs, and made some tea. While it was brewing I undressed and slipped into the river, the cold water setting my blood tingling and freshening me for the day.

As soon as I thought the light sufficient to permit me to see a decent distance I set out again paddling steadily and watching both shores and the river ahead. The stream was now deep cut and there were weird cliffs and breaks, with groves of cottonwood and tangled wild rose bush patches and willows almost stripped of their leaves by the frosts. On most of the cottonwoods there were yet plenty of leaves, yellowed and very beautiful, with here and there a tree having only a few which trembled with each breeze as though they feared to fall and be lost. Deer were everywhere, and twice before noon I saw antelope and several bears. The flocks of ducks and geese and swans were numberless, and over my head their wings whirred unceasingly, while every bend in the river and every eddy I passed were black with them. Whenever I passed close to a swamp cutting into the river, the noise of their rising was beyond belief. There were millions and millions of them all the way.

The night before had been clear and still, with a sky full of stars, and paddling with no thought of channel with my light canoe, the moon had finally come to silver the river, the shadows of trees, rocks and cliffs falling sometimes nearly across from bank to bank. Nobody who has not seen the night breeze dance on moonlit water, especially water that is moving, can ever know its beauty. And now this day, sunny and clear with not a fleck in the sky and with wild things buzzing with the joy of life, was so beautiful that, for a time, I forgot my mission to revel with the rest. Not once, but a hundred times did I warn myself to be more careful, until night came again, as beautiful as the night before. And yet I had seen no human being.

I did not intend to pass Cameron in the night, and I feared that if I camped for daylight he might travel during the darkness and escape me. It was a long, long way to St. Louis, or to any point where I might learn if a canoe had passed. If I found that by camping nights now, I could not catch him. I had time enough to make it up by traveling nights. I could stand as much as Angus Cameron, and a night's sleep would help me, since I was growing sluggish. So deciding, I went ashore, ate supper and slept soundly until daybreak. Then, rested and refreshed by a bath in the river I went on for four more bright, beautiful days and two nights, which I shall always remember, still without seeing Cameron or his canoe. Not once since I set out on my chase had I doubted that I should overhaul him, but now I began to fear I might have passed it somewhere, perhaps at night.

I was about to land and rest a while on the sixth day when, around a bend ahead, a great flock of mallards rose with loud quacking. I knew at once that they had been disturbed and flushed. What had frightened them? Turning my canoe to the shore I pulled it out of the water and into the brush. Then, taking my rifle I slipped along the shore, till finally I cut across a point through a cottonwood grove. I could see the river for a mile or more, but not a thing was in sight, not a living thing. Even the circling mallards, having picked their course, had disappeared. I was turning back, thinking perhaps an eagle had scared the mallards, when I heard a sound, readily recognizable. A canoe was being dragged over a stony beach! In another moment I saw Angus Cameron push out from the shore nearly a mile below me. In another, he was out of sight.

With the intention now of learning the exact course of the river I climbed a tall cottonwood and, from its top, saw that the stream below made a perfect oxbow bend. By cutting across country afoot I could easily beat Cameron's canoe, find a vantage point where the current swept into the bank on my side, and wait for it to come along. Climbing down, I reflected that I would be obliged to travel across open country, but I knew Cameron could not see me from the river. I ran back to my canoe and dragged it into a good hiding place against possible Indian travelers. Then I set out, walking rapidly, sometimes running, to make up the time I had lost with my canoe. I kept my eyes upon a point I had selected while in the treetop, and had not gone more than a half mile when I smelled smoke—and it was cottonwood smoke, too. I stopped beside a juniper bush and knelt behind it, looking carefully up the wind where I saw the tops of seven Indian lodges in a cottonwood grove by the river. I had been so intent upon Cameron's canoe that while in the tree I had not seen them.

Cameron would have to pass them, and I knew that the lodges were of the 'Rees who, at this time, would not fail to attack a single canoe. I was also in great danger of discovery. I waited, fitting my body into the bushy juniper. In truth I was afraid to try to retrace my steps to my canoe, since the lodges were not over a quarter of a mile away. An hour passed, ample time for Cameron to have reached the Indian lodges. And yet not a shot was fired, there was no stir near the lodges, no sounds, except the occasional neighing of a picketed pony near the 'Ree camp. Had Cameron seen the lodges in time to land and hide? Had the wind warned him as it had warned me, or had he successfully passed the Indian camp? I wished I knew.

CHAPTER TWENTY-THREE

 ot until dusk could I with safety leave the juniper bush. Once I had thought I should surely be discovered when two hunters returning to the camp from the plains with antelope rode within two hundred yards of my hiding place. But fortune favored me, and at dusk I returned to my canoe without mishap.

If Cameron had seen the lodges in time to hide he would try to run past them in the night, as I now intended doing. Lunching on dried meat and water I set out once more, being extremely careful not to make a sound. Just where the river turned to flow past the Indian camp I caught hold of some willows on the shore a hundred yards above the lodges and across from them. I could see the lodge fires, seven of them among the cottonwood trees. The shadows were deepest on their side of the river and the banks were higher, so that I considered it safest to go down that side, even though my route would take me very near three lodges which were closest to the water. I first thought to wait until the fires were out, but knowing that then the guards would be more alert and the dogs more apt to be abroad I decided to make a run at once. I let go of the willows and pushed out into the stream, paddling silently across before turning down the river.

There was an unshadowed streak lying clear across the water just above the first lodges, and I was obliged to cross it, which I did, in terror of the dogs barking while I was in the patch of light and giving me away. In another minute I was again in the shadows close under the bank and, scarcely breathing, I guided my canoe with an occasional stroke of the paddle until I could hear voices in the lodges just above my head. I was so close that I honestly believe I could have caught a whispered conversation there if I had known the language. Suddenly, just below me, a woman was dipping her kettle into the river. I caught hold of the boughs of an uprooted tree, just in time to stop until she had climbed the bank with the water. There she called to someone, and my heart skipped a beat–but only one, for now I heard the woman laughing with another. She had not seen me–had given no alarm, and soon I was safely past the camp.

But I did not want to pass Angus Cameron at night, nor did I care to meet him in the dark, and I did not dare stop close to the 'Ree lodges. I was obliged to go on, cheered with the thought that he, too, had gone on. How far? I was determined that he should be ahead of me, and so as soon as I could find a proper place I pulled out my canoe, and rested until morning.

I intended to locate Cameron this very day, and then if the country permitted, cut across and head him off. I soon noticed that no large flocks of ducks were on the river and believed their absence must be due to Cameron's recent passing, so that I was extremely cautious afterward in rounding bends of the river not to come on him too suddenly. But night came again, and I had not seen him. I was now in the heart of the *Arickara* country and knew that any plainsmen would rather chance the river at night. I guessed that Cameron would do this, and so kept on until dawn when, just as I was landing to camp and wait for darkness, a shot rang out and a bullet tore through my shirt at the waist line.

Springing ashore from my canoe with my rifle I saw Cameron, reloading, behind a tree across the river, the stern of his canoe showing in the brush near the water. I had staggered when I jumped ashore, and now I purposely stumbled and fell behind a bush out of his sight and, fortunately, into a sag cut by the high water. Realizing my luck I crawled along the sag to a heavy clump of willows and cautiously looked across at Cameron.

He stuck his head from behind the tree, and listened. He thought I was lying where he had seen me fall, and that I might not be dead. Then for a ruse to make me show myself if I possessed the life to do it, he aimed, or pretended to aim at the spot where I had fallen. But I knew his sights were not on me, and lay still.

The light was not good. I dared not chance a shot. Besides, Cameron kept well behind his tree. I saw my canoe with my blanket and food drifting past me, but one canoe was enough between

Cameron and me, and Cameron's was safe enough on shore. To it I could swim if need be, whenever we had settled. I felt a stinging sensation under my belt where Cameron's bullet had ripped its way through my clothes, and I ran my hand down there to see if I was hit, but I was only scratched. He would not dare come near it before. I was satisfied now, and waited, being careful to not stir even a twig. An insufferable time passed, and my body ached in its cramped position, but every minute was fetching the sun, and both Cameron and I needed good light.

At last as though only half convinced that he had finished me, Cameron began to move toward his canoe, his rifle cocked and ready. I let him come on, wondering at his foolishness, and then when he stopped, suspicious, with the sun's light full upon him, I sent him what he so richly deserved.

I did not wait to see if he stirred after he had fallen, but ran along the shore to overtake my canoe which I found stuck on a sandbar, and not far out from the shore. Wading to it, I paddled up to the place where Cameron's canoe was hidden, and landed there myself.

The iron shirt, wrapped in a robe, was in the canoe's bow, and searching Cameron, too, I recovered the half-crest from a pocket in his hunting shirt. Once more they were mine at the risk of my life!

Every minute spent in open sight was now dangerous. There had been shots fired, and there might be 'Rees anywhere, yet I could not leave Cameron there, and I had nothing with which to dig, nor could I lift him. I finally dragged him into the brush and, unloading his canoe, I turned it over him. Then I took his rifle, powder horn and bullet pouch, and left the place. I paddled hard, the iron shirt at my knees and the half-crest in my pocket once more. At length I found a good thicket near the water in which to hide and refresh myself for the remainder of the day. That night I set out again, and for three days and nights all went well, but on the fourth day I ran amuck.

I had been looking anxiously for a suitable hiding place for more than an hour, but the country was destitute of desirable spots, and now the sun was up. It was high time that I got out of sight for the day. "'Round one more bend," which was just ahead, and take the best that's offered, I said to myself.

Bang! A bullet splintered my canoe. Bang, bang, bang! A half dozen bullets splashed water upon me, and one cut away a chip from my paddle just below my hand. I drove the canoe ashore and, leaping from it, pulled it high and dry. Then, with my rifle, I ducked into the bushes and watched for a shot. When at last a mark offered I did not miss it. My shot brought me several bullets which did me no damage, but which made me realize I was in a tight place, and that I was obliged to stay there. I promised myself that if I got out of this alive I would not, in the future, be so hard to please in camping spots.

Noon came and I had not stirred. All was quiet across the river, and I had not seen an Indian for two hours. I became suspicious of their inaction and, to test the situation, I put my hat on my ramrod and raised it among the bushes. It drew no fire and, after waiting a time, I stood up, half expecting a volley. None came. I searched with my eyes every bush on the other side, which was not more than one hundred and forty yards away, and was moving cautiously out of my hiding place, when I saw an Indian sitting with his back against a tree, and drew back astonished at my blindness. He was in plain sight, even from my hiding place, and yet I had not seen him until I had moved. Why had he not shot at me? In a flash I knew, or I was so satisfied with my guess that I ran down to the canoe, shoved it into the water, and quickly crossed the river to their own side where I pulled my canoe into some thick willows again, so that it could not be seen. Then, in a minute, I found that the Indian was dead, and that his companions, as I guessed, had set him up against the tree to hold me in my former position. I was certain that the whole party had gone up the river and would cross at some shallows I had passed an hour before they had fired upon me. They intended taking me from the rear.

If my guess was correct I was now reasonably safe, since I was hidden within twenty yards of where the Indians, themselves, had been when they fired at me, while they were, or soon would be, occupying my old position. We had exchanged places, and the water left no tracks. Seeing where the canoe had been pushed into the water they would be sure to think I had made a run for it down the river.

I was right, save that they had divided, one party going above, and the other below. Both had crossed the river, and I soon saw them examining the spot where my canoe had been. Splendid shots were offered by the unsuspecting 'Rees, but I was not tempted.

I only chuckled to myself as the party from below met the party from above, and I tried to imagine what was said. They wasted but little time in talk, however, but straightway set out down the stream where I knew on horseback they would ride far. Relieved, I ate a lunch and fell asleep by my canoe. When I awoke, the wind was raw and cold, the sky clouded over, and night was nearly on.

I was heartily glad of all these changes however disagreeable they might prove later on, since tonight I must run past the *Arickara* village, the most dangerous point in all my journey, and my days' work had not tended toward the establishment of friendship with the *'Rees.* I greatly desired darkness, and by the time I got started it was dense. The wind was high and growing stronger, and I could not often see either shore. But my canoe was light, and for a while only snags had any terrors for me, until midnight when I thought I ought to be near the *'Ree* village. By this time rain and sleet were pelting me so fiercely, and the raw wind, a gale now, was lashing the water into such foam about me that I thought if in the darkness and the driving storm, I could miss the hundreds of snags, I would risk the village, gladly. On and on, my clothing soaked, my knees aching, and my hands so benumbed that I could scarcely hold the paddle, I drove the good little dugout, looking blindly ahead—but seeing nothing, save now and then a black, jagged snag flash past, and so near that it took my breath.

At length, upon making a bend that tried my strength, I smelled smoke on the changed wind which was now behind me. Smoke, I knew could come from only the *'Ree* village. My chilled blood bounded happily. The *'Ree* village was past. And I still had the half-crest and the iron shirt, gifts for Jane Strongford, God bless her. My terror of the snags had tided me over my earlier dread unawares.

CHAPTER TWENTY-FOUR

ith the morning the storm lulled. My physical suffering had been acute more than once when in its temperamental turnings the river altered its direction and, instead of having the gale at my back to drive me, it was dead ahead to dispute the canoe's course, and torture me till I ached for shelter, food and fire. But not until nearly noon, when driving clouds were hurrying southward with the strings of waterfowl, and I was sure that I had put eighty miles between the *Arickara* village and myself did I stop to rest. Here, comparatively safe, I dried my clothes before a blazing fire, ate heartily and slept the clock around.

From here on, I felt free to kill meat and build fires whenever I was in the mood, which each day I did. Eleven days afterward I reached Fort Leavenworth and was lucky enough to catch the *Trapper*, a Company steamboat, bound for St. Louis. Upon arrival there, and with some misgivings as to my father's attitude toward me because of my actions, I went ashore to find him.

Entering the office I saw him with his white head and with a long, mottled goose-quill behind his ear, perched upon the old high stool and bent over a ledger. The heels of his carpet slippers were hooked upon the lowest rung, so that his long legs were bent but slightly. Beneath the tall black walnut desk, which had so long been above my head, were his boots, polished and side by side, their tooled tops lopping over as though weary of waiting a trip to our home.

My father, absorbed, did not look up at first, so that it was left to George Washington and Bobby Burns, in their familiar places on the wall, to welcome me. How little things had changed here. Nothing had changed.

183

"Good afternoon, Sir," I said, without advancing.

"Donald, lad!" He turned on his stool, a look of great happiness, shaded immediately, in his fine eyes.

I did not keep him waiting, but even as he took my hand and led me to the setee against the wall. I began pouring out my story, not stopping till I had told him all. It was like him, too, not to interrupt me, even to question, until I had finished. Then, for a long time, he sat looking out of the window, one leg across his knee, the carpet slipper hanging loose from a white-stockinged foot. With what anxiety I waited!

When he spoke it was as though he had been recounting to himself his boyhood days in Scotland. "Mon, mon!" he chuckled, slapping his knee and staring down at his boot-jack, an iron grasshopper whose curved "feelers" would fit any boot heel, "If on'y the auld Scotch grannies could hear this tale over their toddies! I'd like well to be, the nicht, at Strongford castle, for 'tis certain auld Lord John's ghost will walk. Ay, and dance a wee, the mad devil! And mayhap poor, crabbed Duncan Ross will leave off turning stones, and go satisfied to rest in his grave. Ay, and I'd like well to be in the old castle hall, and 'tis too bad, too bad that Mary Campbell cannot know," he sighed.

Brushing his face with his hand he seemed to cast away the past, and both feet squarely on the floor, he chided me. "A bad leave-taking was yours, Donald." Then to remove any sting he added hurriedly, "But I would have done the like, myself, ay, and you are my son, a McLeod, lad. Let me see the auld trash. I doubt not you have it about you."

From my waist I drew the iron shirt–the Moor's shirt, and laid it upon his knee, watching him as his fingers touched it as a fanatic might have laid his hands upon some holy relic of his faith. "Mon, mon! If this could on'y speak," he muttered, turning the tattered thing to see the design, worn and almost obliterated by time.

'Twas there, a crescent. But the shirt had so long been worn between two layers of elkskin that the constant rubbing had all but wiped it away.

"And the other? You have not lost it, lad?" My father's face betrayed rare excitement.

"No, sir, thank God," I assured him, handing out the silver piece.

He took it in his hand and, laying the iron shirt gently on a chair, went to the window where he examined it with spectacles on his nose.

When he turned to me his eyes were wet. "'Tis the half-crest, and none other, Donald. Good God! Found in America. What a tale is here, and we could on'y know it. Come, let us go home, lad. Come away home!"

"But, sir," I objected—

"Oh, ay, go, and ye will. The lass is at the home of Roderick Dunsire, a governess there. The German lady is long gone over the sea. But first, if I were you, I'd tidy mysel' a bit," he added, sagely.

"I cannot wait, sir," I told him, and as I turned to leave him he put his hand on my shoulder.

"Lad, there is something between her and—and Cameron, or there *was*. Mayhap something or other," he finished, lamely, as though he wanted to warn me, to strengthen me, and did not know how.

"What do you mean, father?" I asked, my face reddened, and the thought which had turned me sick in the canoe, returning.

"I do not know *what* I mean, but by your story—by her own words I—Well, lad, go and have done with whatever it is; though it may be nothing at all.

Elated by my father's reception and interest, and yet with frightful misgivings I went out of the office. Good Mr. Bodmer had had the same thoughts, the same fear. Oh, I knew well what both he and my father thought—what I feared, and I believed that never before was a man so sick at heart as I.

The Dunsire house—how well I knew it. Beautiful as it was with its extensive grounds, its broad verandas and French windows, the feature which gave it a permanent place in my memory was its huge brass knocker. As a small boy I had often gone there with my mother, and the knocker, a fierce looking African lion which, to gain admission, a caller seized by the tail and butted the lion's head on the brass plate, had always seemed a marvelous thing to me. I got a thrill whenever my mother, in calling at the Dunsire's, punished the brass brute by pounding his head, although I felt that she was each time too gentle, and itched to do the office myself. Eliphut, Mr. Dunsire's man, who was very black and very fat, always answered the door. Gentle as my mother was with the knocker she seemed always to fetch Eliphut before I had seen enough of the lion. So prompt was old Eliphut when my mother called at the Dunsires that I secretly believed the old black man sat all day and all night just behind the door, and that he watched the brass lion through some peephole. But how well I remembered, too, the iron gate and the lamps (which I had never seen lighted) on its ornate posts.

Entering the spacious grounds I walked toward the white house set far back among the tall elms, its colonial doorway reminding me, because of our visits, of my mother, till I came upon a doll lying on its back, its glassy eyes staring into the sky through the leafless treetops. Then I heard children, little girls, laughing merrily, and saw them darting among the bushes, their bright ribbons flashing color to the gray boughs. Jane would be with the children. Her nearness reminded me of my untidy appearance, and I hesitated, but only a moment as a bright-eyed little girl, racing around a lilac bush, came suddenly upon me. She stared, incredulous, and in another moment had scampered away calling, "Miss Strongford! Miss Strongford!" as though perhaps the premises were invaded by hobgoblins out of her storybooks. And then a dog near the stables began to bark furiously. Fearing to create a panic I stopped in my tracks, waiting, and berating myself now for not having listened to my father who had advised a change of raiment.

"Be still, Bounce!" It was Jane's voice. My heart bounded with joy. She was coming. It seemed to me the sunlight brightened, spreading through the elm tops to touch reverently the green-shuttered windows and the winding walk of the Dunsire place.

"Clar if it aint Mars Don!"

Startled, I turned quickly. Old Mose, a black slave, hat in hand was bowing, and explaining.

"I sca'sly knowed ye, sah, sca'sly. I wuz wo'kin' yonder, an' done heered lil' Miss Lucy call lak somebody come a-pesterin'. Yes, sah, Mars Don. Here dey come, de whole kaboodle!"

Jane, her hair shining in the sunlight, stepped upon the walk and stopped short, unbelieving. The children, hushed by her attitude, clustered close about her, one holding trustingly to her skirt as though even old Mose might betray them.

I saw the blood redden her cheeks. "Why, Donald!" she exclaimed, coming toward me, the children falling behind, but peeping out to see.

"Yesum, Miss Jane, it's him, shore nuff!" Then, "Has you chillun seen de squirrel nes' in de big holler sickamo'? Plum, cram full o' hick'y nuts dat nes' is. Betcha aint, no, sah, betcha aint! Nobody seen it ceptin' me. Come along, den. Mo hick'y nuts in dat ol' tree dan you ever kin shake a stick at."

We watched them, Jane and I, go trooping off after the old black man, whom I paid more than once before he passed away, for this voluntary service.

"They are safe with old Mose," she said, softly, her eyes lingering after the children.

"Yes, Jane, with old Mose, they are safe," I assured her. "Is the garden seat still under the maple by the driveway?" I asked.

"Yes," she answered, stepping off the walk. "Something has happened. What is it, Donald? The garden seat is so far. I can't wait. What has happened?"

"Jane, I have found it!" I said, my blood tingling.

She glanced quickly into my eyes, hurrying her steps toward the garden seat.

"Found *what*, Donald?" she asked as though she feared my answer.

"The half-crest, Jane, the half-crest! And the Moor's shirt, both! Think of it, Jane!"

She took my hand, and I felt her finger on my pulse, "Sit down, Donald," she said, gently, fear in her eyes. "Have you been ill? Oh, have you been hurt?"

"No, no," I denied impatiently, "I have them here! See?" And I laid them in her lap.

CHAPTER TWENTY-FIVE

er breath, stifled by amazement, seemed to stop. She caught up the silver, and I could feel her tenseness as her eyes traced its dim carvings. Her hand trembled–"Oh, Donald!" she cried, her voice unsteady, "It's the crest! It's found! "Oh, Mother, mine," she sobbed, "if you could only know! Do you know, Mother?"

I burned to take her in my arms. Would my story forever separate us? The thought brought me to my feet before her and, standing there like a schoolboy reciting a dreadful lesson, I told it, hurrying, dry-lipped, where I feared most to lose her, but telling *all.* How I thanked God when, finishing, I saw no indictment in her beautiful eyes, no fear of me, but relief! When I saw it come there I bent to put my arms around her and lift her to me. But she restrained me, gently pushing my arms away.

"No, no, Donald! Wait! You do not know," she said, evenly, as though only her will had spoken.

Then, with three words and her manner, she set a barrier between us. "Hear me, Donald," she said, standing up, the half-crest in her hand. "Angus Cameron was a nephew of the Lord Colin Cameron, heir of those to whom, by a ruling of the Lords, the Strongford fief escheated so long ago. He was of a jealous nature, and from early boyhood hated his uncle, the Lord Cameron, as also my mother. Forgetting that the escheatment of the Strongford fief was of another time, and the present Lord in no way to be blamed, she made common cause with Angus, and as a child I quite naturally shared this feeling.

"Although four years older, Angus and I went to school together. His talents lay in other directions than books, and he was a

188

great cheat in all things. This I learned early in our school days, but in all the country 'round there was no other boy so swift at running, so skilled at cricket, or so able a boatman as he, and I believe that these sturdy attainments which were quick to make him leader among the boys, attracted me. I was overawed by his boldness, and always a little afraid of him, but my mother and old Duncan Ross looked upon him as a kind of relation, or at least a retainer. Anyhow we grew up together. Four years make a great difference between boys and girls in early youth, and he came to assume a kind of guardianship over me, my mother rather encouraging his fancy for me, until he, at length, took it for granted that I belonged to him. This I realized, and many an hour it tortured me.

"About the time we were through school there began to be disagreeable talk concerning Angus' doings, especially of the company he kept, and while it gave me excuse for being cool to him, I was careful not to let on that it hurt me in any way. I well remember that I felt its sting to my pride very keenly. Then one day, quite suddenly, he asked me to be his wife. I was not really surprised. I had expected that someday he would ask me. I did not love him. I did not even like him, and I had made up my mind to say 'no' so I had not dreaded the ordeal.

"But he came to me, dripping, out of the sea, where he had just won a silver cup by swimming, and there was something so wild, so romantic about him then, that I made answer in a far lighter vein than I had planned. 'When you bring me the half-crest, I will marry you, Angus,' I told him, thinking of course, there was not the remotest possibility of the crest's being found, and not wanting to wound his pride in the moment of his triumph.

"'A bargain!' he laughed, diving off the high pier, as though to fetch it from the sea.

"I did not see him after that for nearly a year. My mother had died in the meantime, and I was living with old Duncan Ross and his wife, since I could not afford life in the castle. One night Old Duncan, who was always early to bed, did not come home till daylight, arriving just in time for his breakfast, full of mystery and very worn. Soon after this the village folk began to speak guardedly of smugglers, half condoning the lawlessness, as some people will when contraband is being brought to cheat the government. After this there began to be strange goings and comings to and from Deadman's Cove, a rocky, lonely place not far from the castle, and from the number of visitors there one might have believed half the village engaged in some dark conspiracy. All this had been going on for more than a month when Old Duncan Ross was out a second night, coming home this time at twelve, and entering my room with a lighted candle. I started from my sleep to see him standing by my bed with water shining on his white beard, and the candle aloft, shaking so terribly that fear of some dreadful happening almost paralyzed me.

"'What is it, Duncan?' I gasped, my voice unsteady as the candle in his hand.

"'Come awa' wi' me!–'tis found–'tis found! An' in furrin' parts, as God knaws it must ha' been, sin' it could na' weel be here aboots. Dress, an' come awa' wi' me!'

"I thought the poor thing crazed. He was leaning weakly against the wall, and in his agitation, let the candle fall to the floor where its light was snuffed. In the black darkness together we fumbled for it, and at length, disturbed by us no doubt, Duncan's wife came into the room with a much needed light.

"'Now, what are you talking about, Duncan?' I demanded, pushing the old man down on the bed while his good wife, thoroughly frightened also, held the candle over his head.

"'I've said my say, an' I dare na' say more, nor will I say again what I ha' said. Come awa' wi' me, Lady Jane.'

"Coaxing was of no avail after that. Old Duncan Ross would not speak again, except to beg me over and over again to go out with him, and *where*, he would not tell. His poor mind must be gone, I thought, and I pitied him. But when, at last his wife began speaking about the crest, adding her entreaty, I was so thoroughly bewildered to know what to think that I dressed myself and followed old Duncan into a rainy night with high wind out of the North.

"He headed straight for Deadman's Cove, and I thought wildly of smugglers, whom I could never disassociate from bloodthirsty pirates, but I was now too beside myself to protest. The experience seemed more like a terrible nightmare to me, and I stumbled on as though walking in my sleep. At the Cove's edge the wind was shrieking, and I could hear the breakers pounding and sucking in the cavern below us in the rocks, the white foam I knew was there was hidden by the blackness of the night. Then suddenly out a little way where the sea was fiercely wild I saw a green light swinging drunkenly. Old Duncan drew a small, red lantern from beneath his dripping coat, and instantly the green light at sea went out–was gone.

"'All's weel wi' us!' he shouted in my ear, his cracked voice hideous, like the storm. Forging ahead, his frail body bent against the gale which all but prevented his going ahead at all, he put out and dropped the red lantern. I could not see two yards in any direction, yet I knew exactly our whereabouts, and there could be but one destination for us now, the old Jameson cottage, a very decent house, though unoccupied and sadly needing repair.

"With a little more battling we were there, and I beheld a light shining in an uncurtained window. My knees were weak. I began to be truly frightened now, and I have never ceased to wonder why, terrified as I was, I followed old Duncan Ross into that cottage. But I did–and the first face I saw there was Angus Cameron's. There was but one other, a lean-visaged, dark-eyed man wearing a clergyman's attire.

"I had not even thought of Angus Cameron for months. The sudden sight of him now, after the awful night, the strange green light I had seen at Deadman's Cove, together with old Duncan's demented actions, turned everything black for me. I did not quite faint, for I heard Angus greet me, and heard him say, 'Jane, I have brought you the half-crest.' I knew also that he introduced me to the stranger. After that the room swam, and I clutched Angus to keep from falling. And then, oh, Donald, they told me that Angus Cameron and I were man and wife!

"Oh, the awfulness of it, journeying at night of my own free will to meet him thus with a clergyman. How could I explain, even if I dared try? He would tell it, publish it. In desperation I asked him for the crest, although I knew he had lied.

"Of course he put me off, declaring that he would give it to me when I had gone with him to France. 'Why should not your husband share with you the ten-thousand pounds?' he asked, as though he thought I would believe him.

"Then when I spurned him, told him that I hated him, he laughed a scornful, bitter laugh. 'You would not have me, my lady,' he sneered, 'but I have got you safe enough, since you'll hardly dare deny your visit here, ha, ha, ha! 'Twould make uncommon gossip for the crones in the village.'

"His words seemed to soften him a little. He opened the door as though he had relented, and would let me pass.

"'Can't you hear them, Jane, even above the gale?' he asked, stepping aside.

"There was a tone of entreaty in his voice now. But when a gust of wind extinguished the candle and its wick glowed like a coal of red fire in the damp draught he was a demon again.

"'Ha-ha!' he laughed, as I found old Duncan's hand in the dark, 'Can ye no hear Granny Blackburn tellin' that old she hellcat o' Cairn's o' yer visit *here–here* to *me* in the nicht? Ha-ha-ha.'

"His laugh stabbed like a knife. I thought he would prevent my leaving, but thank God he did not, and half dragging old Duncan I fled from the house into the storm.

"Poor old Duncan Ross never spoke again. He died a week afterward. Then I went to live with my uncle in Nuwied. Donald, my dearest, I had not seen Angus Cameron until that night he came aboard the *Yellow Stone*. Now that you have saved me from him and found the hidden half of the Strongford crest, the expressed will of Lord John Strongford may be carried out."

"The rest of the tale you know."

> A quarrel, and by ye king arranged,
> Hath mine from me for aye estranged;
> But pride hath teeth; our line be old;
> Let fate, not I, its future mould.
> My father's crest I now divide;
> One-half I wear, one-half I hide.
> (Armed lions couchant, twain,
> Proper, gules, vert champagne)
> And who of brother's blood, or mine,
> Man or *maid of Strongford's line,*
> Shall find ye half of Strongford's crest,
> That man or *maid shall claim the rest*
> Of Strongford's lands, her castle-hold
> Her vassals, and her store of gold.
> Let none complain, nor cry "Unfair,"
> Since fate alone thus *names my heir.*